CONFESSIONS OF A CYBER SLUT

ALL CLASSIC
— BOOKS —

ISBN-10: 1938759311
ISBN-13: 978-1-938759-31-4

Confessions of a Cyber Slut is available in trade paperback. For bulk discount orders or other questions, contact at randizohr@yahoo.com .

All Classic Books
Printed in the United States of America

CONFESSIONS OF A CYBER SLUT

Randi Zohr

Dedication

To my soul mate—the Universe
really does have incredible timing.

Cast of Characters

Randi — a shy, conservative country girl finally let loose in the modern dating world

The idiot who shall remain nameless — the guy who dumped her for his demon just before the real story starts

Rob — housemate, really just a business agreement

Tim — the voice on the phone who gave Randi a male perspective on the situations she was getting herself into

Robert — sent roses to get her name and address

Rick — fertility expert from England

Ken — traveler who was her first real date

Connor — "wrestler" who taught her how to kiss

Adam — instant messenger friend who needed twelve steps even more than she did

Lawrence — started out like a rose but ended up more like a dandelion

Don — left his mark on her, and it wasn't easy to explain that one to her students

Otto — birthday fling that should have taught Randi not to take so many chances

Alejandra — Randi's teaching assistant

Raul — "Al's" husband who wanted to be naughty

Randy — there was a good reason he didn't want to invite her back to his place

Mark — young'un from back home who just wanted cyber sex

Another knight — the one who got away

High Flyer — Third of July near fling

Mr. Clean — photographer who wanted to take private pictures

Robert — willing to try anything, encouraged Randi to join him

Robin — really enjoyed what Randi learned to do with her tongue

Mike — last new guy in this part of her life

Chapter 1 — I'm a good girl, I am

He was right. I had to face my demon before I could find real love. So did he, but he was afraid to face his. That's the topic of his story, one I can't tell.

Let me tell you *my* story.

First of all, what was my demon, you ask? It's no secret. I never really liked myself. I never thought of myself as popular. I didn't play any sports; in fact I was what most would consider a geek. I grew up in the country too far away from neighbors to have regular contact with them. I was shy and still consider myself socially awkward.

I also never thought of myself as physically attractive. Friends told me I had "mood" eyes that were a subtle gray when I was calm and cobalt blue when I got passionate. I thought they were boring blue and needed my glasses to make them look big enough to actually be seen. My hair was long and what one friend called shimmering chestnut in the sun. I thought it was boring brown and naturally too straight to look good. Those were the features I thought of as my good points physically. There was more that I didn't like.

The polite term used would be "stocky" for my build. My height was average for a woman, but my weight was on the high side for a man. Clothes never really fit right, which only added to my insecurities about my body. Those insecurities constantly fed my demon of not liking myself.

In high school and college I hid it by throwing myself into my studies, or a job, or something for church—anything but dating. God loved me, that I knew and will always know. But learning to love myself would take a lifetime.

For as long as I could remember, most of my best friends were male, but I didn't have boyfriends. Always the eternal "friend" and nothing more. My prom date ended up sleeping on a couch he shared with my best friend—as I shared a bean bag chair with her future husband while watching a not-so-thriller of a movie. I was always the "innocent" one.

It seemed to be a more innocent time back then, at least on the surface. I grew up in a place that was a throw-back to the fifties. Public displays of affection were frowned upon and private displays were kept private.

A country girl at heart, to me a "roll in the hay" meant spending time in a barn with stuff that was baled over the summer. Most of the time that would also include rearranging the bales to build a fort or look for a litter of kittens one of the barn cats had or some other innocent game.

That was more me than the area I grew up in. The only "teenage" party I went to was when I was in middle school. When we started looking for one of the girls we noticed one of the boys was gone as well. The next time anyone saw them her hair was all mussed up and he was picking hay out of his pockets. Since I had never really had a sexual rendezvous like that, the thought didn't even cross my mind.

I didn't date much in college, either; the definition of a date I had from college was that one person had to spend at least 50 cents on the other to count it as a date and since neither of us spent any money, this couldn't be considered a date.

But even good girls have their moments. I learned to talk dirty in college, listening to an international student who was not a native English speaker read from some of "those" magazines to work on her English articulation. I could talk a good game even though I never played. These were small beginnings for what would later grow into more adult situations.

Since I was so shy, I eventually turned to the internet to find someone special. Deep down, I wanted to find my soul mate, and I thought this could be the way to do it, though I wasn't sure if I could find someone to really love me at all. I didn't tell my family about going online. I had previously done and said too much to my siblings about their relationships and you know how cruel paybacks can be. Back home, lots of news you didn't want to share became public knowledge through the local paper that had more space to fill than real news stories. There were also the family members who had nothing better to talk about but just couldn't stop talking.

My internet dating started slow at first. I met several men at restaurants after talking with them on the phone a few times. Pictures on singles websites can't really be used for identification purposes. So finding out what they really looked like was "interesting."

I had a lot to learn about cyber dating.

And I had a lot to learn about myself in the process.

There was one gentleman I met in person just before my 33rd birthday. I left my niece's birthday party early—without giving any real reason—to meet him for the first time. He was tied where he was, and I was about to leave on a three year tour of duty in Alaska—3,000 plus miles away. So it ended before it could really begin. I wondered sometimes if I would ever find anyone, especially in a faraway place like Alaska.

There's a saying about finding a husband in Alaska: "The odds are good, but the goods are odd." Most men up there are hiding something so they don't want to get close to anyone. They find all sorts of "quirks" to hide behind. That made it easy to hide my demon as well. But I was looking for a long-term relationship. Many of the men I met went to Alaska to escape from the permanence of the "outside." The few men my age who wanted to settle down already had, so there weren't many real options for me up there.

Just to give you an idea: there was the guy most known for singing "Happy Birthday" to himself when a friend drove him home from the bar on his birthday; the guy who said he hoped he wouldn't be charged for not rewinding the DVD he rented because he couldn't figure out how to do that; and my favorite, the guy who served fish every time he invited friends over, but said he only ate the ones that told him it would be all right to do so.

Besides weird and slim pickings, I was also too busy to date because I was volunteering for the church. I felt I had to live up to a higher standard in my social life, so I served at church. I later realized it was also a great way of hiding my low self-esteem.

Along the way, there were some men I had met in real life I was interested in but was too shy to do much about it. They were too busy running from their own demons to initiate anything with me.

So instead of pursuing men in real life, where I had never had much luck, I turned back to the computer with full force. On the computer, I realized could hide a lot more than I could in person.

And that's exactly what I did. My true internet experience started out innocently enough. During my first six months up there I had a few month-plus internet "relationships." Basically we chatted online a lot. Since they weren't that serious, I had several going on at any one time. A lot of them didn't go anywhere, and most of them ended the same—the messages got fewer and fewer until eventually they just ended. Not a huge boost to my self-esteem. But I kept going anyway.

I met one guy in real life, once. It was nerve-wracking but exciting at the same time. The messages ended soon after that. Of course I knew it was me. There was something about me that repelled men, or so I thought.

Still, I kept going. I was bound and determined not to give up hope just yet. Eventually I met a guy on a faith-based site. Being a

God-loving person, it seemed a safer place to meet people. He was almost as conservative as my family raised me to be. He seemed just right for me, at least on the surface. And I was so fresh and new to internet dating, I hadn't learned the hard way yet that not everyone is who they proclaim to be.

He kept writing, even after his vacation. I thought there might be hope for us. The messages got more and more deep, including some talk about rings and weddings and children. Most of that kind of talk was from him. I didn't think anyone would want to be stuck with me permanently. Our relationship wasn't typical, but neither were we. Even when we were together for an occasional visit, things weren't exactly right. I thought it was me but he assured me we just had a unique relationship because we were very unique people. Inside, I was just happy to have someone interested in me. I was happy not to be alone anymore. I thought perhaps that is what love was.

Two years later, we were still chatting, and things were changing in my personal and work life. I began to think of life after Alaska. I couldn't stay there and didn't want to go back to my home state. He suggested I come down by him to live. We could get to know each other better before making our relationship permanent. We both assumed it was a matter of time.

Never assume!

So I moved to where he was. Looking back, I can't believe I took that leap. How had I become so trusting of someone I barely knew? At the time, it seemed the natural next step.

For three months we lived under the same roof – though we didn't share a bed or even a real kiss. While we liked each other, still something wasn't right. There were a lot of reasons. We both had jobs, but not the ones either one of us really wanted. I was still recovering from the emotional roller coaster that sent me out of Alaska earlier than originally planned. He was realizing his demon was strong—even if he didn't acknowledge its existence.

I packed on some emotional baggage during my time there. There was a nasty incident sitting together on a couch. Once bitten, twice shy. Actually, I'm always shy or at least I used to be. He had come home early from his scheduled weekly meeting. I was sitting on the couch he usually sat on, because I was doing some stitching and the light was better there. He said I could stay there since I was in the middle of something and he sat next to me to watch TV.

By the end of five minutes he had wiggled himself to the other end of the couch. About that time he decided he would rather sit on the floor across the room than share a couch with me. Really, I have shared couches with friends, male and female, in the past. I took it as an indication that he just wanted me out of his life, which only fed my demon.

Then it happened. One week he asked me my ring size with a goofy gleam in his eye and the next he took me to the park for the "let's just be friends" speech. We had been talking for so long, I had moved in with him, and now this?

What had gone wrong? When I had time to think about the situation, all the horror stories of online dating came to mind. Mine wasn't as bad as the ones that make urban legend status, but it was mine, and it hurt. The really ironic thing was that it didn't stop me from trying again.

It took me a month to find a new place to live. A relative of my teaching assistant had a room he sometimes let people live in to split the rent. He was about 10 years older than I. He was not looking for a relationship, just someone to share the bills. It was a purely business relationship, but he did say that if I left any lace panties in the laundry too long they might disappear. In effect, I had an efficiency apartment on the upper floor of the house with one big room and my own bathroom all to myself. We shared the kitchen but there was rarely a conflict as our schedules were so different.

I was truly alone in the big city. For a country girl like me, it was torture. This time when I turned to the computer I made sure it was with guys from the area, but still I wasn't making new friends like I wanted. He told me I had to learn to love myself before anyone else could love me, and he was right. A Thanksgiving spent rearranging my bedroom was when it hit me. I needed outside help.

I decided to try to work a 12-step program to make myself loveable to myself if nobody else. Giving it to God wasn't a problem once I knew what I needed to do. I quickly went through the steps, pausing at Step 9 because he wouldn't—and still won't—let me do it the way I feel it needs to be done. Even given the events of the year, while I was celebrating New Year's Eve with my family I had the feeling by the end of the new year I would be married. It was just an unexplainable feeling and at that point not looking likely at all.

That brings me to January. A good place to start.

At this point, the only people who were talking to me were the people at work, and I don't like mixing business and pleasure. As you will find, later it was impossible not to mix them, but that was unintentional and somewhat out of my control. The nature of my profession does not mix well with a personal life and most of the people who do what I do try to keep the two separate.

I'm a teacher. The "let's just be friends" speech came near the beginning of the school year but I signed a contract for the entire school year. That satisfied my mom when she asked me to go back to where I grew up since the relationship didn't work.

The "school" I was working at was somewhere between the department of correction and the public school system. Not exactly where you would look for a former church volunteer from backwoods, USA, who doesn't cuss or drink and the only thing I ever smoked was fish. Even though I was almost old enough to be a parent to the high schoolers, they had a lot more experience in what most would consider the real world. They grew up on the streets while I grew up in the middle of a field surrounded by woods. The girls I taught were afraid to take any test—math, urine or pregnancy. The boys didn't worry as much about the last one, but the other two terrified them. This was the big city and I was a tiny, tiny fish in the piranha filled pond.

I figured that somewhere in this big city there might be some guy who would be interested in me. I put a profile on four singles websites. All of them had a picture of me my sister took when I went home that Christmas. Great strides for someone who months before didn't feel at all loveable. I had faced my demon and with God's help overcome it. I was looking forward to experiencing a new life full of action, fun, and romance. What I ended up with was something more than I could have ever dreamed about when I was uploading my pictures for God-only-knows-who to see on the internet. I went from being a good girl because I didn't feel anyone wanted to be bad with me to a cyber slut in a matter of months.

Along the way, I had started writing down my activities, reactions, and feelings each night before I went to bed. Recently I started looking back at the events of this time and realized they are unpredictable to say the least. Just about the time I thought I had things under control, God sent some kind of curveball my way in my social life and other aspects of my life. His timing is so incredible. This story isn't just about how a good girl becomes a computer tramp, but also how God has protected me, until my actions got out of control.

I've gone places angels fear to tread, and with good reason. Looking at my journal entries from this time I see a flexible, creative, and protective Hand keeping me safe. That's the only explanation I can give for the events laid out in my own handwriting. Of course the names are changed to protect the . . . characters. I don't think anyone here would consider themselves innocent, especially me.

No one but God knows the whole story, and you can be sure there are parts I'm leaving out for you. Some of it might be too much to believe. Some of it might just be too much information. Some of it might be too personal to share with anyone but the man who made the memory for me. I'll try not to leave too much out.

Just know this is the truth and nothing but the truth, if not the whole truth. Hope that it doesn't ruin my reputation as a good girl. As Eliza Doolittle said, "I'm a good girl, I am." Really I am.

Some would say I was good at being bad. I'll let you be the judge.

Chapter 2 — January, a good place to start

Back home for Christmas, I had my picture taken to put on the singles websites next to my profiles. In the pictures it looked like I was possessed by some red-eyed demon, so I played around with it a little. Instead of putting black in place of the red I put dark blue. It still looked like I was a little possessed, but the dark blue was almost my real eye color when the picture was taken. Later one of the guys told me that it was my eyes that caught his attention. They say that pictures on websites like these make people more likely to write to you. Little did I know. . .

Within days there were several gentlemen who responded, but nothing really interesting. Many of the guys were throwing out a lot of lines, hoping to get a bite. Some were in broken English and I wasn't playing around until the inevitable, "Can you send some money Western Union" message. I was learning to be somewhat discriminating. What I would eventually learn was men fell into different categories—some potential flings, some potential friends, and some with even more potential than that.

Three of the websites I put my profile on were free for most of the things I used. Singles could send short messages through their secure system, usually just enough to exchange real e-dresses with some amount of reassurance that you were sending it to a real person. Sometimes those people were even like the person in the profile.

A few of my friends from Alaska had sent some Christmas cash my way. As I was uploading my picture I decided to use it to splurge a little. I paid for a six month subscription to the fourth dating website. On that site I then had access to a secure instant messaging system to get to know someone a little better before giving them access to my Yahoo! e-dress. Their IM system was a bit quirky, but when I saw one of the guys I was interested in was online I could start a conversation with them right away instead of waiting for a series of e-mails.

With some things I'm incredibly patient, but not with my social life. That's something I really have to work on. In my job I accept tiny steps made over years. In my social life I want things to happen *now*. You could call me "socially anxious." After waiting 36 years for my social life to start I wanted it full blown instantly. But that's not what God had in mind. I sent out a few messages in the first couple weeks. Eventually I got a standard introductory message to send out. I was just sending messages to guys who lived in the area. I was *not* going to go through another computer relationship ending in a move only to find out he just wants to be friends.

That being said, the introductory message I developed said I was just looking for new friends. I wasn't ready to get too involved yet. What I was looking for was "someone to spend some of my spare time with." That phrase was typed more times than I care to admit. My impatience was always near the surface. The country girl in me kept saying that "friends" meant friends. Later I realized that most of the men on these sites assumed female friendship came with benefits. I never did learn how to deal with that. Not all the first attempts were documented or the record would be way too long.

*****

20

By the middle of January, a couple of guys had given me their phone numbers. The first one wanted to live in my home state—the one I'll never live in again. We decided that since I wasn't going back and he wasn't leaving it didn't pay to get anything started.

The second one was from that state, but he wanted to get out—or so he said. He listed his address as a city in the general metro area in hopes of finding someone here. My guess is that he wanted to find someone to pay for his ride of over a thousand miles and then at least a few months of living expenses. He was living with a "friend" and her mother, and didn't really like either of them. He decided on his dream job from watching TV. He just needed a little more training for it, something he could get from almost any school advertised exclusively on the internet.

At the moment he was living off his friend, her mother, and the money he got from giving plasma. Once a week or so he would say that he wanted to move out here, get a job, and show me the time of my life. Don't know if he ever made it here but twice he said he was *definitely* coming out—once even buying a bus ticket that deep down I knew he would never use.

As it turned out, Tim would be a good friend even though he never came out here. Talking to him kept me going and gave me a puzzle to try to work out when I got *really* frustrated with men. We started with e-mails sent in rapid succession that were pretty much instant messages the first day. He didn't seem to want to type much so phone numbers were exchanged. I didn't have a cell phone or a phone at the house, so I had to give him my number at work. During most of this time I was living out of the school anyway. That's where I had internet access and a phone line. I knew it couldn't last forever, but it got me through the worst time for me.

There were always things I could work on when school wasn't in session. If my classroom was empty, I could check the dating websites and even IM or call using my calling card if the situation presented itself. With no phone, internet, cable or video replay device in the house I was living at there wasn't much to do there anyway. I pretty much used it as a place to sleep and store my stuff while I lived at the school. It was a small facility and they knew my situation. As long as I wasn't using anything but a little extra electricity the current administration let me stay as long as I wanted.

Tim and I talked often. The first week he called about three times every day. He wasn't big on e-mails or instant messaging, but we talked a lot. He tried to call during my lunch but since that was hit and miss, in reality I usually had to call him back. He seemed to be very interested in me and more on my (impatient) schedule. He asked about my family, what I was looking for, and my ring size. The problem was that he was in a different time zone. It sounded like he really wanted to come out here, but I knew that wasn't going to happen any time soon. I've heard the "wish I could. . ." way too many times with very little results.

As long as he wasn't coming out here, I could allow my alter-ego to get naughty when we talked on the phone. The rule I decided on was that I would tell guys my little secret either before we met—if they were coming from a distance just to see me—or the first time we met—if they were from the area and we met after only a little computer contact. What is that little secret?

I was a virgin. Not the "40 Year Old" of movie fame, but getting close. It was difficult for some to believe, especially the way I talked to some of the guys. Being a cyber slut but a virgin in real life was my form of rebellion. Sometimes I talked too good of a game, so good that the guy refused to believe me when I told him of my (lack of) actual sexual experience.

Hey, at least I wasn't a 40-something man pretending to be a 14-year-old to lure girls to some *Dateline* free location. It was my way of taking risks. It was my way of getting rid of some of my sexual tension which had been building up for 36 years.

Those I met in person also questioned it. I'm a Taurus and we love physical contact. I was far away from my family—where hugs from nieces and nephews could somewhat fill that need for basic physical contact. Sexual harassment and other such laws made anything but a handshake at school risky—not that I really wanted physical contact from students or staff anyway. My living arrangements were a business agreement—not that we saw much of each other because of our schedules. In short, I was starving for physical attention.

When I was put in a situation where I could get some I took all of it that I could while still remaining a good girl. Sometimes it was a very fine line between naughty and nice but that was only when I knew the gentleman I was with respected my wishes. I wanted to remain a virgin until my wedding night. If I knew he respected that dream he was allowed to get inches away from ending it—much closer than I would tell anyone in my family. They wouldn't believe me if I told them anyway.

Tim never did find out, because he never became a part of my life in a physical sense. He was just that voice on the phone that made me feel good, or at least made me forget why I should be feeling bad for a while. Eventually I gave him my real name, but he was led to assume that I had experience with men. No real reason to fight that battle with him since I knew I would never be in the same room as him. When the topic came up I would usually just remind him that I was a good girl, and he would ask "good for what?" and I would tell him to use his imagination. His imagination was that of a typical male so of course he thought I was intimate with guys I went out with. I guess I was intimate with them, just not in the way he thought I was.

*****

About this time I got a message from Robert. He claimed to be single and from Boston. Thinking about it later, he gave me some of the signs to look for to protect myself. After only a few messages on the website instant messenger program, he asked for my Yahoo e-dress so we could use Yahoo Messenger. After a while I did the same because the chat program through that particular website was a little tricky, but when guys asked for it that quickly a red flag went off in my head. He changed the IM background soon after switching to that program—another red flag.

One of his first questions to me was if I had a boyfriend. If I was chatting with someone I met on a singles website how likely would it be that I had a boyfriend or was married? Then again, if I was, would I admit it? That might be my conservative upbringing but that question set off another one of those red flags, but I was looking for someone to talk to so I continued the conversation. He was always very flattering. He called me his baby with hearts swirling around in the background of the chat window. I don't remember ever feeling like a baby and no one had called me that before. He was pretty smooth.

For several days we chatted. He would say wonderful things about my picture, and he asked if I had any more. Luckily he would first try to contact me in the afternoon. My job allowed me—all right, made me—use my computer during that time. My boss didn't think too much of me sitting behind the desk typing away. There was always a worksheet to type up since the school didn't use standard texts that have everything set up for the teacher. Some of my school-related contacts were done via e-mail, so I had an excuse to look at that as well. If my boss ever looked there was always another window I could flip to. She wasn't technologically savvy enough to look at the bottom to see that my Yahoo Messenger had a window or two up. As long as I got my other stuff done, everything was cool.

Robert knew I was using a screen name, and he asked me for my real name after a chat or two. I had heard about scammers who could get all kinds of things—like bank account numbers and credit card numbers—by having a full name and current address.

He got my given first name, and asked for my last name and address. When he asked for that I got nervous even though he said it was to send me flowers. Eventually I gave him my work address to send the flowers to. Yeah, right, he was going to send me flowers.

The next day my boss came in the room with a funny shaped box and a big smile on her face. The last time I saw a box like that was when my ex had roses sent to me in Alaska. My face turned a bright red and I forgot how to speak. Yes, he had actually sent me flowers, tea roses, 45 of them in various colors.

It took me a while to get them in the vase. The kids helped when they were done with their work for the day which they took care of in short order on that day. They were sent Fed-Ex and tightly wrapped for a long shipping time. There were three bundles of colorful roses the girls loved to smell. At least one of the boys noticed how happy I looked as they carefully pulled each one apart and handed it to me. My hands were shaking as I cut the bottom of each stem and put it in the water held by the vase that came with the flowers. All the other staff—there weren't very many of them—had to come in to see what was in the box.

During one of my afternoon breaks Robert caught me online. I thanked him many times, and then . . .

Randi: I can't thank you enough.
Robert: You're welcome. Are you an EATON?
Randi: Sorry, I'm not good at this chat speak. What does EATON stand for?
Robert: Is that your last name, Eaton?

When he typed it the first time I thought it was some acronym since it was all in caps. Then I realized that was my boss's last name, and she probably had to sign for the roses. He was using the flowers to get my "full name and address" for God-only-knows what purpose. Yes, God was on my side and protected me from a

25

computer scammer. I got roses out of it though, roses and a pattern to look for next time a guy tries to sweep me off my cyber feet.

He tried IMing with me a few times later that week but things were different. He didn't call me baby anymore. He didn't change the IM environment anymore. He didn't ask when he could come and visit me anymore. Pretty soon he didn't even IM anymore.

By the end of the month his profile was taken off the website. My guess is I wasn't the only person he did that to and someone sent a message to the profile police. But the roses lasted a surprisingly long time on my desk.

*****

This was also about the time I got a message from Rick. He was a doctor in England. We would IM in the morning before school for me and after the last appointment in the afternoon for him. He was quite forward about things. He wanted to have children—and soon. He was the English equivalent of an ob/gyn who helped couples with fertility issues. His specialty was in-vetro fertilization. According to him, he helped hundreds of women get pregnant but none of the children would ever call him Daddy. Right away he started talking about crossing the pond. . .

Rick: Would you like me to come for a visit?

Randi: That would be nice. What would you like to do while you're here?

Rick: Would you allow me to start working on making you a mum?

Randi: Don't want to do that until after I'm married. I DON'T want to be a single mother.

Rick: We could get married while I'm there.

Randi: I've always dreamed of a New Year's Eve wedding.

Rick: Then we will have a baby next fall.

At first the messages were quite instant. As the weeks went on his responses got slower and slower, and I got more and more work done when I got to school early. He always told me when he had to be gone for a day or two for a conference or something, and always sent me a card through the website when he got back. We couldn't connect on weekends so I would rush to work every Monday morning to chat with him. He started planning a trip out to visit in late March when I had some scheduled time off, or so he told me.

Do I sound a little skeptical? Of course I was. I was promised many visits when I lived in Alaska but only one was ever made, and that was only for a very short time. It wasn't nearly long enough to decide if this would be my husband. The more I thought about it the less likely a visit from Rick became. In January, however, it almost seemed like a real possibility, which was probably more my naivety than actual probability.

*****

By the middle of the month I was eager to actually meet someone in person. I had been hiding behind the computer for too long. I wasn't going to put all my eggs in a basket over in England. I started sending out lots of messages to guys from the metro area. Eventually I got some responses from them as well. One response came from Lawrence. He lived in one of the suburbs, but I could deal with that as long as he was living alone there. When I moved last November I almost moved to that suburb. When a seed is planted in the ground it doesn't seem like anything is happening for a while.

*****

Friday I stayed late to call Tim, but there was nothing really exciting from him. He was talking about coming out again. Could I look for a place for him to rent that would be cheap? Would I help him take some classes for the job he really wanted to do? Should I go out with him when he gets here? As usual, he told me his plan for coming out here to live. He still needed to work out how to handle partial custody of his daughter and paying for his way out here. He was spouting off the usual pipedreams.

While I was on the phone with him I noticed one of the local guys I had received a reply from was online, so I invited him to chat with me. We chatted for a bit and found out we had both lived in Alaska for a while. Ken knew the places I was talking about, but he was only there over the summer so he didn't know what the darkness is like over winter. My eyes were getting tired so I asked if he wanted to meet in person.

I think that took him by surprise, but he picked a restaurant to meet me. One of his last comments was that we could meet, get a bite to eat, and see what happens after that. It was his way of saying he was willing to meet me but didn't really trust what he read in our chat. I found that was typical for guys I met on the computer. Later I learned I should have been doing the same thing. My upbringing left me very naïve, but some guys liked that.

Ken was doing laundry so we had to wait until his pants dried to actually meet. That gave me time to run to the house, get a quick shower in and some going-out clothes on. Not that it was much different from what I wore to work but it was something different. Maybe something that didn't smell like the roses that were still in the air in my classroom.

As you can guess, I was incredibly nervous. This was the first time I hadn't e-mailed with a guy for months before meeting him. This time it wasn't even three hours since we started chatting. I got there before he did. I was still using the phone at work so he couldn't call me to tell me he was running late and I almost left. Waiting in the parking lot reminded me of my feeble attempts at dating before Alaska—and the reason I can pick out the tail lights of a Chevy Impala but will *never* own one myself. There wasn't much else to do, so I sat in the parking lot for a while.

Since I had never seen him before, I wasn't exactly sure it was him. He was tall, like his profile said, and I think his hair was kind of curly in the picture. I remember something about a white Camry. If it wasn't him, I'd have a funny story for him.

He called my name as I got out of my Jeep. Must be him.

There was an awkward "Hello," before going in for a bite to eat. He nervously tried to explain that his pants took longer to dry than he thought. He got in the middle of a sentence that should have ended with some comment of him being without pants and turned really red. It was cute how shy he was acting. Maybe he was almost as shy as I was.

The conversation eventually eased into a comfortable "getting to know you" chat. We were both relieved that we didn't have to worry about spelling and could use body language to help tell our stories. We grew up in different parts of the country, different enough to have something to talk about but similar enough that we spoke the same language.

He could have been one of my students if we had met when he was growing up. I understood where he was coming from and the kind of life he had led. As usual, most men from the big city just don't understand growing up in the country—where people had to chop down trees to build a house or get a field ready for plowing. I found it was much easier for me to understand growing up in the world most of the men came from than for them to understand where I came from. Even when I thought I knew the guy, they just couldn't get it that I didn't go to movies every week or play video games and enjoyed walking in the woods. That being said, our conversation went well and he admitted he wasn't sure about meeting someone he just met virtually that evening.

I learned another lesson about dating that night. He must have eaten before he came even though my understanding was that we were meeting for dinner. I hadn't had anything to eat since lunch—and that was on the run between crises at school. So he ordered a bowl of soup and I ordered a burger and fries. It seemed my mouth always had something in it. He ended up carrying the conversation, and soon my left hand across the table. The gentleman that he was, he left my right hand free to continue eating. He was telling me how much he wished there was someone like me to help him when he was high school age. I felt guilty that I was eating. I guess I should have used some of that extra time to grab something to eat like he probably did. Now all I could do was take little bites and swallow quickly to try to hold my share of the conversation.

When we were almost done, he asked if I wanted to go out for a drink after our meal. I never went out much so I didn't know where to go out around my place, so we went to a bar by his place. We had a couple of beers and a lot of conversation. Most of the awkwardness was gone as we shared stories of Alaska and silly things we did growing up. We both had come from bigger families. Now his was spread all over the country and mine—with the exception of me—was within a three hour's drive from where I grew up. We both had stories of things we did to our siblings growing up. Now that I wasn't eating I was able to hold up my end of the conversation better.

Eventually it was time to call it a night. We were both tired, and the karaoke singers killed a couple of otherwise good songs. We had parked next to each other, but he walked me to my vehicle. He would have the weekend off and asked if maybe we could get together again at some point. He put his arm around me. I turned to face him for a long hug. Not bad for a first real date.

*****

The next day, Saturday, I went in to school to get a little more work done, as not all the paperwork got done from an incident the day before. Tim called and asked what I did the night before. So there I was, talking with one gentleman, smelling the flowers from another gentleman, while thinking about a third. I had always thought of myself as a "good girl" but I was becoming a player. Later the line may have become blurred, but at the moment of the three gentleman I was involved with one relationship was definitely over and one relationship would never really begin, so really there was only one active relationship on the table. It only seemed like I was becoming a player.

My work required some computer time, and Ken was back online. He enjoyed the evening as well and was very interested in doing something again. After chatting a bit, he hesitantly asked if I wanted to come over to his place to watch movies. He was worried that I would think he was being too forward. We had just met and going over to his place could imply things, as I realized later. Even at the time I understood his hesitancy but I wasn't worried. Part of it was naivety, part of it was curiosity. Would he try anything if we weren't in public? I was actually hoping he would.

I quickly finished up the necessary school work and stopped at home to put on something a little less "sitting around the house" clothes even though I had the feeling that's exactly what I was going to do. I guess the biggest change was that it wouldn't be my house, and I wouldn't be alone.

He went out and bought the beer I usually drink so I just had to have one as we watched the first movie. He told me have a seat while he played with the remote to figure out what movie to demand. Since he was on the couch, I sat near him, but hesitated–the incident with my ex made me leery of sharing a seat–so I chose to sit on the loveseat.

The couch and love seat made a corner in his apartment. We were sitting as close to each other as we could while still having our own piece of furniture. My arm was strategically resting on the arm rest. When the movie started and he put the remote down, his arm rested close to mine. It was so junior high-ish. As the movie progressed our hands got closer and closer together. I shifted in my seat and "accidentally" hit his arm with my hand. He took the hint.

He put his hand on my arm, and I grabbed that arm with my other hand. We were actually holding hands! Actual physical contact! Physical contact felt really good. I could really get used to this. He ran his hand up and down my arm for the longest time. Who knew something so simple could make me feel so good? But he wasn't done yet.

When the first movie was over, we took a little break from the TV and talked. As the conversation went on I finally got up the nerve to ask him if I could sit on the couch next to him. He quickly shifted to let me in right next to him. As the second movie began, he told me he was wondering if I was ever going to share a piece of furniture with him. I wasn't going to tell him the story of the last time I shared a piece of furniture with a man, mostly because it still made me cry.

When Ken was done fiddling with the remote, one arm was draped over my shoulder. He started rubbing my shoulder, then my back, then reached around to see if there was anything in the breast pocket of my flannel shirt. My hand reached up to keep his hand busy, and away from temptation, or at least as much as I could. To most people this was perfectly acceptable for a second date. To me it was further than any man had ever dared to go.

He started kissing my head. I was *so* glad I decided to condition my hair that morning. Then his lips drifted downward. I didn't know how much he was getting out of the movie, but I kept thinking it was good I had already read the book or I wouldn't have been able to follow it. Soon he had a fascination with my ear. Later I found that many men do. Eventually his lips made it to mine with a real kiss. Not a brush of his lips against my cheek, but a real kiss.

What movie were we watching?

Real life felt so much better for once. His lips were exploring my face and neck while his hands were exploring my chest, through several layers of material but it still felt *soooo* good. Finally I was in the same room with a real man—a man who wasn't afraid of me. He was a man who wanted me. So maybe it was that he wanted anyone he could get, but right now it was me he was after, and it felt good.

Finally the movie was over. We lingered together on the couch. While we were sitting there with my head by his stomach it started to growl so I suggested we get something to eat. He found a flyer for a place that delivered and called in an order.

While waiting for the pizza we stood in front of his French doors, his arms around my waist. Slowly his hands moved to the top of my jeans, and around to the front. When his hands started reaching for the button, I grabbed them.

"Maybe it's time for me to go."

"Too fast?" was whispered in my ear in a voice just barely audible.

"Yeah," escaped from my lips.

"If I slow down will you stay?" he said as his hands moved from under my shirt.

"Yeah."

"Then I'll slow down."

And he did. During the third movie he did more exploring, but with his hand on top of my shirt. His lips continued to explore my face and neck. Good thing it was a classic movie that I had already seen. Finally the movie was over and it was time for me to go home. My jacket magically reappeared and he helped me put it on.

One place I read that if a man helps you put on your coat it means he's willing to help you take it—and any other piece of clothing—off if you let him. It was cold outside, but he walked me to my Jeep.

We talked a little more in the parking lot, including me telling him my little secret. He had a hard time fathoming a woman in her thirties who was still a virgin. That's when I realized how different we really were. He got very nervous and awkward for a few minutes. All he could say was that he didn't know what to say.

Eventually he calmed down a little. He took my hand with one of his, and opened the door of the Jeep with the other. Before I got in there was a long kiss good-bye.

Finally, at age 36, I had an actual date that ended with a real kiss. Not like the high school dates which ended in an awkward pressing together of lips—or so I heard. It was a real, parted lips kiss that lasted for over a minute. It might have gone on longer, but he just had on a pair of shorts in the cold parking lot. His knees were probably as cold as mine were weak.

He said he would call me when he got in next week and maybe we could do something again. I was hoping it would be something like we did today. Maybe next week I would have a little better idea of what to expect and a week to prepare myself to let him go a little further.

Next week would be next month. And what a month it would be.

Chapter 3 — Good girl going . . . going . . .

February was never good for me, especially when Valentine's Day fell on a Wednesday. One Wednesday February 14th evening was spent at the funeral home just after my grandmother passed away. The next time Valentine's Day was on a Wednesday, it was spent chasing kids around when there was a bomb scare at the school where I worked. This year it was on Wednesday again, so my biggest question was what disaster would strike this year.

Maybe it was because I was raised Protestant, but I never understood the significance of celebrating romantic love on the anniversary of the beheading of a monk. I understood sending little messages to friends, like St. Valentine sending last messages to his friends. Outside of that, the allure of Valentine's Day escaped me to the point that I usually referred to it as "VD" and had my "Go ahead—make my day" black heart shaped sticker to wear to honor the day. This year, however, things would be different. This year I would strike back at Cupid and have the best Valentine's Day of my life so far.

The beginning of the month brought the tail end of my relationship with Robert. The glow of the roses was still on my face but they, themselves, were hanging in my bedroom. Tim was still calling and now planning to come out right after celebrating VD.

Ken was still calling and IMing me when he could. His job had him on the road a lot and it wouldn't be for a while until he got a weekend off again for us to spend some time together. We started talking about the possibility of me going out with him next month during my spring break, but that was too far ahead to get too excited about. We never discussed making our relationship exclusive, so I had no guilt in talking with other guys. Rick was still sending messages from England. They were still the "I want to make you a mum" messages but they weren't as regular as they were when we started IMing. He was either out of his office for the afternoon or so busy that he couldn't really chat. I'd seen that one before as well. Work can be a convenient excuse for not returning messages right away. Eventually a message is never returned and the relationship fades away.

*****

It was the first week of that month when I met Connor. We started IMing on the website and quickly moved to Yahoo where he could send all kinds of noisy emoticons and use wild colors and fonts. He wasn't trying to sweep me off my cyber feet. He just liked the different colors, noises, and smiley faces. The good thing was that his job had about the same hours as mine so when the noises came through I was alone in the building with no one to ask questions. If he did get home and on the computer early, I could always plug in the headset so all the "NO WAYS!!!" were not heard by anyone else in the room.

He was definitely experienced. He knew I considered myself on the rebound from a near marriage. He didn't know my secret, but there was time for that later. I knew he was on the rebound. Most of her stuff was out of his apartment but every once in a while he found something else he put in a box in case she ever called again.

Finally there was the phone call on Thursday and we decided to meet for dinner that night. He gave me directions to a pub/brewery near his house. Looking at the MapQuest version of the city, I figured I had a little time to work before leaving. Fridays are usually pretty easy. A few of the kids don't show up and the ones that did didn't want to be grounded or in jail for the weekend so they usually behaved. The lessons were ready and everything was laid out so I could slide in right on time instead of an hour early like usual for me. Rick, from England, probably wouldn't even notice I wasn't on the computer that day.

Eventually I decided it was time to go. I got my map and directions and was off. Since I didn't have a cell phone, his phone number didn't really matter at the time. I thought I had figured in enough time to get there . . . then I stepped outside. The last weather report I heard that morning said maybe a light dusting of snow during the day. The windows in my classroom were above eye level even when I was standing so I didn't see how much snow was falling. It took ten minutes extra just to brush and scrape the windows of the Jeep so I could actually see out of them.

The directions he gave me took me down one of the busiest streets, during the end of a weather extended rush hour. I thought the street he said to take went all the way through town. The map I printed out didn't show enough to tell me that there was a park where the road should be at one point. Once I got off the main street I couldn't see the signs very well and couldn't get over when I needed to. The deejay kept reminding me how late I was and how the Department of Transportation was suggesting that people just stay home. That message came too late for me. I figured, as long as I was this far I might as well go to the pub to see what would happen.

I arrived an hour later than I said I would. As I walked through the parking lot I noticed a car with plates that read CONNOR. I was surprised. Later he told me he got hungry waiting for me and once he decided he was being stood up he ordered dinner. I got there just as it was being served. When I walked in the pub he looked up and missed his mouth with his beer. I've never gotten a reaction like that for a first impression.

He waved me over to the bar where he was sitting, gave me a long, clingy hug and whispered, "You were definitely worth the wait." He knew exactly what to say to ease my tension. Driving in the snow, being an hour late, to meet someone for the first time can be a little nerve wracking—especially all three together.

He told me he was scrawny, and he wasn't kidding. He looked like a blond—and younger—Leo from *That 70's Show.* His beard was more of a scraggily week's worth of growth, but I liked that look. He was also tall, just like he said he was. I've always had something for tall men. Maybe it was because my brothers and uncles are tall. In any case, he didn't disappoint me with his height. He didn't look all that bad all around in a hippy sort of way. That's probably why he would IM with all the colors and sounds, modern psychedelics.

"Sorry I'm late. I didn't know how bad it was snowing when I left." I had no idea what to say. This was totally new ground for me.

"Your picture doesn't do you justice."

"Thank you," was all I could get out of my mouth.

"I really didn't think you were going to show."

"And I thought you would be long gone by now."

"I waited for a while, then I decided as long as I was here I might as well have dinner. Any idea what you're hungry for?" The look in his eye indicated he may be looking for more than a straight answer.

What he had looked good, so I ordered the same. He thought it would be a good idea if we shared his while it was still warm and then share mine when it came out later. At least this time I knew we were both hungry so I didn't feel so bad about eating. There was only one fork to begin with so he insisted on feeding me until the bartender came with another.

While it was in my mouth he looked at me and said, "Lucky fork."

Later I realized he wasn't all talk, but at the time the conversation reminded me of the college English articulation lessons where innuendos flew like paper wads when the substitute teacher turned their back that led to nothing but giggles.

The drive over, with stop and go traffic and three inches of snow, was worth it. I had never been on a date like this before. All right, so there wasn't much to compare it with but I was still really enjoying myself.

When my food arrived, Conner suddenly became left-handed. His right hand started on my knee, and then slowly—bite by bite—moved up my thigh. We talked about our jobs, the weather, where we came from. It was typical first date chit-chat. He moved his barstool over so he could keep his hand moving up my leg. It finally hit me—he was looking for something. This was uncharted ground for me. Even watching movies last weekend Ken's hands stayed above the equator. I really didn't know how to react, so I let him keep going. Most girls in this situation would say they were being young and stupid. Chronologically that wasn't true but the way I look at it, I was a teenager as far as romance was concerned.

Eventually both dinners were consumed. It was getting late for a week night but I wasn't really tired. He looked at me and swept the hair out of my eyes.

"So what do you want to do now?"

Later I came to recognize the look in his eyes but at this point I was too inexperienced to realize he already knew what he wanted.

"Got any ideas?" I hadn't done much in the area so I didn't know what kinds of things there were to do there, especially that late on a Thursday night.

"How about we go back to my place? I have some movies that I haven't seen before. We could watch one."

I was too inexperienced to know the truth. All the signals were there, I just didn't see them. My rule had been "I'll try anything once and if it's fun I'll try it again." This was one of the things I was naively willing to try.

We both drove so he went ahead of me. His car was just like my mother's with his name on the license plates so it was easy to follow. The snow had stopped and it wasn't that far to his place. He lived in an apartment complex but I was able to park next to him. He rushed over to open my door and help me out of my Jeep. He kept hold of my hand as best as he could while opening first the outer door, then his apartment door. This felt good. I could get used to this.

His apartment wasn't all that big. He helped me over to the couch and went to the DVD player to show me what movies he had. I picked the one I wanted to see, but looking back maybe I should have picked another one.

He sat next to me on his apartment size couch. Without excuse or a big yawn he put his arm around my shoulders as the movie started. I could feel his eyes on me as I pretended to watch the opening credits until he took my face in his free hand and turned it toward him. "I really got lucky tonight. Hopefully you will, too."

It was time to tell him my secret. Actually it may have been too late already. By now I was realizing what I had done in accepting his invitation. Of course he was surprised to hear I had never gone all the way before. I told him, with a few tears, about why I moved to this particular metro area and what happened in the months that followed. He said he had just left a long-term relationship as well. He couldn't believe that a man would invite me to live with him and then never touch me. That seemed to be all Conner wanted to do, touch me, any part of my body with any part of his.

Then for a while we didn't talk. His lips were too busy pushing against mine to allow any conversation. His tongue started to explore my teeth and eventually started wrestling with mine. I could tell he was a smoker, and waiting an hour for some chick he met on the Internet probably made him smoke more than usual that evening. It didn't really matter that much. Usually I react to tastes and smells more than other people but this time it was the touch that consumed my thoughts. I was absorbed by the feeling of his tongue running around mine, then mine chasing his until a giggle escaped from my throat. He moved his lips to my neck, but his tongue didn't stop. When it ran down from my ear to my collar bone, I couldn't help but moan.

"So, you like that?" Any tone above a whisper would have been too loud, which told me he had done this before.

"That feels really good."

"Let me make you feel even better. . ." he said, as his hand stopped over my breast. "How many shirts are you wearing?" I guess he was taken off guard by the way I always dress in layers to keep warm. My body is bigger than most, but my blood doesn't circulate right. I'm usually cold. Growing up near a place known for cross-country skiing and then moving to Alaska, I learned to dress in layers.

I had on my usual three shirts and sports bra, but even through all that I could feel his fingers trying to find the center of my breast. His tongue started to creep to my collar and I could feel my body falling to the side. It wasn't like I was trying to keep some kind of distance. It was more like I was melting with all the heat we were generating.

"How about we go to my bedroom so we'll have more room?" By this time I knew exactly what he had on his mind. I may be slow, but not stupid.

"No, I think we better stay out here." I had to start actually thinking and that wasn't so easy with his breathe cooling down my tongue-dampened neck.

"Then how about we move to the floor?" That I could handle. More accurately, that was what was going to happen in a few seconds anyway. He was pretty much sprawled out on top of me and my back was twisted. My legs were in the sitting position but my shoulders were pushed against the pillows he used as armrests for the couch. I don't think my body could have taken much more

41

on the couch so I slipped down to the floor—with him on top of me. Another giggle slipped out. I has seen this on daytime soaps, but never experienced it in real life.

He gave me a couple of seconds to arrange my legs, and then he separated them enough to sneak his wiry little body between them. By this time I could really feel what he had on his mind, and what head he was thinking with. I was beginning to think it was time to go.

"Are you sure you don't want to go to the bedroom?"

"Yes." If I had said any more he would probably sense my temptation.

"I'm not asking you to do anything you don't want to, but I would really like to see what you have under all those shirts."

"But then I'll get cold." If you haven't guessed, my mind was beginning to think again and my libido was cooling down. I have the habit of getting silly with words when I get nervous and don't know what to say. I had worked with kids enough to be able to act like one when the situation called for it. Now I needed to act like the naïve little girl I was in order to get out of this situation with what was left of my innocence intact. What was going on in the movie? Maybe we should be watching it like he said he wanted to.

"I'll be able to keep you warm. I've got plenty of covers on the bed."

"But then you won't be able to see anything anyway."

"I've got good night vision so I can see in the dark. And I have the feeling you would really like it if I let my hands look for my eyes."

"You're doing that already out here."

"But my bed would be more comfortable than the floor." He started to get up on his knees and reached out for my hand.

"We just met, and I don't think I should." That he understood, or maybe he had paused long enough to get the blood flowing to the head on his shoulders. In any case, he lowered himself back on top of me and started kissing me again.

I started wondering if he ever wrestled in high school. His hands were in places only wrestlers could touch each other in public and he was using his body—scrawny as it was compared to mine—to keep me on the floor. Then his hands moved up my chest, stopping for a good long grope of my breasts before shooting down my arms. He gently but forcefully held my wrists to his carpet. Something about that kind of excited me, so I let my guard down again. His lips were on mine, our tongues doing a dance first inside my mouth, then his. I was starting to get the hang of this kissing thing, I think. After a few more giggles from me, his mouth moved to the left, inching down my neck, then up to my ear.

When he got his mouth right by my ear he dropped the bomb.

"Maybe you should let me make love to you. Then when you go back to your boyfriend you'll have some idea what you can do to make him want you."

That cooled me down instantly. My mind started to run away with itself. I was never going back with the loser that I lived with last summer. What time was it? I have school in the morning. Did the snow start up again? The roads will still be bad enough that I'll have to drive really slowly. How far from home am I? Being new to the area I wasn't really sure how long it would take to get home under the best of road conditions. How late is it getting?

"Maybe it's time for me to go."

"The movie isn't over yet. You really should stay at least until you see the end." Not like I had seen the beginning or the middle of it either. "You are incredible, and I can't imagine someone could live with you for any amount of time without even a hint of wanting you." He was good, stroking my ego to go along with the stroking of my breasts. Then his hand moved down to brush against my fly. "You are really warm, and I bet pretty wet."

I couldn't disagree.

"Let me find out. We can go to my bedroom and I'll undress you."

My guess is he could feel my body tense up with the mere thought of someone seeing me naked even if he didn't know exactly why I tensed up.

"You don't have to do anything. I just want to see you naked and I'll take care of the rest myself. At least I can show you what a real man can do. Then maybe next time we can do it together."

Next time? Who said anything about next time? My first reaction was shock, and then my ego took over again. He likes me. Maybe he really likes me. My mind wasn't working enough to realize what he really liked—something I wouldn't do for him. For the moment I was enraptured by the thought that someone might actually want me for something more than just a friendship, something physical, something sexual even if not at all romantic.

He must have felt my body relax again and started stroking me and himself with one hand while the other hand held both of my wrists.

I was getting caught up in the feeling again. It felt so good to have someone touch me, especially in the places he was touching me. We continued wrestling there on the floor for a while before we realized the movie was over. The crash of static after the DVD player timed out shocked us both back to reality.

"We both have to work tomorrow and I have a drive ahead of me."

"You could stay here overnight. The offer of my bed is still open."

"And what would they say at work when I come in wearing the same clothes? Kids notice things like that." The boy who had a crush on me commented on my clothing often.

"They probably wouldn't say anything to your face, but when you leave the room I'm sure they would start talking." His smile said he understood and was willing to let me go.

He helped me up off the floor and walked me to the door. I had taken my shoes off so he offered me a chair to put them back on.

"What, you don't want me to put these on while sitting on your bed?" The playful side of me was coming out again.

"No, the bed is for taking clothes off, not putting them on." He was being playful as well, I think.

By that time both shoes and my jacket were securely on.

"Can I get one more kiss before you leave?"

I guess I could give him that. I didn't really have the choice, anyway. He quickly took it only to slowly let it go. He was significantly taller than me and after the wrestling we had done he couldn't bend his back for too long so eventually he had to straighten up.

"I really had fun tonight, and maybe next time we can actually watch a movie."

"Maybe."

He opened the door for me and followed me down the hall.

"I'll try to get online right after work tomorrow, hopefully you'll still be at your computer." I had heard about the "I'll call you," line but now I was actually hearing it for myself. Another first for me, but unfortunately I would hear that line many times again.

The snow had stopped but the air hadn't warmed up. The cold air quickly brought me back to reality, and trying to remember how he said to get back to the interstate. At least this time he didn't have me driving through town. It didn't take me all that long to get home. No one was on the roads this time, except for a few snow plows that were cleaning up the sides of the road and other assorted leftovers of the storm. Only a few hours to sleep before work. After an evening like that who could sleep anyway. This was a story I would have to tell my journal.

*****

Of course Tim didn't believe me the next morning when I said nothing really happened. He said he could hear the smile on my face over the phone. The smile in my voice was from a night that was fun, and way out of my ordinary. Tim was a typical male and obviously thought I took up this "other guy" on the offer of his bed. Since I got to bed late and to work late there wasn't really a lot of time to talk to Tim in the morning, and during the day we could never talk. That night I didn't stay long at work. I was tired and there was no one interesting online the one time I looked. I needed a night off anyway.

I ended up taking the whole weekend off from dating. Since I was still addicted to the Internet I went in to check my e-mails and see if there was anyone interesting online. There were just the usual people waiting in a few of the chat rooms. Tim was still asking about what happened Thursday night. I was just mysterious enough to keep him guessing without out-and-out lying. I don't like to think about my ex but one of his rules of the truth was "two out of three ain't bad." Then he would say that you have to tell the truth and nothing but the truth, but the whole truth was optional. There were even cases—usually dealing with kids—where they really can't handle the whole truth so it worked. Tim seemed to enjoy filling in the gaps with his imagination. It was probably a better fantasy than his reality so he was living vicariously through what he thought was my social life.

There was a short chat with Connor. My guess is that he didn't get what he wanted so he wouldn't be calling or IMing much anymore, if at all. In the short time we chatted he asked a couple of times if I was ready to become a woman. I thought I already was. Maybe not in every sense of the word, but I definitely passed the little girl stage long ago. Life in the big city hadn't made me into a person who would jump into bed with anyone anytime. I may be a cyber slut, but when it comes to reality I'm a good girl—I am. Really, I am.

The next week was quiet as well. Daily chats with Rick were getting shorter and shorter. He kept up the line about coming to see me during spring break, but messages were getting fewer and further between. Messages from Robert were less than daily, trailing off to never again.

Tim asked for my address to send a Valentine's Day card. After the near miss with Robert, I wasn't about to give out my real address. It would be different with Tim because I had talked to him so much, but I still wasn't ready to tell him where I really lived. Tim got my work address and when the card got there I had some more explaining to do. The kids already pegged me as a player, a reputation I really wasn't used to. All the other staff members were in long term relationships, which seemed boring to the kids who regularly hook up and break up on a weekly basis. Of all the staff, my social life seemed to be the most interesting to the students. It was one of their favorite topics of conversation when there was time to chat. There were already a lot of reasons for the students not to trust me. By making myself like them in at least one way I could make a connection with them that might help me actually teach them something.

*****

The week of Valentine's Day finally arrived. Multiple daily phone calls from one guy, the smell of flowers lingering in my classroom from another guy, and the promise of a New Year's Eve wedding leading directly to a fall baby from another guy. Did I mention I wasn't a big fan of VD?

With Valentine's Day coming up I didn't know what to give my co-workers. The old roses from Robert were hanging upside-down in my bedroom to dry. A friend of mine, who used to be a florist, said if you dry them that way you can use them for dried flower arrangements. My decision was to put a few in a vase for each of them to put on their desk. I taught at a small school and my flowers were a major conversation piece. This way each of them could share my flowers for a while.

The staff thought the dried flowers were neat. They all knew where I got them from and that my social life was getting, shall we say, active. All of them were much more experienced than me. They all had advice. Most of it was this: "be careful." Well, I had been careful all my life. I was looking for some danger. I was ready to live on the edge with my social life. There was one thing I had to take care of yet, and I did that with my Valentine's gift to myself. Not exactly careful, but not as over the edge as I was earlier with this situation.

My gift to myself was a message to my ex. He had sent me an e-mail saying he was ready to talk to me, as long as we avoided certain topics of his choosing. He didn't think we ended the relationship that badly so he thought we could really be friends. This is after I moved 3,000 miles to be with him only to get the "let's be friends" speech after about three months.

I waited until late on the 14th to send a message back. Timing is everything, and I needed time to think of exactly what I wanted to say and exactly how I wanted to say it. When we were together we usually understood what the other person was thinking even before they said it. Since he was probably still on my wavelength, I had to say things carefully.

My reply was civil on the surface, but full of innuendo. I not only pointed out his demon (again) but also added another characteristic, one I never mentioned before because I didn't realize it until after I moved out. That one was probably worse in his mind than the original demon. I also included several topics that I wouldn't talk about. Knowing him, he just wanted to know how I was doing. He was a news junkie and had to have as much information as possible. All the things he wanted to know about me I had on the list of things I wouldn't talk about. Between the things I wouldn't talk about and things he didn't want to talk about, there was nothing for either of us to say. I ended it by once again pointing out his demons in a civil but sarcastic way.

After I sent the message, I called Conner again. I thought would be nice to have a real date for Valentine's Day once in my life. But he was on his way out to meet someone. My guess was it was his ex-girlfriend and he was looking to get lucky that night, unlike the night I came over to watch a movie. Tim was busy with a Valentine's adventure of his own. So there was no one for me to talk to. But the night wasn't over yet.

Alone with my thoughts, I was feeling a little nervous about how my e-mail to my ex would be received. Once before he got so angry that he threatened a restraining order against me. He gave some lame reason that could have been spun to make me sound a little like a stalker, maybe, if it were added to other things that I thought of doing but never did. The real reason for the threat was that he didn't want me to talk to his family, and possibly mention his demon to them. He spent a lot of time and energy to hide it, so to have some angry "friend" bring it out in the open to his family would be disastrous for his reputation.

There was a lot of satisfaction that I sent a message I knew he would understand but on the surface looked harmless. Knowing him a response wouldn't take very long. I wasn't disappointed the next morning.

He must have understood the various layers of meaning. He shot back three quick and cruel messages that night, according to the time the messages were put in my in-box. He was so mad he couldn't think or type well. If you put the three messages together he ended up calling me a fat, drunken heathen. All I could do was laugh!

Later in the morning there was a fourth message. This one was a little more cohesive. He typed it out at work where he had to be composed. There were still some typos but more complete sentences and it made more sense than the ones from the previous night. Just the fact that he said everything in one message told me he was thinking things through a little better. That one proved he understood what I was implying. This time he said the restraining order was written out and a judge who was the boss of a friend of his would sign it. He still couldn't really do anything on his own, but that was only a tiny part of his demon. This time he didn't give any real evidence for needing one, other than the unspoken fact that I knew his secret and he didn't want me to tell anyone who knew him. The ironic thing was that the only threats made in the past couple weeks were made by him. If he sent *all* the recent correspondence to his attorney friend, as he claimed, the restraining order would be against him, not me. I knew he was bluffing, or so angry that he wasn't able to use logic. He was grasping at straws because I won.

This had turned out to be the best Valentine's Day I had ever experienced. There was still no date for the day itself, but I won against the idiot. He was scared now, maybe as much as I was hurt when he gave me the speech. I may not have hurt him, but he was feeling pain just like I did. Really, I'm not usually a vindictive person. In this case, however, I wanted him to know how much he really hurt me. Love was a game to him and I wanted him to realize that game wasn't for me. Based on his response then (and no more responses for two months) he felt a little pain and knew I was serious about the relationship when we were in it. Maybe he realized that love wasn't a game, or if it was he was the big loser. In any case, I had finally won.

Me, the good girl, had won at love.

I had finally broken a heart, making this my best VD ever. It may have taken a total of three years from start to finish, but I finished it. It may have hurt me in ways I thought I could never hurt, but at that moment I felt good. It may have taken me away from everything I knew and loved into a cruel and lonely city, but I survived it, and gave some back.

Maybe I wasn't the shy, quiet girl who was embarrassed to see a man in a towel anymore. I had changed. Now I was a heart breaker making a new reputation for myself in a new place with a new attitude. I wasn't back home with people gossiping about my love life. And now, since the last real tie to my good girl past was broken, I was ready to start my life as a different person. My family would never know.

I had been a good girl for so long, I was ready to see what it was like to be bad. If the date with Connor was any indication, I was sure there would be men willing to help me walk on the wild side. I was known to say that I was willing to try anything once, and if it's fun I might try it again. I tried the date with Connor and it was fun, fun enough to try it with someone else if the opportunity arose. Actually, fun enough to go looking for someone else to have fun with. It took me a while to realize that my definition of bad girl was only about a step away from what most men on the dating websites would call a prude. But it was wild enough for me.

*****

That was Wednesday, and by the weekend I was ready to go on the prowl again.

Tim didn't appreciate my Valentine victory. Even he didn't understand how different I was becoming, mainly because he didn't understand how different – how innocent – I was to begin with. His Valentine's was a romp in a van he borrowed for a night, typical for him. I didn't want to listen to his pity party. After all, I got what I wanted to celebrate the holiday.

Online there were lots of guys disappointed with how the holiday went. One in particular was Adam. We started chatting the usual way. When he found out I was a teacher and sitting in my classroom, he asked if I would put certain school supplies in certain parts of my body. There was no webcam involved so I could indulge his fantasies through the chat bar. The memory of articulation lessons from college gave him the impression I had done just about anything he asked me to. I let him think I was enjoying everything, and he gave me the impression he was enjoying things, too. I learned that there are some things men want to see women do but refuse to do themselves or have done to themselves. It's not exactly fair, but reality isn't always fair.

That first weekend with Adam, it was all about cyber sex. Basically, talking dirty and being intimate with words. It took a little while but he let me know about his past. In the next few weeks I learned that five years previous he had been cheated on by the love of his life. Since then he had been involved with a series of one night stands. His real hope was that his ex would want him back. She had moved on with her life, but he was stuck in his past with her. I thought I was bad about losing the idiot, but that had only been four months ago—and I was now pretty much over it. He was feeling the same hurt for five years. We chatted off and on for about three months. Never again was it purely sexual like that first weekend.

One of the twelve steps is to help others who are where you were. I was like his sponsor. By the time our chats ended he was going out and at least talking to other women. He talked about a few dates that didn't involve sex. That's what he really needed. He lost his friend when she jumped in bed with someone else. Now he needed to find another woman who he could see as a friend and not just another sex partner. For a while that was me, but I knew that couldn't last. If my other relationship taught me anything it was that long distance love affairs are likely to end in pain. He needed to find a woman he could physically be with without having a purely physical relationship with him. My training as a counselor was paying off.

As with most of the men I met during that time I never really knew how things turned out for him. We chatted pretty much every weekend until the summer. The really weird times were when I was chatting online with him and on the phone with Tim. Two guys I would never really meet talking like we were old friends. I was always better at being a boy's friend than being someone's girlfriend.

Eventually came the summer and my trip. I was a week away from that IM program. During that time we lost track of each other. This time it was my turn to take a vacation and never send a message back. Yes, I had become a repeat heart breaker.

*****

Remember that seed planted last month? It was watered, and almost ready to sprout.

Lawrence sent me messages occasionally, some on the computer and some on the phone. He was busy finishing up a job out of town most of the time. He was back long enough to do some laundry and catch up on some sleep, but then it was back to the jobsite. I thought nothing serious would come of it. I should have stuck with that, but hope springs eternal. At this point we were still doing a cyber dance around the subject of sex without really talking about it. There were lots of hints and innuendos on both sides with no action on either. The seed needed a little more time to germinate. Maybe if it had taken longer the plant would have lasted longer. Maybe it was a hint of what was to come.

*****

One more weekend before February was over. Thursday night I got a call from Connor again. "Sorry I blew you off on Valentine's Day. My girlfriend called me and we went out. That's probably the last time I'll see her. I should have gone out with you. How 'bout I make it up to you by making dinner for you tomorrow night?"

It was hard to concentrate at work that next day. Luckily it was Friday, a good excuse for very little to get done. As I finished up my last tasks, Connor was online again. I got directions straight to his apartment this time—using the interstate rather than the surface streets that messed me up last time. Real directions, no snow, maybe I could make it at the time promised.

I started questioning if I should really go through with it. Last time he just wanted to get me into his bed, and then he blew me off for what he thought would be a sure lay, now he asks me to his place—no public meeting for me to wiggle my way out of it before-hand. I had on several layers of clothing, as usual. Last time he had asked, begged, pressured me, but he didn't force me to do anything I didn't want to do. I was praying this time would be the same.

A quick stop at a liquor store to get the beer he drank and I was on the interstate in no time. Friday rush hour starts early and usually gets done early. Traffic wasn't bad this time so I got there about when I said I would. My nerves were at the surface, but I wasn't going to drop the bag with the glass beer bottles in it. How do you knock on the door in a situation like this? Too hard and you seem too eager, too soft and if he's in the back getting ready I'm left standing in the hallway looking lonely. Just knock, silly!

When he answered the door he didn't have a shirt on and his hair was wet. "I was going to be showered and ready but I had some, uh, technical problems."

I was a little confused and he picked up on it as he took my free hand and ushered me into his apartment. "The pan I used for dinner was supposed to be oven safe. I was in the bathroom, getting ready for my shower and I heard something breaking out here. The cat was with me in the bathroom, so I had no idea what it was. I came out here but couldn't find anything out of place. As long as I was out here I thought I should check dinner. The glass baking pan broke in the oven so I had to clean it up and get something else out for dinner."

"It's times like this that I wish I had a cell phone. I could have picked something up for dinner along with this," as I showed him the beer.

"That's more than you needed to do, but now you have to join me in one. You won't be driving for a while, so it won't hurt." I knew he was hoping to get me to stay the night. One beer this early in the evening would be all right. I had never had the fancy beer before so I was willing to partake. "Let me go and get a little more presentable and I'll join you." He raced to the back and came out with a t-shirt on while I took my shoes and my flannel shirt off. Now I was down to two layers of shirts and a sports bra.

The place was pretty warm. Being the shy, innocent girl I was, my first thought was that the oven had been on a while and he just got out of the shower. I've been known to turn the heat up while I'm in the shower to keep me warm, why wouldn't he do the same? Thinking a little more, I realized his plan was to make it so warm I would have to take my clothes off to be comfortable. So far only my shoes and flannel were off, and that's all that would come off as far as I was concerned.

"Dinner's going to be a little late, and I hope it's done. Luckily I defrosted a whole package of meat, but only used half the first time." He was in the kitchen, stirring something. "I could put the movie in if you want something to keep you entertained while I finish dinner." He walked over to the DVD player and put in the movie we didn't see last time.

He came over to where I was sitting on the couch. "We've got a little time before it's done, got any ideas what we could do to kill time?" By the end of the question he was close enough for me to feel his breath on my neck, and his lips weren't far behind. He started off right where he left off last time.

I know he just took a shower, but the smell something like silage came along with him. It wasn't his shirt, more like his hair. Come to think of it, he was quiet in the corner for a minute or two, then needed a cigarette while in the kitchen. So maybe the smell was a little sweeter than silage. Living on a farm for a while I know what the stuff they feed cows smells like. Being such a good girl for so long I didn't know what the stuff humans smoke smells like. I bet if I looked into his eyes they would be all bloodshot, but I didn't want to open my eyes. I just wanted to feel his kisses on my neck.

"Want something to help you relax?" he whispered into my ear before running his tongue around the outside of it. The thought of it made me tense up. "Or is that something else you've never done before?" It was hard to look him in the eye and talk about this.

"Would it surprise you if I tell you I've never smoked anything but a fish—and even that wasn't really me, but a grill with wood chips?" The line slipped easily off my tongue. The kids I work with are curious and not afraid to ask questions about such things. An answer like that usually made them laugh and change the subject, maybe even back to schoolwork.

"You have been a good girl too long. Maybe it's time for you to be bad. I have plenty if you want to try some tonight." I usually say I'll try anything once, but I just wasn't ready to try that. There was enough good girl left in me to know I would feel guilty if I partook in something like that. And besides, I would probably end up coughing up everything instead of inhaling. I would like be thought of as overly innocent rather than a coughing fool.

"I'll stick with the stuff in the oven tonight. I still have to drive home you know."

"Well, you don't really have to drive home tonight if you don't want to. We don't have to work tomorrow, so we could stay up late and do whatever comes up tonight after the movie is over. And then you could go home in the morning if you still want to go." His hands were back on my chest, but still over layers of clothing.

Oh, yea, there was a movie on. The previews and opening credits were over already but I don't think we really missed much. This was a movie I had never seen before. It was some kind of science fiction type thing from the 1970's—judging from the hairstyles and clothing. Or maybe it was just made to look that way. I think it was a movie he had on hand for just such an occasion. Something you could only laugh at for a bit, before starting to look for something else to do while it finished up.

"That 'stuff in the oven' as you put it should be done by now. I'll get it for you."

"Sure you don't want any of my help?" He was banging things around in the kitchen, maybe his mind wasn't exactly on what he was doing. The stove and sink were on the other side of a small breakfast bar separating it from the living space. Every time I looked over there for no reason he was looking at me. Every time I looked because of a noise he was turning his attention to something on the stove or counter and hunching his shoulders like he was fumbling something with the hands I couldn't see.

"No, you're the guest. I'll take care of everything." By this time I was thinking of what else he wanted to take care of, and how far he was willing to go to take care of it. Maybe I did bring the beer, but he insisted I drink one knowing I have to drive to go home, and then he offers me something smokable before inviting me to stay the night. Even a good little country girl like myself knew what he had on his mind. He was male, do I really need more clues to point to the fact that he didn't want me to leave until he got some satisfaction?

"Wasn't sure what you wanted, hope you like it." He handed me one plate and kept the other for himself. Then he sat back down on the couch. The meal was good, and I was trying to eat slowly to stall for time. He probably didn't even taste any of it, he ate his so fast. He put his plate on the floor and his hand on my leg. My hands were holding the plate so I couldn't do anything about what he was trying to do, and I was willing to let him do a little more than last time. I don't think Connor and I had the same idea about dessert.

His cat must have smelled what we were eating. Since I still had some on my plate the cat was trying to get friendly with me. I think Conner was getting a bit jealous because I was petting the cat and not him. He put his plate in the kitchen and grabbed the cat, taking it to his bedroom. "I don't want the cat to bother you while you finish up." Actually, I think he knew I was playing with the cat to take longer to finish dinner. I was getting nervous as he sat next to me again. He started the movie again, but he wasn't watching it. I finally finished up my dinner and he took my plate.

When he came back from the kitchen he sat right next to me on the couch. There was no question what he wanted. "I'm really sorry about what I did last week. I should have gone out with you, but I already promised someone else the evening. It didn't work out the way I planned." An evening with me wouldn't have worked out the way he wanted it to either, but right now he wasn't thinking about that. "So what did you end up doing for Valentine's Day?"

"I had a quiet evening at home."

"No date or anything?"

"No date, but it wasn't all bad."

I didn't think he would understand my little victory, or even care about it right now. One hand was sliding down my back while the other lingered in the middle of my front. His tongue started caressing my neck again. I was getting lost in the moment, tipping my head to give him more area to work with. I was feeling a bit selfish, but he didn't seem to mind pleasing me, at least for the moment. My guess was that he wanted to pleasure me even more with something that would please him as well. That wasn't going to happen tonight.

He took the hand that was at my back and turned my face towards his. His lips pressed against mine and his tongue was checking out my dental work. Without a word his hand went down to my hips, pulling them towards him. "Let's go back to the floor again." He was going a little faster tonight.

He must have noticed I was tensing up. "Are you sure you don't want something to help you relax?"

"What you are doing is helping me relax. Right now I don't think I could walk to the bedroom if I tried." Maybe that was the wrong thing to say.

"So, you've thought about my bedroom? Are you ready to go there?"

"No, I just said I'm so relaxed now I can hardly move."

He helped me to the floor again. This time a little more gracefully than the tumble off the couch the last time. One hand was going through my hair and the other was taking off my glasses. "You're not going to need these."

We started tongue wrestling again. This part made me feel good, maybe too good. I was beginning to like it. For a couple seconds I wondered what his bedroom looked like. He must have sensed my inhibitions melting away. He took my hand and started to pull me up.

"No, I'm not ready yet."

"Really, you don't have to do anything. Just lay there and look pretty, I can't imagine you looking any other way." His tongue was back on my neck and his hands back on my chest. "I can slowly take all your clothes off, rip mine off, and then you can watch me. . ."

Was he really saying what I think he was saying? Would a man really be able to do something like that while looking at my naked body? Was that movie still playing?

"Maybe I should be going."

"But you haven't let me really do anything."

"You've done more than you know."

"You're still wearing a shirt—I didn't do anything."

"Well, if you want to get technical, you have more on now than when I first came over tonight."

He laughed. "You got me on that one."

I was starting to sit up. "I really better go now before things go too far." They probably had already, but I wasn't going to let things get out of control.

"Neither of us has to work in the morning. You could stay here, even if we don't do anything."

"No, I better get going. Just for the record, I did take my shoes *and* my flannel shirt off."

"I really wish you would take more off. I wouldn't make you do anything you don't want to. I just want to see your beautiful body."

I'll give him points for that line. I never thought of my body as beautiful. Yes, I better get out of there while I could still think straight.

"One last kiss?" He probably knew it would be since I was so set on not letting him get what he wanted. That's exactly what we had—one last kiss.

The night air wasn't as cold as last time, but his apartment was warmer so there was still some shock when I walked out the door of his complex. While the Jeep warmed up a bit, I had time to cool down before heading back to my house.

Connor sent a couple more messages in the weeks to come. Mostly they were asking me if I was ready to let him have his way. Since the answer was always no, he never asked me to come over again. He should have taught me that some guys only want one thing, but sometimes I'm a slow learner.

One thing I did learn from Conner was how to kiss. Some girls practice with a pillow. I heard of one boy who practiced with a balloon. I got to practice with a real, honest to goodness man. And it wouldn't be long before another man noticed my new skills.

*****

Saturday I went back to the school to check my messages and do some of the things I didn't do on Friday because I was so distracted. As usual, Tim didn't believe I was still a good girl. He was using his imagination as he told me about his weekend frolic. I just smiled and remembered my weekend wrestling match. I was ready to play along. I told him that one of us had our shirt off during the date. He assumed it was me and I let him think that. He was never coming out here, so why not give him something to think about?

His new plan was to come out around Easter. He asked me to find out how much a bus ticket would cost. Well, he had free time on the computer, maybe he should do that. What I really think he wanted was for me to offer to pay for his ticket, but that wasn't going to happen. I could scope out some places for him to live if he would actually come out here. At one point he suggested living with me until he found a place. That wouldn't happen and not just because he wasn't going to leave his home. But of course he kept saying he was coming out right after Easter. It was already Ash Wednesday so Easter wasn't all that far away. And the calendar turned to the month of March.

Chapter 4 — Good girl gone bad

I was beginning to think of my social life weekend to weekend. The first weekend in March, Ken was home. He called and texted his way back to town, sounding excited to meet me again. This time asked me over to his place with no hesitation. We had been talking about what we could do on a real date. Neither of us had anything better to do, so I went over to his place before noon. This way we had a chance to talk face to face instead of chatting online or texting before deciding what else to do.

When I got there he was doing something online. He stopped long enough to get the door and then went back to it, explaining as he was surfing. "You said you liked football, what about arena style?"

"I've never been to a game, but it could be fun." That would be something new, going out for a date. I've been to dinner many times, but never to an actual event. And I've never been to any type of sporting event unless you count the high school games my brothers and sisters were in.

But watching the event on TV, that was typical for my family, though usually we were participating in other activities at the same time. I remember one Super Bowl in particular where my mom wanted to get rid of a chair and offered a reward to anyone who could break it so she would have to get it out of the house. That Sunday we broke two light covers in the living room and various parts of a couple of bodies, but the chair remained solid. That was more my family's style of entertainment.

"I'm checking to see if there's a game in town today."

I knew he was driving a lot this week, and sitting by the computer must have been hard on his back. I walked up behind him and started massaging his shoulders.

"If you're going to keep that up I won't want to go out today." His muscles were pretty tight. Usually when I gave someone a back rub I was too rough to do much good. He seemed to like what I was doing. At first he tensed up but as my fingers worked over his muscles he started to relax. Maybe I wasn't so bad at this after all. In the computer I could see his reflection. His eyes were closed and he was definitely enjoying my attempt at massage therapy.

For a while his hands were still on the keyboard. The site for the local arena team was on the screen with a calendar across the top. They were out of town this weekend. "Guess we'll have to find something else to do today. I've got some ideas, but I'm not sure if you're up to it." The look on his face told me it was something he was thinking about for a while. "Let's see what movies are on today." The TV is usually a good, safe stand-by for entertainment.

There were a couple of movies we could watch. Then he remembered all the videos he bought but never had time to see. He put one in the DVD player and let the credits roll. He was ordering pizza online and I didn't know how to run a DVD player so the opening credits were background noise. Soon he realized we weren't quite ready to watch the movie so he hit pause and went back to the computer.

I was still massaging his back. By this time it wasn't just his neck and shoulders. I was sitting on the arm of the love seat. It was a bit of a stretch to reach him from there, but I was doing my best with my shorter than average arms. Over the time I was there he had moved back from the computer a little, especially when I started rubbing his back.

While all this was going on, we were doing a little more getting to know each other chatting. He had been married before. It lasted three years and then his life on the road got in the way. They didn't have any kids. He wanted some, once he found a job where he could be home more. It sounded like his childhood wasn't all that good and he didn't want to bring a child into the world until he knew he could be home more to help raise his own.

Speaking of his work, there was a woman at work he had dated off and on. He thought they were just too different, but she thought he was the one for her. She knew he was now seeing someone so she let up on him for a while. I shouldn't be worried. According to him, she wasn't a stalker or anything like that. And she had no idea what my name was or where I lived anyway. He had to see her every time he went into the office and didn't like how she made him feel. When she knew he would be home a couple of days she would make sure to mention that she didn't have any plans, stuff like that.

On the computer, he was switching back and forth on several browsers, checking for something fun to do besides watch movies and keeping an eye on the progress of our pizza. He was trying not to let me see the background on his desktop. I'm guessing he changed it often, and may have gotten the picture from a soft-core porn site. He knew I could see over his shoulders. Glimpses of a couple strips of clothing on some skinny blond occasionally flashed when he switched between screens. If I remembered right, that matched the calendar in the bathroom last time I was here. It made me a little nervous, but last time he was a gentleman and only went as far as I would let him. My biggest concern is that I would never measure up to the woman on his screen. He didn't seem to mind. Maybe it was one of those "love the one you're with" kinds of things. I was getting too thinky again until the doorbell interrupted my thoughts.

He must have been hungry, probably didn't have breakfast. This time we finished the whole pizza and a six-pack. I guess he didn't want me to leave any time soon. He didn't log off the computer before we ate so he had to take care of it after. I knew it wouldn't take long, but I started rubbing his shoulders again.

"That feels good, but I think it's time I return the favor." He turned his head to look at me with a grin I had seen a couple weeks before. One last button and the computer was put to sleep for the moment. He stood up, pushed the chair under the computer table, and stood right in front of me. I was still sitting on the arm of his love seat. He flipped around me to kneel on the love seat and put his hands on my shoulders.

"You don't have to do that." It felt good, but really it was his shoulders that needed some relaxation.

"I'm not just returning the favor." I could feel his breath on my ear. He *really* didn't have to do that. "You rubbed my back, but how about I rub your front?" His voice was barely above a whisper. He didn't really give me a chance to answer. His hands were moving from my shoulders to my chest before I could say anything. It caught me off guard. He pulled me toward him. We both tumbled onto the love seat. I was giggling and I could feel the smile on his face. My feet were up in the air and my back was on the seat cushion. "From what I remember you probably haven't been on a couch with your feet up in the air before."

"No, I haven't."

"I shouldn't make fun of you. It can't be comfortable to sit like that." In a way I was sitting, with my back on the seat the loveseat, my thighs going up the armrest and my knees on the top of the armrest with my feet hanging over the side. He helped me to my feet. "Here, sit down." He sat next to me with his arm around me, one of them anyway. "I'm still trying to figure out why someone like you has never been with a man before."

"I've been with a man, just not in a sexual kind of way." At least not to the fullest extent, and I wasn't going to share with him exactly how far I had gone. To me sex included taking clothing off and I hadn't done *that* with a man. The smile on my face went along with my words to show I was in a playful mood.

"You know what I mean."

"Yeah, I know what you mean." I went on to explain more of what happened between my time in Alaska and now. Then I went back a little more to explain what happened before and while I was in Alaska. It was unbelievable to him. I was wondering what he thought about me. He probably figured I was a stuck up who didn't want to try anything or something like that. He must have thought I'm some prude stuck back in the days when a couple's first kiss was in front of God and witnesses after he lifted her white veil at the altar.

He said he grew up on the streets. I'm sure he had a lot more experience by the time he was 20 than I have now at age 36. Then I realized I should stop thinking about what he thought of me and concentrate on the conversation at hand.

My thoughts were distracting me and when I came back into the present his hand was under my shirts—all three of them. Not quite high enough to realize I had on a sports bra, but still under my shirts. His hand was warm, which is probably how he got away with putting it under my shirts while I wasn't really paying attention. It felt natural and good. His warm hands were caressing the soft, sensitive skin of my torso. For some reason I wasn't afraid of what might happen next. Last time he stopped the second I asked him to. I'm sure he would this time as well.

"Is this too fast?"

"Not really."

"Just making sure. Is it all right if I go a little further?"

"A little."

"I'll go slow and try to be gentle." His voice was playfully sweet.

"You are being very gentle, and it feels good."

"Are you warm enough?"

"Yeah, why do you ask?"

"Well, you're wearing three shirts, and I was wondering if you would be willing to take some of them off."

"Just some of them?" Now I was trying to be playfully sweet.

"As many as you are comfortable taking off."

"Are you willing to help me?"

"If you want me to, I think I remember how to." His hands were already lifting my three shirts all at once.

"That was fast, but I'm not complaining."

"I'm not complaining either. You are beautiful." His hands were starting to feel my sports bra. My mind works in weird ways. All I could think of was that he was boldly going where no man had gone before. No, I'm not a Trekkie, really, I'm not. I didn't want to say anything like that. He already probably thought I was weird. Why should I open my mouth and prove it?

His hands were gentle, caressing my breasts now with just one layer of clothing covering them. One hand went around to my back and pulled me closer to him. His tongue started to caress my lips. I was getting lost in the moment. At that point I don't think I could have told you my name and I didn't really care what he did next. When I came back to my senses, what little I had left, I was laying on his couch totally topless. This was definitely uncharted territory for me, but he seemed to have experience at this.

He was kneeling next to the couch. His tongue was moving down my body from my lips. He moved my hand to feel how I was affecting him. That was even more new territory for me. It was obvious I didn't know what to do. I could feel that he was excited, but had no idea how to deal with it.

"I want to go down on you so bad right now."

I had no idea what he meant by that, but I'm sure it was something sexual. I didn't ask him to clarify, but I didn't know how to respond to it either. He must have gotten a sense of how little experience I had.

"How does this feel?" His tongue was on my breast when he wasn't talking.

"It feels good." Honestly, it felt so good I could hardly speak.

"Do you want me to keep going?"

A moan slipped out, but I couldn't come up with an actual word. He took that as an indication he should keep going. I was enjoying the experience, maybe a little too much. Is this really what a good girl does? For the first time in my life I was topless with a man. Last time he tried to take my pants off. This time he took my shirts off. It felt so good, but this was as far as it could go. His hand went down to the waist of my pants again. I took it in my hand and without a word he stopped kissing me.

"Is this really the first time you've gone this far?"

I think he was afraid of the truth. The look on his face said I was disappointing him, but his lips never said those words—on that date.

"I'll be a good boy. Maybe I should start that movie."

The rest of the date was pretty much like the first time I came over there, with my shirts staying in a pile on the floor. We sat together on the couch. He explored my body with his hands and tongue when the movie got boring. The thought that I was selfishly enjoying what he was doing kept going through my mind. Then I realized he was fully dressed. If he really thought I was being selfish some of his clothes would probably be off as well, hoping I might get the hint. My hand was guided to the center of his shorts once, but now there was no sign of excitement from where I was sitting.

We talked about our work and other things. I told him how I used to travel around the country by bus on various church trips. He suggested I come with him sometime on one of his work trips. The idea sounded good to me. I hadn't been on a road trip for a while. The last week of this month was our spring break. Rick said a while ago that he wouldn't be coming over from England to see me then, so I had no plans for the week. He didn't know where he would be going until the week before or so, but he was sure he would be going somewhere at some point in the week and would like company.

It was an uneventful walk to the Jeep. Again he was still in shorts and a t-shirt but this time it wasn't quite so cold outside. I was getting used to ending dates with a kiss, as used to it as you can get after only a few actual dates. Ken was still flabbergasted that I had so little experience. "A beautiful woman like you, I'm sure you've been out more than just a few times." One would think so, but sadly that was not the case. One more kiss good-bye and I was off again.

*****

The next week I was trying to sort out what had happened at Ken's apartment. The kids would wonder what took me so long to be topless with a man if I would ever share that story with any of them. Some members of my family would scold me for doing that if they ever found out what I did, or allowed someone else to do to me, on the third real date. Neither one would know about it in any case.

There was another guy on the website who had sent me some messages. The last time I was in this situation it turned out all right. I didn't think there was a real relationship with Ken, so why not spark up a conversation with someone else? Don was online while at work. He worked as a dispatcher for a towing company. Occasionally there would be a message that took a while to respond to, but then he would tell me what the phone call was about so I didn't get the idea he was ignoring me. Usually there was a funny story he shared when he could turn his attention back to me.

We talked about our adventures with cyber dating. There was one question I was dying to ask, but I wasn't sure how he would take it. Our chat was getting graphic. Not wild, hot cyber sex like with Adam that first weekend, but still not something I would talk about to my family and if my students were here, I would be blushing big time. He knew I had met in person a couple of the guys I met online, and he had a good general idea of what we did. I told him of my lack of real sexual experience and mentioned there was something I was wondering about. He seemed up front about things, so maybe I could ask him.

Don: Really, you can ask me anything and I'll try to answer it.

Randi: You're going to think I'm pretty weird that I don't know this.

Don: Actually, I think I'm very lucky to meet a woman without a lot of relationship baggage.

Randi: Oh, I have baggage, just not as much as most people my age.

Don: So go ahead and ask. Don't worry, I'll be gentle ☺

Randi: I was with a guy and he said something. I think I know what he meant, but I'm not sure.

Don: Just type it already.

Randi: All right, the guy said he wanted to "go down on me" and I'm not sure what he meant by that.

Don: That has to do with putting a tongue an on intimate part of the body. You really haven't had that much experience, have you?

Randi: That's what I thought, but I wasn't sure. You still want to chat with me?

Don: Well, what I would really like to do is talk to you over the phone. Any chance I could get your phone number?

I gave him my number, and explained it was my work number, directly to my classroom. He called and we got to know each other a little better over the phone. He worked the late shift most nights so he was sleeping when I was working and working when I had free time. We could talk over the phone, but with lots of interruptions when his job got busy. He said he wanted to meet me in person. Part of it, by his own admission, was out of curiosity.

On Fridays he worked an earlier shift, one that ended at 7 p.m. We chatted online until about 6:30, and then he asked if I would mind meeting him that evening since he could sleep in the next morning and he was dying to see if I was for real. Later I found out that guys usually don't believe me, so they ask to meet at a coffee shop or something like that. If they don't see anyone that matches my picture on the website they are only out a little time and an overpriced coffee. Don had a different idea. He wanted to meet me at work. I could stick around for a little while longer. We wouldn't have to be there all that long anyway. The school was on his way home from work, sort of, so he would be there as soon as he could. He logged off at about 6:45. At 7:08 he called and said he was outside the building.

I jumped up on a chair near the window and saw his truck. Then I had to run back to the phone to tell him to come to the front of the building. The administration said I could "work" as long as I needed to but when I was alone in the building it had better be locked. Of course my key wouldn't work right when I unlocked it from inside. By the time I got done with that he was on the steps at the door. It was dark and a bit on the cool side, so he quickly came in as soon as I opened the door.

The picture he had on the website was just of his head and his body caught me off guard. I'm a big girl so I'm not really saying anything bad, but his body was oddly shaped. He was pear shaped, but with a really big bottom half. He was the shape that can only wear sweat pants to be comfortable. They just don't make jeans for people shaped like him.

The smile on his face said he was happy with what he saw, or maybe he was just happy to be inside, or that he found the place. In any case, he couldn't hide the smile on his face. I noticed he walked a step or two behind me as we walked to my classroom. Later I was told some guys like to look at my back side. There was one guy in Alaska who would come into the store I worked at just to see it. He didn't say anything to me, however, until the day before he flew home for the winter when he had to explain why his hand was on it as I reached for something on the top shelf he just *had* to have me get for him.

The hallway to my classroom wasn't all that long, but long enough when you really want to start a conversation. There were doors that had to be kept closed and every footstep echoed for a while. Don didn't say a word until we got to my classroom.

"This doesn't look like the classrooms in my high school."

"Were you in juvie for any reason during that time?"

"No, why?"

"The kids I teach were. Some of them still have ankle monitors and probation officers and stuff like that." The walls of my room were cinder blocks painted with an odd shade of light blue. One wall had a white board on it that was also used as a screen when I wanted to use the overhead projector. The poster on the wall by my desk marked good behavior. Most days it only had a couple of smiley faces for the all 16 of my students. Anything put on the wall was likely to be destroyed when there was a fight or someone had to be physically restrained. There were only 12 student desks. The room wasn't big enough for more than that and we only had 8 students at most in the room for any one class. If there was a meeting for all the students it was in one of the other rooms or the first student who sat on a desk was asked to get a couple more chairs from another room. "But I'm sure you didn't drive all the way over her just to talk about my students."

"No, I came to see if you were for real."

"Why does everyone want to know if I'm for real?" I was beginning to realize just how much of a freak I seemed to be. Eventually I learned how much the average person stretches the truth when dating, online or in person. Bit by bit I was losing my innocence.

"Because you seem too good to be real."

"I'm not Mother Theresa."

"No, but most of the women I've met on dating sites are nothing like you."

"What do you mean by that?"

"Most of them know what it means to go down on someone."

He had me there. I put my head down a little embarrassed.

"That's exactly what I mean."

He gently tipped my head back up so he was looking in my eyes. "Most women are on there for a date which may or may not lead to sex, so they are eager to talk about it. People say that sex is all men think about. I think we all think about it the same. Men just talk about it more in public."

We talked openly and honestly about a lot of things for the next hour or two. When he was talking about where he was living a huge red flag went off in my head. His living arrangement was too close to that of the idiot I was done with. He had a different excuse, but I was done dealing with excuses on stuff like that. In general he wasn't that bad of a guy. I just didn't see any long-term potential with him. Later I found out that he was busy with thoughts of his family situation so he may not have been giving me the best indication of what he was really like.

We noticed it was late and neither of us had been home since leaving for work that morning, so we decided to call it a night. I grabbed the usual stuff for me to take home on a Friday night and warned him that I usually walk out in the dark since the light switches were not very conveniently located. The street light through the glass door at the front gave me enough light to unlock the door to let him out, set the alarm, and quickly get on the other side of the door to lock it. I only had 15 seconds from pushing the last button of the alarm code to having the door locked. I had plenty of experience, but each night I made sure I was fast enough that the alarm didn't silently go to the police station.

It had warmed up outside. Or maybe it was just that my room had cooled down so the difference wasn't as bad as it was two hours ago when I let Don in the school.

"I'm tired, but I don't want to say good-bye." His arm was around my waist as we walked to my Jeep parked right next to the school. His truck was on the other side of the street but he followed me first.

My hand with the key went to the lock, where he grabbed it and held on to it. He was just holding my hand, but it felt good. Then he brought his other hand to cover my other hand. This was getting interesting. I opened the door of the Jeep and threw my purse and book bag into the passenger's seat. It wasn't quite time for me to jump into the driver's seat. Don was driving this encounter.

When my head came back from tossing the stuff in, his was there breathing down my neck. He still had my left hand in his resting on the side of the door. With his right hand he brushed the hair off the back of my neck and pressed his lips to it. Then his right hand slid down to my waist. He wasn't trying to go anywhere with it—for the moment—it was just resting there where my shirt covered up the waistband of my jeans.

In my head I couldn't stop laughing. For some reason that morning I put on what I jokingly called my "first date shirt" under my flannel. The shirt was made of thin denim—thin if it would be made into jeans—but still thick for a shirt. The buttons going down the front were about ¾ of an inch in diameter and placed about an inch apart. There must have been 14 buttons going down the front of that shirt. It would take a while for a guy to unbutton every one of them. Since the men I was meeting weren't very patient, they would probably give up trying to take my shirt off. That was probably a good thing as we stood out there in the street. The street was empty because it was in an industrial area on a Friday night but I still wasn't going to let someone disrobe me there in public, after meeting him only a couple hours earlier.

He didn't try to unbutton my shirt, but he ran his hand up and down the buttons. Eventually he paused about half way up and let his hand linger there for a while. His breath was hot on my neck.

I turned to face him, shifting slightly so I was leaning on the back door and could turn the dome light off by shutting the driver's door. His mouth remained hovering above my neck until finally he lifted it enough to press it to my lips. This wasn't even a real date and it was ending in a kiss.

His lips moved to my cheek and started down to my neck. So he was more of a neck man. My contemplations distracted me for a bit until a strange feeling on my neck snapped me back to reality. He was sucking on my neck!

"I can't come to school Monday morning with a hickey on my neck." Could you imagine what the kids would do if *that* happened?

"So I guess I better be a good boy."

"Yes," was all I could say as I was trying to decide if I liked the feeling or not. His hands were massaging my back and I knew that felt good. I just wasn't sure about what he was doing to my neck. He was still working it a little harder than I would like. For some reason sometimes I bruise really easily and that would be one bruise I couldn't hide.

"It's getting late and you've put in a long day," I said, trying to turn my body back to the unlocked Jeep door.

"Wonder what your kids would say if they saw us out here in the street like this." He seemed to be enjoying the idea of making out in public, which I didn't really like either. Some things are meant to be done in private.

"Hopefully they will never know. I'm supposed to be the good teacher."

"Maybe I'll have to change that. I bet you could be very good at being bad."

"I'm making out with someone outside on the street. They know about some of the guys I've been talking to, especially the one that sent flowers for me to the school. They already have the impression I'm a player. I don't want to encourage them." I had told Don about the flowers and about some ill timed calls from

Tim when we were talking in my classroom, so he knew I wasn't all that innocent in their eyes.

He helped me open the door. Since I'm not all that tall, I usually have to do a little hop to get into my Jeep. His hand was right there to make sure I jumped high enough. And he was quick enough so it didn't get caught under me on the seat.

"Maybe next time we can actually go out and do something."

"Maybe."

"One last kiss?"

He got his request and closed the door for me. I started up the Jeep and waited for him to start his truck. We both put our headlights on at about the same time. I had to go down the street to the nearest opening in the sidewalk to turn around and he waited until I got past him to pull out. He followed me up the deserted street the school was on and got lost in the traffic on the main drag I took to get home. He mentioned doing something again. I wasn't so sure I wanted to. By Monday I was sure of it.

*****

The next morning I looked in the mirror and saw the most horrible sight I could think of at the moment. My neck had a huge, dark bruise on it. I was glad I hadn't made any plans that weekend. Of course I would call Tim and tell him about it. He would get a good laugh about the good girl with a hickey. At church I didn't take my coat off and leaned my head to the left if I was talking to anyone.

Monday morning it was still there for the entire world to see. I never liked turtle necks because it always felt like they were strangling me. I had one sweatshirt that had a higher neck line. Not even a mock turtle neck, but a little higher than any other shirt I owned. I could wear a polo shirt with the collar out over that and hopefully the kids wouldn't notice the mark of my indiscretion.

The first group of kids wasn't really awake most days. On that Monday I liked that. They were each busy with their individual math assignments. When they had a question I would go to the left side of their desk to help them. We both looked at the sheet they were working on. If they looked up at all they wouldn't be able to see the left side of my neck.

The second group of kids was older, and several of them were at the same place with their math. I had to explain something using the board. Unfortunately the windows were on the same side as the bruise on my neck as I stood in front of them. The kid who regularly comes to school with hickeys on his neck (and when he's on the "skins" team playing basketball there are usually some visible on his chest) acted up the week before so he was required to sit in the front of the room for a while, between me and the light of the window. He was actually looking at me while I was explaining percents. Usually he's drawing or practicing his tagging during any teacher talking in class. All of a sudden he stood up.

"Miss Randi has a hickey!"

Of course my face turned red. The boy who had a crush on me put his head down but the rest of the people in the room, including the teaching assistant, all turned to see my neck. I knew we were done with math for the day. My hand went up to my neck and I thought of the line from *How the Grinch Stole Christmas*. I thought up a lie, and I thought it up quick.

"No, this weekend I was decorating for Easter." It was only a couple weeks away. "The boxes with the decorations were all on the top shelf of my closet. To get them all in there, I had to stack them on top of each other. I wanted to see what was in one of the bottom boxes and the box on top fell forward. My natural reaction to a box coming at my face is to turn my head and when I did a corner of the box hit my neck." That sounded plausible, but my previous reaction said it wasn't the truth. The pantomime I was doing while the words came out of my mouth made it look possible, if not what actually happened.

78

The teaching assistant, who was the one who found the place I was living and knew the shelving situation in my room, stifled a giggle long enough to think up an excuse to go out in the hallway. Once she got out there we all heard her laugh, and the kids started laughing all over again. No, there was no way math was going to get done any more that day. Luckily it was near the end of my explanation and the kids already knew their assignment. Some of them were actually working on it between giggle fits.

During the next class, the students were separated by gender instead of by class. By lunch everyone—students and staff—was looking at my neck with silly smiles on their faces. The last part of the day we would take the kids to a recreation center for P.E. It was my turn to drive the van. While the kids were busy on the basketball court or playing pool, the other teacher came up to me for a chat. He was significantly older than me. He wasn't quite old enough to be my father, but much closer to retirement than I was. The sheepish smile on his face gave me a hint of what he wanted to talk about.

"I heard you had some problems with some boxes this weekend."

"Yeah, decorating can be dangerous."

"Just hope you had fun doing it." The look on his face said he had a good idea what the truth was. This proved I was a player like the kids were saying. I was just hoping no one at school would find out where I really was when I got that bruise.

Did I tell you my bruises take a long time to heal? For a couple of weeks the kids sitting on my left side would occasionally giggle when they looked at me. The only one who got in trouble was the one who referred to it as a "tramp stamp" when he thought I wasn't listening. I may not be the good girl everyone thinks I am, but I didn't think of myself as a tramp. Eventually the bruise faded, but the memory took a lot longer, and I don't think my reputation at school ever got over that.

*****

The next weekend I didn't have any plans. The bruise wasn't quite healed so maybe that was best. It was light enough that the kids stopped commenting on it, but a man would be closer. At some point he would see it and ask. I wasn't hiding the fact that I wasn't seeing anyone exclusively, but I don't think any man would want to see proof like that on a potential new girlfriend. Maybe I needed a break from the physical stuff, anyway. A little time to catch my breath and try to figure out exactly what I was trying to accomplish might be helpful.

Tim understood needing a little break from dating. He said he needed one also. Easter was only three weeks away and he was still talking about coming out the week after. He didn't want to start a new "relationship" and he had pretty much ended the latest one, or so he said. Now he was going to figure out how to deal with the custody of his daughter when he came out to live in the big city. He said there was too much he had to do to even think of dating.

While I was talking with him I was also checking out some chat rooms. On Saturdays there were usually people who were lonely, besides me. There was one guy who said he was "hot for teacher." He described his bedroom to prove to me he was in it, alone. He asked if people outside could see me in the classroom. He asked what I was doing with my hands since no one knew what I was doing. He asked for a picture of me to see if it went along with my suggestive chatting.

I was hesitant. This guy was from a general website, not the one specifically for women like me. After chatting a while I broke down and sent a picture. Suddenly his computer was having problems. He said it was because he was in his bedroom, doing things with one hand and trying to type with the other. He said he would have to quit chatting with me because of technical difficulties. Last time this happened to his computer it went down for a week, or so he said when he told me he couldn't chat any more. A half hour later he logged into a different room on the same site, probably hoping I wouldn't notice. That's what I'm used to. Guys who say they want me, until they see me.

Soon after that, Ken was online. He was in town tonight, but had to go back out tomorrow. Some of his buddies had a poker game they invited him to. Of course he said he would rather be with me, but they were some of the guys at work who could get him that job that kept him in town more often. It was just an overnight stay anyway. At this point, the plan was that he would make this run and be back on Tuesday. He would have Wednesday and Thursday off, but of course I had to work during that time. Then Friday he would take off for another run and be back on Sunday. Monday he would have off with another run from Tuesday to Friday.

He asked if I wanted to go with him on that run since that was during my spring break. He would be going to the general area where I grew up, but not close enough to see my family. He thought it would be a good change of pace to have someone with him. His ex-wife went with him occasionally, but that was a long time ago.

I asked him what I should pack. He said I didn't really have to pack anything with a suggestive emoticon on the end of the message. Since he is in the truck most of the time either driving or sleeping he didn't worry much about what he wore. Even during the required time off the road he would be in his truck with a laptop where he would text me and other people sometimes. His suggestion was that I pack something slinky and lacy and have one other set of clothes to wear if we got out of the truck. I said I didn't have anything like that. In that case, he would be willing to pick out something for me and do all the packing. Usually I would have sent back some flirty message that would turn into some form of cyber sex, but this was different. I had seen him, and he expressed interest in a sexual relationship. Now I was planning on spending several days alone with him away from home. We would be sharing a bed in his truck when he wasn't driving. I realized there would be no way out for me once we started on the road so I had to be careful not to encourage him too much. For the first time I was getting nervous about the trip.

Once I traveled 3,000 miles to meet someone in a strange town with no way out other than my plane ticket back to Alaska, but this was different. Ken knew I wanted to be a good girl, but he thought of himself as a bad boy. He didn't understand my experiences. He was still trying to wrap his head around the fact that I was only a couple years younger than he was and never had sex. He probably thought I wasn't being totally honest with him. He didn't come out and call me a liar but he kept hinting that he didn't believe I've always been a good girl. After all, I was willing to let him take my shirts off on our third date, that wasn't all that good was it? I was beginning to question the wisdom of such a trip.

When Tim called again, I didn't tell him what was happening on my computer or in my head. He probably knew I was chatting with someone but didn't ask any questions. My voice started getting down and he asked what was wrong. Of course I said there wasn't anything. He started saying what we would all do once he got out here. He was going to take me out to any bar that was open and show me how to make my troubles disappear. Somehow he knew I was feeling insecure. Between the almost routine rejection after seeing my picture and the change in feelings about a spring break road trip, I was getting more than a little down. He was really a good friend to have for times like this. He made me almost wish he had gotten the courage and the money to move. At least with Tim I would have a slight advantage, and if things went bad I could get lost in the city with all my stuff. On the road with Ken there would be no place to run to and no place to hide.

That night I went to a wine tasting event. It was a group of singles, but we met just to hang around. We could just share our everyday experiences of our jobs, our pets, and the wines we were sampling. My glass was never really full. An hour or so before the end of the event everyone who was driving switched to soda. I had only a few sips of each wine. The host lived about a half hour's drive from town. Most of the other people lived within five minutes of the host so it would be easy enough to get a ride home and drive (or walk) back to get their vehicle the next day if they couldn't drive home.

The house we were in was dark and my bruise was almost healed so no one asked me about it. It was just a nice evening of good conversation. The other singles would ask about how things were going in the big city. Most of them also knew I lived in Alaska. Between those two topics, there was plenty for me to talk about without revealing too much of my personal life.

Back at my house, Rob, the guy who I shared the house with, was sitting outside drunk. I go to a wine tasting and come home to a drunk. Yes, my life is full of irony. We had never really talked and it was a nice night to sit outside. It was fairly late so all the neighbors were inside and their kids were sleeping so no one really could hear us. I would have a good hour of being wide awake after the drive, so I stayed to talk.

"I can't believe how lucky I got to find you to share my house with." His words were a little slurred, but heart-felt. We chatted about where I was from and his work and stuff like that.

Eventually he decided he was cold, so we went inside. I was starting to get tired. It was hard to find some way to excuse myself to get some sleep.

He took my hand and said, "We'll have to do this again sometime. You really are a sweet girl." He laced his fingers with mine and we just stood there for a while. He was almost a generation older than me and we had a business agreement in sharing the house. That's all we would have. He gave my hand one last squeeze and I went up to my bedroom. That was the closest thing to an intimate moment I had with Rob. Of course he didn't remember it, but he did continue to say we should do something together sometime.

*****

Sunday, Lawrence was online for a while. He was talking about his job way out in the country. This week wouldn't be that busy and maybe he would be able to take an extra day off. He thought he would be coming into town for supplies also. That would mean he would spend at least one weeknight by his computer. During the week he had his cell phone so we talked occasionally. He saw my picture on the website and was very interested. He said big girls like me were always good to him and he found them very attractive. That's why I was on that site. I was looking for a man who would appreciate my unique build. He said he wanted to see more soon.

At school we were getting ready for spring break. Some of the kids were worried about being grounded during that time, so they were good. Some of the kids were scared of the idea that they would have to spend an entire week without the routine of school, so they were not so good. Every night I had to stay late to write up something on an incident during the day. Not another word from Ken. I guess I wouldn't be going on a spring break trip after all. Maybe that was a good thing. Most of the nights there were, however, a call from Lawrence. The seed was about to sprout up from the ground.

We told each other where we were coming from. He was taken care of by a native nanny when he lived in Puerto Rico for a while, where he learned to speak Spanish. English was my only language so what he said to prove he knew Spanish could have been anything, but it sounded like what I heard when some of the kids at school would speak it. Luckily the teaching assistant with me was bilingual. Since she was there primarily for behavior—it was her job to remind the students to watch their language. Lawrence's father was supposedly a very high level executive with buildings named after him and everything. He was an architect, working with high end houses right now. On the website it listed his profession as construction because he didn't want to attract women who were just looking for someone with money.

By this time, he had my real name. He knew I didn't have much experience with men, and he said he had enough experience for both of us. We talked a little about where I grew up and what I did before moving to the big city. He was interested in meeting a real country girl. Maybe that's what he was really looking for, a simple, old fashioned country girl. Now he was ready to meet me in person. Plans were beginning to be made for the weekend.

He explained that he was having car problems and wouldn't be able to get his fixed until after they got the money from the job they were finishing. He was living in the basement of a friend's house. It was more storage for his stuff and a place to crash on weekends, so not a place you want to take or even show a date. Maybe this should have set off some warning, but not to my naive mind. You would think that with all the online "dating" I've done I would have been an expert in such things. For some reason I wasn't learning my lessons, probably because I wanted to believe them that they were different from all the other guys.

*****

Friday he came back to the city earlier than normal. The job he was working on was almost done. There were just a few finishing touches and it would be ready. He wouldn't get paid until it was all done, but he wanted to celebrate with someone. The guys he worked with were all celebrating with their families, but he didn't have one. The phone conversation took up most of the evening. He said he wished I had a phone other than the one at school. I was thinking of getting a cell phone. Despite the amount of time I spent on the computer, I considered myself technologically challenged. If I got a cell phone it was going to be one that would allow me to call my friends in Alaska and my family in back where I grew up, but I didn't have a lot of money to spend on a plan or a phone. Anyway, a cell phone was something I could do without for the moment.

He asked if I had any plans for the weekend. At that moment I didn't, but that quickly changed. He thought it was time we finally met in person. My bruise was gone and I was ready to go on the prowl again, and prowl I did.

He wanted to take the evening to do laundry, and it was already too late to go out. I had put in a full day of work and he ended his workday with a long drive back to town. He said he would call me when he saw me online the next morning to arrange for a meeting. He was looking forward to seeing the person behind the voice he said he was falling in love with.

His use of the "l" word caught me off guard. Last time someone used it he later said he never meant it. Actually it was more like he was incapable of feeling it. The idiot was the first to close an e-mail, "With love," years ago. Several times during our relationship he asked me if I was in love with him or in love with being in love, indicating to me he wasn't sure of the concept. Part of this year's Valentine's Day rant was that he never really loved me. It may have been a reaction to my comment that his demon had closed off the romantic place in his heart, making it impossible for him to feel real love. I finally went home that night with visions of a new relationship dancing in my head.

*****

I slept in the next morning, and as it turns out that was a good thing. Eventually I made it to the school a little after noon. Lawrence was at his computer waiting for me, or at least it didn't take him long to see that I logged in. He called just like he promised he would. We decided to meet at a Starbuck's near his place. While we talked, I looked up the address and Map Quested the place. It didn't seem that hard for me to find. He said he didn't do his laundry the night before like he planned so he had to do some before he met me. Last time I had to wait for laundry it didn't turn out all that bad. Since next week was spring break there was really nothing for me to do at school, so I decided to take a drive while waiting for Lawrence's laundry.

There was no one at the lookout park, which was odd for a Saturday afternoon. The park was on a hill just west of the city. It was high enough that you could see the grid of major streets. The real reason I went there to think was that it had trees. I grew up in a rural forested area. In high school when I wanted to think I took off to the woods. The city had some trees, but not like these. The lookout had century old pines with lots of pine cones and a smell that took me back to my childhood.

The morning had been cloudy, perfect for sleeping in. Maybe the planned picnics were postponed because of the weather. It was, after all, late March, when the weather changes quicker than any outdoor plans can. Soon the sun was out, but looking at the sky that probably wouldn't last long. There was so much for me to think about, but I didn't feel like thinking. I wanted to take some time and just enjoy the moment. The air was washed fresh that morning and the sun had dried everything. I had a week to sleep in if I wanted to, and I wouldn't have to deal with the kids for a while.

Eventually it was time to get back on the road to meet Lawrence. I had to drive to the other side of town and then try to find the place. I wasn't going to be late for a first meeting again, especially since this time there was no excuse for it. The roads were fairly empty, which was typical for this time on a Saturday.

I hadn't been to that part of town before, and I wanted to make sure I was on time. The corner where the little strip mall was located was at the intersection of two main streets, so it wasn't that hard to find. I got there about a half an hour early. There was a car wash on the back side of the strip mall. The Jeep hadn't been vacuumed or washed in a while and there was some time to kill.

Finally it was time to enter the Starbuck's and wait for him. Since I don't drink coffee, I ordered a hot chocolate while a table opened up. Wherever I sat, it had to be in a place where I could see the door and be seen by whoever came in. A couple of college-age girls were sitting at the table that would be perfect. Just as my drink was handed to me, they got up to sit on a couch that just opened up. I got over to the table as soon as I could and sat facing the door.

Now what do I do? I didn't want to make it too obvious I was waiting for someone. My purse hadn't been cleaned out in a while, so maybe I could occupy myself with that. The notebook I used for lists had several old ones I put together, slowly, into one list. All the while I was sipping the hot chocolate. Everyone else there who wasn't talking to someone had a computer or a cell phone they were using. I had a laptop, but no wireless card so I left it at home. It was too cold outside so the tables there were empty and the ones inside were full. Funny the things you think of when you're trying to kill a little time.

The cup in front of me was getting empty and the clock on the wall said it was just about the time we said we would meet. Good thing the floor was solid, because my leg was bobbing up and down like crazy. Hopefully that was the only sign that I was nervously awaiting someone. Every time the door opened I looked up, so it was obvious I was, but everyone else seemed busy in their own little worlds, and hopefully not talking about me.

Then the door opened and a tall, scrawny, older man walked in. That was him—it had to be. I thought I would have a little time to compose myself while he got a coffee, but he walked straight over to my table. His hair and beard were grey and he had on a leather bomber jacket to match. As he got closer to my table I noticed his eyes were bluer than mine, also behind glasses. He was wearing a musky cologne that made it to the table a couple of steps before he did.

"I'm hoping you're Randi."

"Yes, and you must be Lawrence."

"Yes." He sat down across from me. We started chatting, finishing various conversations from the weeks on the phone and IMing with follow up questions. I was wondering why he wasn't getting anything to drink. My hot chocolate was gone, but with the cover still on I could pretend to drink for a while and he never asked when I arrived.

All of a sudden, he took my hand. "Would you like me to take you to dinner?"

It took me off guard. All I could get out of my mouth was a half-hearted, "Sure."

As I was collecting my stuff from the table, and my thoughts, I asked, "I thought you wanted to meet here for coffee."

"No, really I just wanted to make sure you were who you said you were before I went any further."

"And am I?"

"You are exactly what you said you were, but I thought that was too good to be true so I wanted to meet you where I could easily get out of it if you weren't. I've chatted with a lot of girls who said they were like you only to find out they were making it all up." He told me in previous conversations he had been married twice before and made no secret that he was involved with many casual relationships. Of course he said he was looking for something more substantial after I told him I was looking for something long term. "There's a little Mexican place I like to go to, but not alone. Think you could go for some authentic Mexican food for dinner?"

"Sure." This time it was a little more convincing.

Soon I had everything put back and rearranged in my purse. I picked up my empty cup and tossed it in the nearest receptacle. He let me go ahead, pretending to be a gentleman. After we got into my Jeep I got the real reason.

"Has anyone ever told you how nice your ass is?"

"As a matter of fact, yes." I was thinking of the guy in Alaska who said good-bye to me with a second long kiss and a minute long massage of the area around the back pockets of my jeans.

"Well, whoever it was he was right." I could feel my face starting to turn red. "And your face is so cute when you're blushing." His hand reached over to pick my chin up so he could see my face. "And your eyes are such an incredible shade of blue. I liked your picture on the website, but I love what I'm seeing now."

He gave me directions to another little strip mall with the restaurant at one end. I don't know if I'll ever get used to men opening doors for me, but he was eager to please. He even pulled out my chair and helped me get it situated. That was new to me, but I could get used to it as well.

The menu looked like the average little family-run establishment. Lawrence wanted to order for both of us. To really show off, he started off a conversation with the server in Spanish. I had no idea what they were saying and all I could think of was Elton John's, "A Word in Spanish." Soon what tasted like a Diet Coke was set in front of me and something that looked like a beer was set in front of him.

We chatted more about nothing for a while. He kept his eyes on me, which made me nervous. I kept wondering if there was something on my shirt. He was usually looking at my face, but every once in a while I noticed him looking down at my chest. Our conversation had passed the awkward stage back at the coffee shop. Now it was much more natural, more like it was when we talked on the phone. He told me about his kids, two grown daughters and a teenage son. I talked about my family and what brought me out here so far away from them. We also talked about our online dating experiences.

Our food arrived. Every conversation with the staff was by him and in Spanish. Yes, he knew Spanish and he was making sure I knew that. About half way through our meal he got quiet, stopped eating, and focused his gaze on my face.

"Would you mind if I kissed you?"

Not a good-bye kiss or making out on some guy's couch, but an unexpected kiss in the middle of a very public place.

"Sure." Again, I was taken off guard. I think he was doing things like that just to see my reaction. He wasn't teasing me; I think he was enjoying my reactions to his forwardness.

He stood up and slowly took the step he needed to in order to be standing right next to my chair. I started to get up, but he put his hand on my shoulder to keep me seated. He bent down—since he was so tall that wasn't easy. Again he took my chin into his hand to tip my face to his and planted his lips on mine. It wasn't really long since he probably couldn't bend over that long. Then he quickly went back to his seat without taking his eyes off of me. He was probably checking out my reaction. In any case, I wasn't used to people looking at me all the time like that.

"That wasn't so bad, was it?"

"No, in fact it was kind of nice. I'm a little confused about it, but it was nice."

"Confused about what? I'm sitting here with a beautiful woman and I wanted to give her a kiss. They say you can tell a lot about a person by their kiss."

"And what does that one say about me?

"It says you're for real and I'm a very lucky man to find you."

We continued eating, slowing down with our tummies getting full.

"What would you think about getting a hotel room for the night?"

"I don't think so." Maybe he was hoping I would come out with another, "Sure" but not this time.

"So what do you want to do tonight? I really don't want this to end a minute before it has to."

"I'm not the one to ask for suggestions. I've only been in this neck of the woods a few times, and I really don't know what there is around here to do."

"I gave you my suggestion, so if you want to do something else you'll have to come up with an idea." Yes, he was enjoying this.

There was a huge grin on his face between his graying mustache and beard. "I'll be a gentleman and give you some time to think."

We both went back to our nearly completed meal. I was simply playing with the rice at this point. Now what was I supposed I do? I'm a good girl and good girls don't go to hotel rooms on the first date.

The server came around again and set down another soda for me. He asked if we wanted dessert, or I think that's what he asked, or maybe he asked if another beer was needed. In any case, Lawrence shook his head no.

"Are you sure you don't want to join me for the rest of the evening at a hotel?" His hand gently took mine. "We could watch a movie and get to know each other a little better." The movie line seemed common. I grew up an hour's drive from the nearest movie theater so for me it wasn't something done regularly. These city boys seem to be watching movies all the time.

There was nothing for me to go home to really. Sunday morning meant church, but that could still happen, maybe. When the words came out of my mouth I couldn't believe it.

"As long as you don't expect too much."

His face started to beam. Immediately I was having second thoughts. My rule had been that I'll try anything once, and if it's fun I just might try it again. This was one of those things that I probably shouldn't have done. I'm pretty stubborn about keeping my word so once they left my mouth I felt like I was bound somehow to do what I said I would.

He must have felt my hand start shaking. "Don't worry. I won't make you do anything you don't want to do. Really, we can get a room and watch movies and stuff." He was studying my face, and it probably started to look incredibly nervous. "I think I told you that I live in my friend's basement. I don't want my time with you to end, but I don't want you to see the storage area I sleep in when I'm in town. Pretty soon I'll have to get a real apartment. For tonight, though, a hotel room will have to do for us."

What he said made sense. Much later I learned that sometimes things conveniently make sense even if they are just good excuses for what was really going on. I knew what it meant to get a room after a date, but Lawrence promised this would be different. It had worked for me in the past, a promise that things would be different from what usually happened in similar situations. I had been talking with Lawrence for over two months. He knew I'd never gone all the way. He knew I was a good girl. He knew I was nervous about what would happen next—or at least I hoped he remembered all that from various conversations.

He pulled out his credit card and put it on the table. As Lawrence held my hand, the server came over and took the card. Soon he returned with the slip for Lawrence to sign. The impressively large tip was left on the table in cash. Lawrence kept hold of my hand to lead me to the door and all the way to my Jeep. Maybe he thought I might change my mind, so he wanted to get me going and make sure we were both going to the same place.

After closing my door, he ran around to his side and jumped in. I could figure out how to get out of the parking lot, but from there I would need directions.

"Can we stop at a 7-Eleven?"

"Sure, but why?"

"I'm feeling lucky and I want to get a lottery ticket." I thought the smile was still from my acceptance of his offer, but he had something else in mind. Lawrence motioned me to drive straight across the main road to get to the parking area for 7-Eleven. I shut off the Jeep out of habit. Usually I was the only person in it so when I stopped, it meant I was getting out. "You're coming with me? Good, you can help me decide what kind to get."

When we got in the store, I was expecting him to go right to the counter. After all, that's where lottery tickets were kept. Looking back, how naive could I be—really? His legs were longer than mine and he was on a mission. He ended up pulling me down one of the few aisles in the store. He went straight to the condoms.

93

"I told you not to expect too much." Now I was sure this wasn't such a good idea.

"I told you not to worry. These are just in case." In case of what? In case he wanted to smuggle cocaine into the country? In case he felt like making balloon animals? In case we needed first aide? I think I might have visibly started shaking. "We won't do anything you don't want to do." He whispered into my ear as he started to the check stand.

We got back into the Jeep. Maybe someday I'll get used to gentlemen opening doors for me. This time it was more of an excuse to touch me again. Hopefully he didn't feel how much I was shaking.

"You've really never done this before, have you?"

"No, I told you I've never done anything like this." Later I learned that the afternoon with Ken was what he had in mind, but I wasn't exactly thinking straight. The only time I had ever been in a hotel room was for the church trips, family events and things like that. I was either alone or with family members. Never with some guy had I met face to face for the first time only a few hours earlier and bought condoms only minutes ago. Remember what I said about going where angels fear to tread? This was one of those places.

He gave me turn by turn directions to the hotel. I can only imagine how we looked as a couple, holding hands, with no luggage, walking up to the front desk.

There was no line so we walked right up to the front desk. He asked if there were any suites available. The person behind the desk started typing something into the computer. Lawrence put his credit card and ID on the counter and tapped his index finger to attract the attendant's attention. He turned away from the computer screen to the counter top and took a long, hard look at the ID. The attendant's eyebrows went up a little and very soon he found a room for us. He quoted the price, which wasn't bad for a suite, depending on what it actually looked like. He asked if we needed any help with our luggage. I stifled a giggle. The inexperienced country girl in me was showing. The clerk didn't react at all. I'm sure this wasn't the first time a couple like us came to him this time of night with no luggage asking for a room for just one night. He was being paid to not ask too many questions.

Our room was on the fifth floor—high enough to see the night lights of the city, and the black hole that was a lake in the middle of it. But I didn't notice that for a while. Lawrence didn't let me leave the entry room. I took a couple of steps into the room, followed closely by Lawrence. I heard the door close and felt his hands quickly reach around to grab hold of the edge of the flannel shirt I had over my polo shirt. I tipped my head down to see what was going on. I could feel Lawrence's breath on my neck. He took one hand back to sweep the hair away from my neck. The other one started to pull the flannel off my shoulder. He started kissing my neck while engaging both hands in taking off the first layer of shirts.

His hand went to my jaw and gently turned my head, with my body following, to face him. He must have felt how much I was shaking. After all, his hand was on my jaw, where most of the activity was happening. My eyes were closed, my head down as far as I could get it with his hand pulling it up to face him. "Don't be scared. I'm not going to hurt you. I just want to see what's under all those shirts." His lips were inches away from my ear. Soon I felt them again on my neck. All I could do was to tip my head and enjoy the sensation.

His hands found the bottom of the back of my polo shirt and started pulling it up. He pulled his head away from me long enough to pull that shirt off as well. His hands ran down the bare skin on my arms to squeeze my hands. I was half-way to topless only two steps into the room. This was going way too fast.

Lawrence must have noticed my trepidation. He took his shirt off and threw it in the pile. He was standing so close to me it seemed he was taller than he actually was. I had always fantasized about a man who was so tall that my face was at his chest level. I let my head rest on his bare chest while my hands started to run up and down his bare back. The feeling of skin on skin felt good. This was something I could get to like—maybe too much.

While my mind was distracted, his hands went down to take off the last real shirt. He made sure I felt his hands run all the way up my back, pausing ever so slightly when he hit my sports bra before finishing off the shirt pile with my gray athletic shirt. His hand went back to my chin. This time my eyes were open and solidly met his. "You are beautiful on the inside and the outside. I'm a very lucky man."

He reached down for a kiss. Actually it was more than just a kiss. We were melting together for a moment or two. His hands were caressing my back, inching upward to the last covering of my breasts. He backed up slightly, to give his hands enough space to slide to the front, keeping them under my bra. The feel of skin on skin was spellbinding. I just couldn't get enough of it. At that moment I didn't care what he did as long as he kept making me feel good.

With his arms around me he started to move forward, backing me up. Finally we were what most people would consider inside the room. Slowly he moved me back to the couch. He sat down first, probably so I didn't collapse onto it. When I sat down, he kept backing me up until I was lying on the couch. The coffee table was pushed back to give him room to kneel beside me. Ok, so this was the second time I was in this position, but this was different. Sure, we talked for months before meeting, then we talked over dinner, but we were alone in the room for mere minutes before we were both topless. He wasn't wasting any more time. The seed was sprouting now, and growing quickly. For a few minutes I just laid there, enjoying his exploring hands and mouth. When he reached for the button of my jeans I immediately tensed up.

Looking at the clock on the TV, we were lost in each other for longer than I thought. He let me sit up and we started talking again.

Most of it was, one more time, me crying about how lonely I was before moving to the big city. He was patient with me, and a bit hungry. He called room service and this time I could actually understand his side of the conversation.

While we were waiting he explained to me why he was getting such good treatment. It seemed his father used that particular hotel for business conventions. He brought quite a few people at different times. When they saw Lawrence's last name, they knew whose son he was and gave him a good deal.

Now he was using his name and reputation to get something good from the chef on duty. When they brought it up, he had a conversation with whoever brought it. I could only hear part of it since I had to run into the bedroom. My shirts were still on the pile that Lawrence almost tripped over on his way to the door. There was no way for me to put one on and I wasn't going to give the hotel employees a show. While there, I was exploring the bedroom and looking out the window. We were five floors up so no one would see me topless from the ground level. And it was dark so no one could see much, anyway. I left the lights off so I could see all the city lights. I was paying more attention to them than what was going on in the other room.

"He's gone, Babe. You can come back in here now." He called me Babe? Probably couldn't remember my first name off the cuff like that. Still, it sounded good to me, and something smelled really good.

When I came back in, there was a tray with grilled shrimp and what looked like beef tips with some potatoes and steamed veggies. What I heard of the order it was just for them to cook up a little "late night snack" for us. Maybe there was something to his story about being the son of someone who did a lot of business with them. In any case, the shrimp was *really* good. He was more of a meat and potatoes guy, so I got the shrimp and veggies. Eating it topless was a new experience. Lawrence seemed to be enjoying it. I was trying to be ladylike and not eat too much or too fast, so he decided to start feeding me.

Eventually our "snack" was finished. Lawrence turned the TV on. "Why don't you see what's on while I jump in the shower?" Now he decides he needs a shower? I was too innocent to realize what he was really doing in the shower. The TV was loud enough to cover any noise that came from the bathroom. I was getting cold, so I dug my flannel from the bottom of the shirt pile and covered my arms and shoulders. There was nothing really on TV this late, but I flipped from commercial to commercial so it made enough noise for him to hear it in the bathroom when the water stopped.

He came out wearing just a towel. There had been an uncomfortable incident last year with a man coming out of the shower wearing just a towel, but this time it was different.

"I took all the trouble to get naked and you put more clothes on."

"I was cold."

"At least you didn't cover everything up." He noticed that I didn't bother buttoning the shirt. For some reason, that shirt never seemed to get buttoned.

He sat next to me on the couch, still just in his towel. "Now we'll have to work on getting you naked. I could help you if you wanted to shower."

"I'm a little cold, that's why I had to put a shirt back on."

"There has to be a blanket around here besides the ones on the bed." He got up, clutching the towel, and went into the bedroom. There was a small closet space but in the dark I didn't see any blanket there. It took him a while to find the light, but he came out with a typical hotel blanket. He put the blanket over me, and again took my flannel off. "What good does it do to have your shirts off if you have to be covered by a blanket?" He walked over to the heater and cranked it. Back on the couch he sat back down, sharing the blanket with me.

We started talking again for a while. Eventually we were interrupted by a knock on the door. Room service brought something for us to drink. I don't know if he talked to them when the snack was brought up, but it was impressive that they came up again just to bring up a bottle of champagne. They stayed at the doorway and I was covered with the blanket so I didn't have to run and hide this time.

We ended up drinking the entire bottle in a very short time. Since I didn't have to drive anywhere, I didn't think there would be any harm in having a couple of glasses. Lawrence was trying to get me to drink the whole bottle myself. I guess he wanted to get me drunk. I was half naked, and maybe with a bottle of champagne in me I'd let him finish the job. Our conversation turned to just that topic.

"You aren't going to sleep in your pants are you?"

I hadn't brought any pajamas. In Alaska I had what I considered a kit that had something for any emergency. If there was any chance I would be spending the night somewhere I had a pair of jammies in the Jeep with me. When I left home that morning I was sure I would be home at some point in the evening so I didn't have any jammies in the Jeep.

"At least take your socks off now."

My shoes had come off at some point with my shirts or before. In Alaska it was customary to take your shoes off when you enter someone's house. Most people have shoe holders or something like that right by the door. My socks, however, have always stayed on. Usually I even sleep in at least one pair of socks. Now I was realizing I may be taking my pants off in front of a man for the first time in my life, but I started with my socks. I don't think *anyone* had ever seen my bare feet, except the doctor and X-ray tech when they were trying to figure out why my foot turned five shades of purple after a simple fall.

He was only too eager to help. He stood on the tip of my sock, careful not to stand on my toes, and lifted my leg to pull my foot out of one sock, then the other. Instantly my feet started to get cold so my toes crinkled under, opposite the way the feet of the Wicked Witch of the West's feet curled up.

"You have such cute little toes." My older sister referred to them as tater tot toes because they were so short and round when they would stick out of a hole in my sock. I was glad I had put on a good pair of socks that morning. She also said that if someone tickled my feet in my sleep I would start talking. That little tidbit was not going to be made known at this point.

My mind was going crazy trying not to think about what Lawrence had in mind for the rest of the night. Now that my socks were off, the next thing would have to be my pants. There wasn't much clothing left to take off of me.

His hands followed the seam on the outside of my jeans. I knew exactly what was on his mind, but he was being graciously slow. The condoms were in his jacket pocket last I saw them, and his jacket was over the arm of the couch. This is exactly where angels would fear to tread, but I was there with no real way out. We were both still sitting on the couch. Our shirts were in a pile at the door, my socks were tossed in a little pile in front of the TV, and the blanket was going between the floor at my feet and back on my shoulders.

As the room warmed up and the champagne kicked in, it was possible to keep it on the floor longer and longer each time. Lawrence was also trying to keep me warm in any way he could. Mostly it was just rubbing the exposed area which by now was the majority of my body. His beard and mustache tickled the sensitive skin on my breasts. His hands were warm and he kept them in constant contact with some part of my bare skin. He must have had some idea of how nervous I was. He was going fast for me, but probably painfully slowly for him.

Instead of a giggle, it was a yawn I couldn't stifle.

"You must be getting tired. Maybe we should go to bed now." The look on his face was a bit mischievous, but something about it said I was still safe with him. God would take care of me, even if I was going to a forbidden land where, yes, the angels feared to tread.

He helped me off the couch and to the bedroom. For the first time both of us were in the bedroom at the same time. I looked at the bed, and then at him. The towel never made it off the couch. He was totally naked and I had two pieces of clothing left, my pants and my underwear.

Oh, yes, my underwear. I'm a very practical person. I want things that are functional, not frilly. When I bought underwear it was in a package of at least five—sometimes there would be a bonus pair. They were always cotton and most recently always white. I was living alone with a fear of dating. No need to have lacy panties.

Rob, the guy I shared a house with, had a collection of lacy panties he stole from various women—I think from their dresser drawers when they weren't looking or from cars when he worked at a car wash—so I was careful to collect all of mine from the washer and dryer when I did laundry there. Not like mine were of any interest to Rob. He wanted panties and I only owned underwear. I guess they are sometimes known as granny panties.

Now it was too late. Either I was going to sleep in my jeans, which I had done before, or a non-medical man was going to see me in my underwear. He slowly solved my dilemma by unbuttoning my jeans. That time I let him. He was slow, deliberate, and very careful about everything he did for the next few minutes. He unzipped the fly and started pushing my jeans to the floor. They stuck around my hips, but he gently nudged them down. Once they hit, he kicked them off to the side and started walking to the bed. Since I was directly in front of him, we ended up walking together to the far side of the room. At that point he didn't say a word about my underwear. Actually, I don't think he even saw them. There were sheer curtains over the windows, but I could see the reflection of his closed eyes. There was only a quick glance at his eyes as he buried his face in the crook of my neck. I closed my eyes also. Part of it was to enjoy the new experience, and part of it was I didn't want to see my reflection in the glass the night turned into a mirror. In case you haven't figured it out yet, I didn't really like mirrors.

He pulled back the comforter, the blanket still left on the bed, and the top sheet for me. My eyes opened long enough to see the bed and sit down on the side of it. Still without a word, he bent down to kiss me. The kiss was designed to last, and to ease me down so that I was soon lying in bed. Lawrence was on top of me, sliding his feet under the covers with mine. Still being very slow and deliberate, he maneuvered himself to the other side of the bed. His legs slid under the sheets, which he pulled up to cover us both.

"You've probably taken off all the clothing you plan on taking off tonight?"

"I've taken off more than I planned already."

"Have you always been a good girl?"

"You probably won't believe me, but this is the first time I've done anything like this." In my mind this was so far beyond making out or even being topless on some guy's couch. I was in bed with a man and there was one piece of clothing on between the both of us. This was definitely a place where angels fear to tread.

"I can feel you shaking. Of course I believe you." He had his arm around me. The feeling of skin on skin was something I don't think I'll ever get tired of experiencing. "You're probably such a good girl you never stay up this late except maybe for New Year's Eve."

"I am usually an early to bed, early to rise person. But this morning I got up late and didn't really do all that much before coming over to meet you."

"I'm kind of getting tired, too."

I don't know how long we laid there. His hands, lips and tongue were all caressing different parts of me at different times. I was too tired to resist, or reciprocate. I never could sleep on my back, so I rolled on to my side facing him.

"I had a really good time tonight, and I'm glad it's ending with you in my arms."

"You say that now, wait until you see what you wake up next to in the morning." I hadn't brought a tooth brush, comb, or any of my morning toiletries.

"I can't imagine you looking anything but beautiful no matter what time of day it is. Now, get some sleep. I promise I'll be a good boy tonight."

"Maybe if I were a good girl I would believe that."

"As far as I'm concerned, you are a good girl, and always will be."

"You are such a smooth talker. But I believe you that you'll be good tonight. If you really would have wanted to do something you would have gotten me drunker and done it already."

"Now it's time for us both to get some sleep. You obviously don't need it but I need all the beauty sleep I can get."

I was too tired to argue. He continued to caress me as I drifted off to sleep. At some point he fell asleep as well, but I have no idea when he stopped moving his hands across my body. And there we were, two pretty much naked bodies in the same bed, one of which was mine. There's a first time for everything.

The next morning I woke up a little before him. I'm used to lingering in bed for a while before getting up. I lay there, looking at him and wondering how I let myself get this far. Then I rolled over to look out the window. Things looked a little different, or maybe it was me. The lights were gone and the mess of the spring melt by the lake was what kept my attention. Early spring, with dirty snow and brown grass, is not the prettiest season. Luckily it quickly changes to colorful flowers and green grass.

Lawrence's hand pushed its way under my arm and reached down to surround my breast in a good morning squeeze. He wiggled his body against mine, probably to tell me he was awake.

He mentioned something in one of our conversations about not being all that talkative before he has a cup of coffee in the morning. Luckily there was a coffee pot and some coffee in the room.

"You stay right there while I get my coffee going."

I lifted my head to see what time it was. I could still make it to church if I hurried, but in reality I knew this would be the first week in a *long* time I wouldn't be going to at least one Sunday service. While in Alaska I regularly went to two different services each Sunday. When was the last time I didn't go to church on a Sunday? I think that was the day I had a migraine so bad that I barely could walk from the bed to the bathroom, which was only about 10 steps away at the time. For me going to church was the way to start off every Sunday morning. This was just another indication that my "good girl-ness" was wearing off.

Soon Lawrence was back in bed with me. "How did you sleep, Beautiful?"

"It usually takes me a while to get used to any bed, but for a hotel bed it was pretty good."

"No dreams of some big, bad monster coming to turn you into a bad girl?"

"No, that's what happened before I went to sleep." I rolled over so he could see the smile on my face.

"I feel kind of like a beast waking up next to a beauty like you."

"You are way too kind."

"And you are incredibly beautiful, any time of day, with or without your clothes on."

His coffee didn't take long, but it wasn't the coffee he was hoping for.

"Maybe we should go out and get some real coffee before we do anything else." He walked back into the other room and must have called room service from there. I heard him say something about a cup of coffee and hot cocoa. There was just enough time for him to put his jeans on before there was a knock at the door.

He came into the bedroom with a big cup of coffee in one hand and a cup of hot cocoa in the other.

We took our time getting ready. We got out just before the 11 a.m. check-out time. When we found our way to the Jeep he asked if I wanted breakfast. I'm used to eating as soon as I get up, and getting up earlier. Yes, I was hungry.

He gave me turn by turn directions to a restaurant by the lake we could see from the hotel. On weekends they didn't open until noon so we had time to wander around a bit. I told him about the lake we used to go swimming in as a kid. He talked about swimming in the Caribbean as a child. It was a couple minutes to noon by the time we got back to where the Jeep was parked. There was a little bait shop next to the restaurant. That would make me wonder if they served sushi. As we stepped out of the bait shop they were unlocking the restaurant and asked if we were waiting to go in.

We decided to eat outside. It was a beautiful morning and they had a deck that looked out over the lake that was still in the shade. He had a burger, but I had a breakfast burrito. I had always wondered what it would be like to get up this late on a Sunday morning. Then again, I always wondered what it would be like to wake up in bed with a naked man. I was still in shock from the latter.

Lawrence finished his burger and was playing with his fries as I was finishing up my burrito. "Did you enjoy the evening?"

"Yes, and the morning as well."

"Even though we didn't really do anything."

"I've done more last night than I ever have in my life."

"You really mean that, don't you?"

"I try not to say anything I don't really mean."

"Well, I try to say only what I mean also, and I have something important I need to tell you."

I put my fork down. He immediately took my hand with one of his and my chin in the other. He tipped my head so I had no choice but to look him in the eye.

"I want to marry you." He paused a little, maybe to let it sink in but that wasn't happening. "You are an incredible woman and I want to spend the rest of my life with you. I told myself after my second marriage dissolved I would never marry again, but I've never met anyone like you."

It still wasn't sinking in for me.

"You probably don't believe me, but I do want to marry you. Would you be willing to marry me?"

"Sure," was all I could get out of my mouth at that moment. It was a bit too much to handle after the events of last night. Good thing I had next week off of school. I would have time to really think about what happened and the possibilities for the future.

"I have some things to do at home this weekend, but maybe next weekend we can look for a ring for you. We won't be able to put any money down on it until I get paid from this last job, but we can pick it out at least. Got any ideas about what you would like? I'll go with whatever you like, no matter how much it costs."

I'm a simple girl. I always said if someone presented me with a diamond on a gold band I would turn them down no matter how big the diamond was. Sounds a little cold, I know. But my theory was that any man who wanted to marry me should know me enough to know that I wanted sapphire and silver. He was just going to let me pick it out myself. Somehow I knew it would never happen but at that moment, anything seemed possible.

He pulled out his credit card just before the server came over with the bill. It didn't take long for us to get back to the Jeep, and he had me drop him off at his dad's place. Thinking later, that might have been where he was actually staying. He probably didn't want to admit it, but every time I dropped him off that's where he wanted to go. In any case, he came over to the driver's side of the Jeep when he got out. My window was down already. "I had a wonderful time with you. Hopefully we can do it again soon. I may have to do some things at the jobsite late this week to get it ready for the final inspection, so I may not be coming back next weekend. But I want you to remember that I want to start looking for an engagement ring for you. I'll call you when I can. Speaking of that, when are you going to get a phone so I can call you whenever I want to talk with you?"

"Maybe I'll start looking for something this week since I don't have school."

He started talking about his phone, which was fairly inexpensive. Nothing fancy, but it let him call and text when he needed to. I told him I would look into it.

"I really do want to marry you. I enjoyed waking up next to you and want to do that for the rest of my life." He reached into the Jeep to pull my head close to him for a good-bye kiss. "I'll call you when I can, or at least leave a message on your school phone."

The seed planted months ago had grown into a plant. Right now it was still green, but there were some buds showing. This relationship was going to places I had never been before.

The last time I was in what I considered a "relationship" it took us over a year before we met in person. We never even sat on a bed together and the only time we weren't both fully clothed was when he ran from the bathroom to his bedroom wearing only a towel after a shower and I happened to be in the room between the two.

With Lawrence we met after two months of internet and phone communication and the first night we were together we slept in the same bed wearing one pair of underwear between the two of us. How big was this plant going to get? Actually, what I was really thinking about was what the flowers would look like. Maybe I should have been thinking about how long they would last.

I was trying to sort things out all the way home. We had been talking for several months now, but to say he wanted to marry me after the first real date, not that probable. For some reason I had the feeling this would be the year I got married, but was it really going to be that easy? I don't think I would call this situation easy in any case.

The date ended late on Sunday, but since there was no school that week it didn't really matter. I went to various libraries that week to check my e-mails and such. There were a couple of e-mails from Tim, which was odd for him. It sounded like he was suffering from withdrawal without daily talks with me and was e-mailing as a last resort. I went to the school a couple of times to use the phone and the computer.

There were some changes at school. The staff was small, but still full of politics. The school's funding was always questionable so when one staff member gave the "it's him or me" ultimatum, it was easier to replace her. Her replacement, however, had a different idea of how the school should be run. I knew when they told me what happened things would change, I soon would find out how much they would change and how those changes would affect my social life.

The few times I did talk to Lawrence, he was still saying he wanted to marry me. He used the "l" word to end our phone conversations and the brief e-mails he sent. He sent me a couple pictures of parts of him, saying he'd never sent anyone pictures like that. I almost believed him.

He would be stuck at the jobsite again that weekend. He said that he was the only single person in the group who was working on the house. Since all the others had a family to spend the weekend with, they told him he should stay to be the contact person and in case there were any problems. The lines these guys come up with always sounded logical; maybe that's why I actually almost believe them.

The end of spring break was also the end of March. The last week was pretty lamb-like compared to the weeks before. It was definitely a month of changes for me, and not just from winter to spring. I was becoming a good girl who could easily make some bad choices, but I wanted to be good.

Chapter 5 — Getting good at being bad

The week of spring break was over before I realized it. Back at school the kids and staff asked about my break. The truth was the week wasn't as eventful as the weekend before, but the glow of that weekend was fading. The kids were busy swapping stories of their exploits of the week. As long as they weren't talking about gang or other illegal activity I let them. That way I didn't have to go into details about my weekend. If they did ask, I could easily change the conversation to some hook-up or break-up they talked about to get them off of my social life.

Tim was still talking about coming out the week after Easter. I told him a little of my adventure with Lawrence, but not everything. Since I knew deep down he was never coming out here I didn't mention that the date ended with a proposal. Sometimes I just needed someone to talk to and if Tim knew Lawrence asked me to marry him he may not want to talk with me anymore.

He said he bought his bus ticket already, but I wasn't sure he actually had. He said something about the people he was living with received their tax returns, so they didn't bug him about food money as much. Since they weren't hounding him about helping out with the bills, he said he used the little money he had to get his bus ticket out here. He was still talking to his ex about how they would handle custody of their daughter. I wasn't in a hurry to look for weekly rentals for him. Most of the calls with him were during my lunch or in the afternoon when the kids were gone. There was no reason to keep our conversations private. The conversations with him weren't as full of x-rated innuendo like the conversations with Lawrence.

Things had started to change. Now I wasn't staying at school as late as I had before, but still well after school hours. I looked at the website. Lawrence had hidden his profile, maybe he was serious about me being the last woman he would be dating. Mine was still on, but I wasn't spending evenings trolling for men like I had. That was the main reason I was leaving work earlier than I had before. I usually left before the new staff member, but apparently not early enough for her.

Lawrence and I communicated via e-mail for the most part. I called him the few minutes between when the kids left and when I left school. The days were getting longer and now there was enough time to make a quick run to the lookout after work occasionally. After my weekend with him there was a lot to think about and going to the lookout gave me time to think while driving there and walking around once parked.

He was still talking about marrying me. I had been through that before, but that was after a year of e-mails, not a weekend of sexual frustration for him and something that should have made me feel incredibly guilty. I wasn't planning a wedding yet, at least no more than I had in junior high when my best friend and I were dreaming of when we grew up. Those plans were missing the groom, but now that was about the only thing that was set for this shotgun type wedding.

Marriage. It was a nice dream. In losing my innocence, I lost the ability to believe everything people told me. But it was fun to dream. I was still thinking about what ring I would get. I let myself dream about that.

*****

By that weekend, he wanted to meet again. That was Good Friday. Usually than meant a somber night at church, but Lawrence had other plans. He wanted me to pick him up at the coffee shop again. This time he suggested going to my place for the evening. After the last date, I wasn't sure what to expect. I did, however, remember that he didn't do anything I didn't want him to. In the hotel room he stopped when I asked him to even after I fell asleep. I was sure he would do the same at my place. I should be safe there.

He told me to call him when I was ready to leave on Friday. He said had already eaten dinner, but wanted to just spend time with me. This time I stopped for a bite on the way. I was learning from my mistakes. Later I realized it should have raised a red flag for me. So I wasn't learning fast enough to keep me out of trouble. Maybe I was so tired of being a good girl I was looking for trouble. In that case, I was doing everything right. Good girls always seem to be attracted to bad boys.

We were to meet at the same coffee shop as we did for our first meeting. He arrived just a few minutes after me this time. Again he didn't get coffee, just came over to my table and told me he was ready to be alone with me again. As we were walking to the Jeep he asked if it would be all right if he went to a liquor store for something to drink at my place. He knew me well enough to know I wouldn't have any alcohol at the house. There was a liquor store in the strip mall with the coffee shop, so he ran in as I got things arranged in my Jeep. I had always used it as a mobile office; now there were old newspapers and fast food wrappers that need to be bagged up to be tossed next time I got gas. The one from my dinner on the run still smelled of burgers and fries. I was getting nervous. It was a good thing I didn't eat too much on the way there.

He was out with a 12-pack before long and we were off to my place. He talked about how close they were to finishing that particular job, but the money would be at least a month away. His birthday was next Friday, but he wouldn't be able to celebrate much because of his money situation. The friend he was staying with was going to move at the end of this month so he had to find another place to live. He wasn't hinting at my place, even temporarily, since it was all the way across the big city from the suburban neighborhood he wanted to stay in. Eventually we got to my place.

Up in my room he wasted no time. We cleared the steps, so there was no way anyone would see or hear us, and he started undressing me and himself.

"This time maybe I'll see a little more of you?"

"There's only a little of me that you didn't see last time." I didn't know what to say. Last time I took off more than I had planned, and this time he wanted me totally naked?

Our clothes made a trail from the top of the stairs to the bed. As usual, I had more layers than he did so he was naked before I was. This time we were both totally naked. His hands only left my body long enough to take something off. He was being careful, gauging my reaction each time he touched a new part of me.

It was hard walking to the bed with him. Our mutual strip tease slowed our progression to a snail's pace. I was enjoying all the sensations, the cloth brushing against my skin as it was taken off and his hands treating every inch of exposed skin as it was uncovered. It was only about ten feet to the bed, but it took us a good 15 minutes to make that distance.

I made sure to let him know how much I was enjoying this. Each little moan or giggle that escaped my lips put a smile on his. At least it did when I could see them, some of the time his lips were causing the sound. I was making what I thought was a feeble attempt to reciprocate. He didn't seem to mind my hands fumbling around his body. He knew this was my first attempt and said he was happy that I was at least trying.

Now that we were fully naked he was exploring my body with his hands and his lips. It was like we were in a different universe.

This was the second time I saw the guy, and already we were naked now and both lying on my bed. This is *not* what a good girl does. But at this moment I didn't care, I was caught up in the moment. He was careful while undressing me, but now his hands were getting braver. They were wrapped around me, getting lower and lower down my back. His knees were getting higher and higher up my thigh. He was significantly taller than me, so he must have been pretty flexible.

"You're doing all the work again, is there anything I can do to help?"

"You're doing everything you need to. Just keep letting me know how much you are enjoying this. Let me guess—this is the first time you've been naked with a man."

"You know it is." I was having a hard time saying anything. Not that I was embarrassed or looking for the right words, but enjoying the sensations doesn't lend itself to carrying on a conversation. Feeling his hands running up and down my back, the skin to skin contact was too much for me to keep to myself. As my back arched toward him, he took the opportunity to tease my breast with a quick kiss.

He definitely had more practice at this than I. Practice, what's that? I really had no idea what I was doing. I think in some ways Lawrence liked that. He had total control. He knew exactly how to act to get the right reaction from me. He explored every part of my body, pausing occasionally only to have a drink or two and let me catch my breath.

At some point he paused, and I was curious as to why. "Do you have any pictures of yourself dressed like you are now?"

"I think you know the answer to that."

"Yes, but maybe by some chance you took some at some point."

"I don't have a digital camera and those are the pictures you don't want to have someone else develop."

"Would you mind if we took some, so I have something to remember you during the week? Next week I may be staying out by myself most nights and would like to have something to look at when I'm missing you. Just sit there, I'll get my camera." He went over to his pants and pulled a small camera out of a pocket. He came back over to the bed and sat on the edge, grabbing a sip or two from his can. "Let me get some of just you first." He snapped off a couple of pictures before I could really comprehend what he was doing. He was taking pictures of me with no clothes on. As you've probably guessed, that was also something new for me. I pulled one of the sheets up over my chest, but not before he had at least three pictures that he later showed me. "Don't tell me you're getting shy now."

"Not just now, but the last time pictures showed so much of my skin I was wearing a diaper and don't remember much about the pictures being taken. They're just brought out every once in a while to embarrass me."

"Your bare ass, that's what else I need pictures of." The smile on his face let me know he knew better than to try to get pictures of that. My arms may not be all that strong, but he was holding a camera and only really had use of one of his. I was no match for that. "All right, how about some pictures of the two of us? We could call them our engagement pictures."

"Dressed like this?"

"If I had my way this is how you'll be dressed most of the time once we are married."

"Even when you're not around?"

"Well, then I guess you could get dressed. I wouldn't want you to catch a cold. When I'm there we can use body heat to keep us warm. Here, sit on the edge of the bed with me."

I sat behind him, peeking at the camera over his shoulder. The camera was on the TV just at the end of his reach. He tried to look as natural as he could with his arm stretched as far as it would go to get the pictures he wanted.

"If we need any more pictures we can take them later. Now, you seem to need some body heat." He turned around and flipped me back on to the bed. He followed with his body before I could even catch my breath. He was doing everything he could to create friction between us to keep me warm. It sounded good to say friction, better than saying he was groping me. It sounded better than saying we were doing everything just shy of wild monkey sex. It sounded a little more like something a good girl like me would do.

Time seemed to stop for a while. He continued to touch me, and I did nothing but enjoy it and try to do things that he would enjoy. Before I knew it I looked at the clock and it was getting late for me. Of course by now everyone had silently and soberly filed out of church. As if he knew I was distracted and coming back to reality, he ran into the bathroom. There were some noises coming from there, but I wasn't about to ask. It took me a while to realize what he was doing in there. There was still a little of the innocent girl left in me. When I finally realized what he was doing I *definitely* wasn't going to bother him in there. A few minutes later he came out, quietly walked over to the bed, and silently lay down next to me.

"Our wedding night is really going to be something. I bet you can't wait." He rolled over to his side so he was facing me. "I know I'm looking forward to it." The look on his face made it obvious what was on his mind.

He was still talking about getting married, even when he was with me. Maybe there might be something to it. Maybe there was good cause to dream about a ring. Maybe someone might actually want to marry me.

"Then we'll be able to sleep next to each other all the time. Think you could get used to sharing a bed?"

"I've lived a long time alone, but I think I could handle it."

"Is it all right if you try tonight?"

115

"I'm not going to drive you home now. As long as we're already in bed and comfortable. . ." He put his free arm across my chest, to go with the one that was already under my neck, and squeezed a little, just enough to let me know he was hoping I was enjoying this as much as he was. "We may as well stay here for the night."

Like there was any question about that when I picked him up earlier. We slept together after our first date, why should this date be any different?

"I can definitely get used to sharing a bed with you." His arms squeezed me again. Somewhere in the next few minutes we both drifted off to sleep. My last thoughts were about how good girls don't lay totally naked with a man they've only met twice.

Saturday morning came slowly, like they did for me recently. I woke up at my usual time and after remembering that I wasn't alone, I looked over at the other side of the bed. He was still asleep so I decided I could go back to sleep as well.

What seemed like only a couple moments later, I felt someone brush the hair off my face. "Good morning, Sunshine."

"Good morning, yourself." We lay there for a few minutes. Both of us seemed to be just enjoying waking up next to someone.

"Don't suppose you have any coffee here, do you?"

"I think I heard Rob leave already. He has coffee and I don't think he would mind if I made you a cup or two. But that means I have to get at least a little dressed to go downstairs."

"If it's for coffee, I'll let you do that."

I put on a long shirt and socks. "You'll have to remind me how you want it." After I said that, I realized I had no idea how he drank his coffee. We met at a coffee shop where he never ordered coffee.

"I prefer it hot, at least right away."

"You know what I mean."

"How about I come with you, or do you think that Rob will be back?"

"When he leaves in the morning on Saturday he usually doesn't come back until Sunday night."

He put on his pants and we went down to make the coffee. Luckily there was enough that we could make what Lawrence needed and it didn't seem like any was taken out of the canister Rob kept it in. It didn't take long for the coffee to start dripping into the carafe. While it did, he kissed the back of my neck to the beat of the drips. His arms were wrapped around me, his right hand on my left breast and his left hand on my right. Of course it was over my t-shirt, but still it felt good. I could really get used to Saturday mornings like this.

Finally, the coffee was ready. I watched as he put sugar and milk in his coffee, so that the next time he would come over I could make it for him. What was I thinking, next time?

He started sipping the coffee on our way back upstairs. "I'll have to get your recipe for coffee."

"I'm sure you'll get it down eventually. It's not that complicated, and when we get married you can quit your job so you won't have anything to do but take care of me." At that moment it sounded good. Thinking about it now, what was I thinking!?

We talked a little more about where we came from and what was going on now in our lives. As he drank his coffee he got more sociable. He was still talking about what it would be like married to me—how it would be different for him and for me. I mentioned I was going to Alaska again for a couple of weeks in June. He said he might be able to join me if I wanted him to.

That would be interesting. Introducing him, the man I went to a hotel with the first time I saw him, to all my friends at church up there. Me, the good little church girl, with him, a man who cussed like a sailor, drank like a fish and smoked like a chimney. Yes, that would be interesting. There was one older lady in particular who threatened to take care of any man who hurt me. She was a surgical nurse who did most of her own veterinary care for her animals. In short, she knew how to get the right materials and how to use

117

them. Maybe it wouldn't be such a good idea to introduce him to all my grandmothers up there.

His birthday was next Friday. He wanted to go out, but only if at least some of the money for the job came through. Even if it was his birthday he didn't want me to spend a lot on him or make a big deal about it. He said by my birthday he would definitely have the money so we could celebrate them both together. It was only a little over a month away and he was willing to postpone his celebration so we could do it right.

Soon he was awake enough to remember all the things he had to do today. I took the hint and asked if he wanted me to take him home. Once we got to the area by the coffee shop he started giving me turn by turn directions to his father's place again. He gave me a long kiss good-bye in the Jeep, jumped out and got what was left of his beer in the back seat. He walked across the street and to the door without even a look back. I should have taken that hint as well, but I was still so inexperienced about this stuff. Looking back, there were so many hints that this wasn't going to last long. I just didn't know what to look for and wasn't thinking well enough to put the pieces together.

The flower was starting to bloom. It didn't look like anything I've ever seen before. Now the question is what to do with it. I once got an aloe vera cactus to bloom and didn't know what to do with it. I took pictures so people would believe me, which was good because the flowers didn't last all that long. The flowers were tiny white petals with no smell that I could find. The novelty of this flower was like that. I didn't notice the things about Lawrence that I didn't like. But in my defense, there were some things that I hadn't seen yet. When I was looking at the buds getting ready to blossom on that aloe vera all I could see was the potential. Rose bushes have thorns before the buds have a fragrance or you can see the velvety petals, but you put up with them because you know what the bud will turn into. There was hope that this flower would be as beautiful and aromatic as the rose. The little thorns I had seen

118

so far were easily overlooked in hopes that the end result would make it all worth it. It can be dangerous to focus on the potential and not take into account what is right in front of you. A lesson I would have to learn the hard way.

*****

The next day was Easter Sunday. A few people at church asked where I was on Friday. I just told them I got out of work late and it had been a long week. Two-thirds of the truth isn't bad. It was the truth and nothing but the truth, just not the whole truth. They probably wouldn't believe me anyway if I told them I was in bed with a man at the time. They still thought I was a good girl.

At work I was distracted the entire week. With his birthday, my birthday, the trip to Alaska, getting—GULP—married, there was a lot to think about. My New Year's Eve premonition was looking almost possible. Maybe it was that idea that had me blinded to the red flags that should have been obstructing my vision.

Even Tim told me to watch out for him. Maybe he was jealous that Lawrence was with me and he was in a different time zone. He kept telling me about "men like him," meaning Lawrence. My guess was that he knew so much about them because he was one. He claimed to have his bus ticket already. He would be out here the middle of next week, if he could make arrangements to still have his daughter on weekends. That wasn't looking all that promising so I wasn't going to hold my breath or make arrangements to pick him up from the bus station. Funny how I totally dismissed what he said, but was seriously thinking that Lawrence might actually marry me. Lust can do a number on the mind.

Lawrence made it seem possible. He was to the point of sending pictures of himself, well, parts of himself, along with the pictures he took last weekend. I quickly realized that I couldn't download any attachment he sent unless I was totally alone in the room. The kids couldn't see the computer screen if they were in the "student area" of the room. One problem was that they didn't always stay there. Another problem was that when I would see the pictures I would start to giggle. Then they would ask to see what I was doing on the computer. If even one came back to see the screen (probably one of the girls) they would announce to everyone in the room what I was looking at and that would probably end my internet access at school for good—and maybe my job as well.

My access was being limited anyway. The reason is longer than I care to share, but the short version was that a new staff member, who was looking to work her way up quickly, had a real problem with me staying so late. She said it was for my safety, but really it was a way to look like she was in charge. I decided to get one of those "pay as you go" phones. I couldn't look at the pictures while I was at home, but I could text and talk with Lawrence any time.

We talked a couple of times on the phone. He was at a new jobsite, one with very limited accommodations. Actually, he had to bring his own but it was so far away from his "home" and at the moment he couldn't justify getting a hotel room for just a few hours every night to sleep. As long as he was willing to rough it they had someone to keep an eye on the equipment and supplies that were already there. It was while he was alone in his tent that he would call me. The calls came too late for my personal preference, but it was the only time he had to talk. At least that's the story he gave me and at that time I didn't feel the need to check up on it any further. If I really thought about it, if he was out that far from civilization would there be cell phone coverage? It was possible, but something in his story should have had me asking more questions.

*****

Soon it was Friday again, Lawrence's birthday. I sent him a birthday card in hopes he would get it on Friday. Since he refused to give me his address—because it was changing he said—I sent the card to his father's place. I couldn't get him a real present, but at least he knew I was thinking of him even before his birthday.

I'm not a big fan of my own birthday, but I think everyone deserves something special for their special day. Lawrence said just hanging out with me would make it a good birthday for him. I picked him up at the coffee shop again. This time I didn't even bother getting something to drink. It was too warm for hot chocolate, and I'm not a big coffee fan.

I arrived right at the time we were going to meet. Now that I had a phone with me, we could coordinate things better so I didn't have to wait around. Lawrence opened the door about the time I sat down. He only took one step in, just enough to be out of the doorway, and we were out the door before it could close all the way. Without a word we walked over to the Jeep.

He opened the door after I unlocked it. "Happy birthday." He smiled and gave me a quick kiss before I could say any more. He pulled the card I sent out of his jacket pocket to show me he got it. He must have picked it up from his father's place before meeting me. At least that's what I told myself at the time. Later I realized this was another hint that he was actually living with his dad and wanted to make it look good. In any case, the card stayed in my Jeep for quite a while as a reminder.

"Mind if I get something to drink again?"

"It's your birthday. You should be able to do whatever you want."

"Whatever I want?" His eye brow arched up as his lips shifted into a sly grin.

"We'll see how the evening goes."

He quickly got what he needed and we were off. Rob's vehicle wasn't in front of the house when we got there. Lawrence asked if it was parked in the garage or if my housemate was gone—and for how long. Rob wasn't in the house and his Jeep wasn't in the garage. Then I remembered he said something about staying at the computer lab at the school where he was taking classes. Last time he said that he got home pretty late and went straight to bed. He sleeps with a breathing mask so once he goes to sleep he said he doesn't hear anything besides the machine. Tonight we were going to put that to a test.

"How about we stay down here and watch a movie or two while we are alone here?"

"Works for me, Rob said we could watch anything he has. I'm not sure what he has, but we can look." At least we would be in a somewhat public space for a while. That would be a little safer. I was getting nervous about how far he was expecting to go. He said he respected my decision to wait to go all the way, but the ride home was full of ideas of what could be done short of that.

He picked out something to put in the DVD player while I went up to get out of my work clothes and into my sweats. It was one of those movies you had to watch all of, and it still didn't really make sense the first couple of times. I had seen it before for a class I took so I could pick it up if we got distracted. And get distracted I did. His hands stared roaming over my body.

"Your skin feels cold."

"It usually is, but right now I wish I were a little warmer."

"So I'm not enough to keep you warm?" His hands were continuing to explore all the places he could with the knowledge that someone could walk in at any moment.

"I'm cold blooded. Maybe I should get a blanket for us."

"That sounds good. I'm a little chilled as well." We both looked at the fireplace, but that would require more work than just getting a blanket. He had ideas of what could be done if we were under a little cover and I was thinking that there was no wood in the living room for us to use to start a fire.

There was a blanket on the back of the couch we were sitting on, but it was full of dog hair from Rob's husky. The truth was I didn't remember it was there until I came down with one from my bedroom and saw it on the back of the couch. The one I brought down wasn't all that big so we had to sit close together to get it to cover us both. That was only part of his plan for asking for a blanket. The blanket gave us some measure of privacy. If Rob walked in he wouldn't be able to see where Lawrence's hands were. Now his hands could go anywhere he wanted them to, which was probably his plan all along.

He started by pretending to pull the blanket up to my neck from underneath and then letting his hands come to rest on my chest. But they didn't rest for long. Why do guys even bother putting a movie on? His eyes were on the TV, but his hands were in constant motion on my chest, not that I was complaining. His right hand moved down my torso, and started to gently lift the waistband of my sweat pants. As usual, I was too busy enjoying the feeling to really think about what would be happening next, or what he was thinking would happen next.

Maybe that was it. I would get so caught up in the feeling and the moment I would let things go too far—to that place where angels fear to tread. Luckily God was still there and keeping me safe. Well, as safe as you can be with a sex-starved male in a pretty much private place. He knew my intentions, and I should have had a good idea of his. Unfortunately, it wasn't likely both of us would get what we wanted. In fact, the two were probably mutually exclusive, but I would never pretend to know for sure what someone else was thinking.

The movie was continuing, but really I could have cared less. His hands were exploring my body below the covers, and below the waist. We weren't saying a word, just getting comfortable with each other's company. From what I remembered, the movie was about half over when there was a noise at the lock of the outside door.

Rob opened the door, saw us on the couch, said a quick hello and good night, and went to the back of the house. It took a few seconds for Lawrence to get his hands out of my pants, me to get my sweats situated right, and then head off to the kitchen. By then

Rob was almost done eating something quick before going to bed. "Didn't mean to bother the two of you," he said with a smile after he swallowed.

"Hope we didn't bother you."

"No bother. I'm going to bed now and you know I can't hear anything once I turn my machine on, so you guys have fun and watch any movie you find over there." He used a breathing machine for his sleep apnea. I usually didn't go downstairs at night, but when I did there was a rhythmic hum from Rob's room when he was sleeping.

"I was hoping you wouldn't mind if we put in one of the DVDs you had."

"I told you any time you wanted to you could watch something down here. It's about time you took me up on it."

"It's Lawrence's birthday, so we wanted to do something different."

"Between work and school, it's been a long day for me, so I'll let you two to 'do something different' or whatever they're calling it these days." He could hardly keep from bursting out in laughter, his smile was so big.

I got a beer for Lawrence so it looked like I had a real reason to go into the kitchen and Rob went to his room. Soon I heard the rhythm of the breathing machine. Later I would question if he was really sleeping or hoping to hear something from the living room, but that night I believed him. Then again, that night my mind was on other things.

Luckily Lawrence knew how to use the DVD player. I'm not real good with remotes. It took only a couple of minutes for Lawrence to get right back where he was, under the blanket with his hands all over me. It was his birthday, but he was giving me quite a present. The movie got a little loud, and he didn't seem to mind that I was getting a bit loud as well. The rhythm of the machine only added to the rhythm of the moment.

The first movie was done. While Lawrence changed the DVD I got him another beer. There was no noise from Rob's room except for his machine, and his light was out. I don't even remember what movie he put in. It didn't really matter anyway since neither of us was really watching it. Then again, all I can say is that I wasn't watching it. My eyes were closed as I was enjoying every moment of Lawrence's explorations. We were pretty much alone, with covering if we should get company, and taking full advantage of it. It was his birthday, but I was getting all the presents. The way we were sitting I couldn't even pretend to practice making him feel good. His legs were straddling my body and his arms were making it impossible for me to move mine. I could feel his breath on the side of my face. I was in no position to do anything but enjoy what he was doing. He was in total control.

The movie finished before we knew it. There was another movie, but Lawrence suggested we go upstairs. He shut down the player while I got another beer for him. He waited for me by the stairs with my blanket over his arm. About halfway up the stairs I figured out why he waited to let me go first.

"Even in sweat pants your ass is the best I've ever seen." I felt his hand on the back of my knee. "But it would be a better birthday for me to see it without the sweats." He was starting to unwrap his present.

My sweats didn't make it to the top of the stairs until the next morning. At the top step he stared quickly peeling away the layers of shirts. In seconds all of our clothes were on the floor and he was maneuvering me to the bed. If I had thought about the situation, things would have been different. My mind was totally gone, lost in the magic of the moment. Lawrence knew what he wanted, and how to get it. I didn't give much resistance. Part of that was that I didn't know what to do, part of it was not caring what was happening because it felt so good.

I hit the bed first, and Lawrence carefully adjusted my body into position. Positioned for what? Now it's time for you to use *your* imagination. All I will say is that Lawrence got something like what he wanted for his birthday, and I could still say that I was a good girl by at least one definition of the word "good." After it was over, we both fell into a well deserved sleep.

*****

The next morning I got up before him and snuck down to make coffee. Rob was gone for the day again. I stayed downstairs until the coffee was done and fixed it like I remembered Lawrence doing it the week before. He was just waking up, or maybe he heard me picking up my sweats from the steps and woke up.

"Hopefully this is the way you like your coffee."

"It's exactly how I like it, from your hand." Even half asleep he was a charmer. He sat up on the bed, giving me a space to sit next to him. "I could really get used to this. Rolling over during the night and seeing you next to me, waking up to see you with my coffee in your beautiful hands, sitting here chatting with you as I'm waking up. Think you could get used to waking up next to me?"

"I think I could get used to that. The hard part might be getting used to sharing a bed with someone. Hope I didn't crowd you out last night."

"I slept just fine. Then again, all last week I was sleeping in a sleeping bag on the ground in a tent. Exercising like that just before going to sleep usually helps me sleep pretty well." Either it was the caffeine kicking in or he was just in a good mood. Then again, most men are in a good mood after "exercising" like we did last night.

We started having a real conversation, like the ones we would have on the phone. It sometimes got a little flirty, but usually it was about things we really did need to talk about if things were going to go any further between us. Sometimes he got serious, maybe a little too serious for me at that moment. As the conversation went on it was more of the serious and less of the flirty type.

He told me about some of the jobs he had in his past. Some of them he could talk about, some he said he couldn't say any more than the vague description he gave me. He kept saying there were things about him his wife would have to know, but never ask about. That was part of the reason his first marriages didn't work. One wife didn't trust him and the other was constantly asking too many questions and then not keeping the information to herself. At least those were the excuses he was using now. My job required confidentiality, but not high level security clearance like his supposedly did.

Time flew by again. Eventually he realized he was hungry. He asked if there were any little places that we could walk to for something to eat. A few blocks away was a small shopping district with several different types of eating establishments. We decided to get a big sub and go back to the house to share it. That way Lawrence could wash it down with a beer instead of the beverages they offered.

This time when we went back up the steps, we both kept our clothes on. Then again, he went right upstairs while I went to the fridge to get one of those beers for him. The bed was the only furniture I had, so we had to sit on it to eat. Once the sandwich was gone, he started talking again. He kept telling me about schools I should apply to so I didn't have to teach at "one of those schools" again next year. Apparently his kids went to a private school. That was one he told me to apply to, saying he could be a reference for me. I was thinking about how I would explain that I knew him, but that would be something to think about another day if I ever decided to actually do that.

He started talking about all the times he ended up in the hospital. A few nasty wrecks with different types of vehicles—a car, a motorcycle, a boat—he crashed them all. A couple of times it was after a fight. He admitted to having a pretty bad temper. I hadn't seen it yet, but there were flashes that made me wonder. Anyone with the passion he showed when we were "exercising" was likely to have the potential for a nasty temper. I was trained to see behavior problems before they happen, and he definitely had some of the signs. I was a big girl and I could handle myself so I wasn't worried. It was, however, something to think of with all the talk he was doing about getting married. Once I had a dream that I married someone like him. Needless to say it wasn't a good dream, but that wasn't the reason I didn't date.

Yes, sprinkled in there was more talk about our wedding. This time it was more than just what we would do that night when we were finally alone. He knew my family lived out of state and that I was pretty close to them. He remembered I wanted a simple ring. He said I could do all the planning. He wasn't all that close to his family, including his own kids. He would do anything I wanted, even a church wedding if I insisted. We would be talking about that more as the time came closer. There were a lot of other things to do before we needed to worry about that. Or at least that's what he kept saying.

Lawrence told me to pick out a ring and he would take care of it once he got paid for this job. I was beginning to notice a pattern with this. All of his promises hinge on getting paid for a job that was supposedly done weeks ago.

Of course those weren't the thoughts running through my head while he talked. I was thinking about how good it felt to be sitting next to a man on a lazy Saturday afternoon. My hands were caressing his arm. This is the longest I had been just hanging out with a man since high school. We were just sitting there, talking about nothing, and enjoying each other's company. Yes, there were some flirty innuendos sprinkled in the conversation but it would be rated "G" for the most part.

Eventually we turned the TV on to see if there was anything to watch. There weren't many choices since we didn't have cable, satellite or a good antenna. I couldn't even get all the local channels up in my room. The usual Saturday evening movies and stuff were starting. Things for kids who didn't know what it meant to go out and lonely adults who didn't have anything better to do. We didn't fit into either category so it didn't stay on that long.

We spent the entire day together just talking. Now it was almost time for bed. He was still talking about meeting me up in Alaska during my visit up there, but he added that he had a trip to take in between now and then. It would be one of those trips I couldn't ask about. He couldn't say much other than that his destination was somewhere in the mid-Atlantic area. He wasn't sure when it would be, but probably around the middle of next month.

Conveniently he would be gone around the time of my birthday. He said he would make it up to me somehow. I wasn't expecting something like I gave him for his birthday, but he was saying it would be well worth the wait. By that time he would definitely have the money from this last job and he would make up for all the bad birthdays I had in the past. Of course I told him it wasn't necessary, but this year I was thinking of actually celebrating my birthday. In any case, we had a month to discuss it.

We were both getting tired, so we decided to put on our pajamas and get in bed. Well, we got naked and under the covers. Lawrence must have been tired because he went right to sleep. Either he was tired or he knew he wasn't going to get what he really wanted—and would not get as close as he had last night—so he wasn't going to push it tonight. It was still nice to fall asleep with a man next to me.

The next morning he asked to get his coffee on the road when I took him back home. It was probably his way of saying he had enough of me, but that was one hint I didn't get right away. There was no long good-bye at his father's house. He thanked me for the birthday present and keeping him company for the weekend and said he would call again next weekend when he got back into town. Again there was the hope that he would be back in town before Friday and the money would come through for that last job. He also mentioned that it was good that I got a cell phone so he could talk to me more often.

129

A quick kiss good-bye and he was gone.

*****

Tim was wondering why I hadn't answered my phone since Thursday night. Lawrence didn't answer his phone when his brother supposedly called, so I wasn't going to answer the phone when Tim called. The messages were just that I should call him when I got a chance. On Sunday afternoon I finally got a chance. His ticket was for that Wednesday, so I should be ready for him. He didn't exactly say what that all entailed, but I was guessing he was going to need a place to stay right away. Do you ever just have a feeling that something is (or is not) going to happen? With Tim for some reason I knew he wasn't going to use that bus ticket. For the moment, however, he was so concentrated on his intended move that he didn't really ask what I was doing that was more important than talking with him. I got away with, "It was the new guy's birthday and we were celebrating." I tried not to use names with Tim when it came to the guys I was seeing. I would describe them like the peripheral characters on TV shows. Usually he would start off as "new guy" and moved on to some other category as I got to know him.

Not surprisingly, Tim decided not to get on the bus on Wednesday. He called to complain about losing all the money for not using the ticket. They said he could use part of it at least if he wanted to use it for a ticket for a different day, as long as it was in the near future. He said he was still going to try to come out, but he had been saying that for four months now and when he finally got the ticket he couldn't do it.

As it turned out, my gut feeling was right.

*****

Lawrence said he was moving to a different friend's basement the next weekend. I left a message, all right—maybe more than just one message—that weekend letting him know I would be willing to help. When he finally called back late the next Tuesday he said he didn't want me to see how he was living. Most of his stuff was in plastic totes so there wasn't much real packing. The stuff he kept with him was just what he needed so there wasn't much. Most of his time was spent at various jobsites so "his place" was more a place to store his stuff and crash on weekends or nights he was in town. It didn't take him long and he had the help of the friend who he was staying with and the one he would be staying with. He didn't need my help and didn't want me to think less of him because of how he lived. At least that was the story I was given.

Family birthdays were the next week for Lawrence. As he was listing who was celebrating when, I mentioned that I could attend some of those events. If he really wanted to marry me, I needed to meet his family and this would be a good chance to do that. At least that's the way I saw it. I realized, and explained to him, that he couldn't meet my family without a plane ride. My mom was planning on spending some time with me during the coming summer so he could meet her then, but the next time I planned on heading back to where I grew up was for Christmas. He was starting a new project and it would be hard for him to take time off. He was still talking of coming to Alaska, but that was more as a vacation, which is very different from a family meet and greet. Here was a chance for me to meet his family even if he couldn't meet mine for a while.

He didn't see it that way. Finally he came out and told me he thought I was moving too fast. I was moving too fast? I was moving too fast? Finally, I saw a red flag waving.

He insisted we go to a hotel the first night we met, but that wasn't moving too fast for him. He undressed me without a word before I could stop him the three times we were alone, but that wasn't too fast for him. And I was moving too fast? We obviously

131

had different ideas of what the pace of a relationship should be. Then again, on his profile he mentioned he was looking for a wife as an afterthought.

Finally, I realized what he really wanted was a friend and a lover. Those I could be without meeting his family. In fact, it would probably be best if his family didn't meet me if I was only a friend and a lover. A sick feeling when straight to my heart.

April stared out with such promise. I missed church twice for Lawrence, but he would never know what that meant to me. To him it was par for the course. There were times I went to church sick. That may have even been why he was in such a hurry to leave the day before Easter, knowing if he spent that Saturday night I would be attending a service since it was a special Sunday.

I was thinking the vibes might be right, that some time in that calendar year I would be married, but that was the beginning of the month. Here at the end of the month, things weren't looking so good for a wedding this year. I had blown another chance at a husband by seeming too needy.

The bloom was fading. It looked good for a week or so, but then I noticed all the thorns on the plant and realized the flower wasn't all that pretty anyway. It definitely didn't look like the picture on the seed package. It wasn't the color I was expecting and didn't smell all that good. The bloom didn't last all that long either. The plant was still alive so there was hope it would bloom again. I tried to keep it well watered to help it along. Maybe I watered it too much. Maybe it didn't like the way I tried to take care of it. Maybe I wasn't the right one to try to save it. In any case, it wasn't growing like I hoped it would.

Now at the end of the month everything had changed. I chased off a guy by wanting to spend too much time with him and trying to be a part of his life, like he said he wanted me to become. When he did call back he said he wanted to get together at some point but right now he was busy with work and family. After all those family birthdays he would be going on that trip he couldn't talk to me about.

April ended very different than it started. Back at square one.

Chapter 6 — Sometimes lucky is better than good

May was finally here. There was about a month and a half left of the school year. Things weren't going according to the plan made at the beginning of the school year so we were trying a new approach with the kids to see if we could survive the year with our sanity intact. To add a little tension for me, the day after the teachers' last day I was going to fly back to Alaska.

Lawrence was saying he would be flying up the week after that, so while I was on my vacation time he would be there. The problem was that he only wanted to talk about that in the wee hours of the morning. It was a good thing my ringtone wasn't anything like my alarm. I don't know if he was calling before going to sleep or because he woke up early. In any case, he would call while I was asleep, which didn't help me think clearly during the conversation or during the day when I was supposed to be teaching.

I felt like I needed to answer whenever he called. I reasoned that he may not call again for a while and I wanted to talk to him as much as possible since we probably wouldn't see each other for a month or so—maybe not until I picked him up from the airport in Anchorage, if that was actually going to happen.

The pattern that was developing didn't thrill me. He would call somewhere between midnight and 3 a.m. on Thursday. We would talk for a bit and he would say I should call him on Saturday morning so we could meet somewhere. I would call him when I got up on Saturday and left a message saying I was ready to go. Then I would leave a couple more messages that day. It may have seemed to him that I was a little too persistent, but he said he wanted to talk to me or see me so I kept calling him.

If he called back at all, it was sometime Sunday afternoon or evening, too late to do anything that weekend. He would still say he wanted to marry me, but that was looking less and less like something that would ever really happen. I wasn't sure I wanted to marry him anymore given his recent—and probably more typical—behavior. This was a little more than being "independent together" and I was getting the impression I was more of a sex toy that he was tired of playing with since I wouldn't go all the way.

Occasionally I would get some blocks of time with no students in my classroom. Late one Thursday afternoon I checked my account on the dating website. Without something besides a promise from Lawrence over a month ago, I wanted to keep my options open. I wasn't sending out messages, only responding to the few that came in. Most of them were going nowhere fast anyway.

Wait a minute, there was a message from Don. I hadn't heard anything from him since he left a bruise on my neck. He happened to be online, so I thought I would say hello. I'm one of those people who never wanted to burn bridges, and I never really said good-bye to him.

He remembered me, and he asked how my neck was the morning after our last meeting. He could tell I was a little agitated about that and apologized several times. Right after our meeting his father got sick and family business took precedence over his social life. He couldn't believe I was still available. I didn't let on that some might argue if I was or not. He asked what I was doing this weekend. The last I heard from Lawrence was that he was preparing to disappear. It would probably take longer than a weekend to do whatever it was that he was doing, come back, and find time to see me again. This would give me something to do this weekend.

Don didn't sound like he was on the prowl for a quick sexual encounter. He mentioned going to a movie in an actual movie theater. I haven't done that since . . . since . . . since my first trip to town when I came to visit the idiot who shall remain nameless. It sounded safe enough to try again. We agreed that he would pick me up the following night after I got home from work, and we would catch up on things. That would also be something new. A date was coming to my place to pick me up. A date where I didn't have to drive—that was something different.

The rest of the day and all of the next went pretty fast at work. The new plan for the kids was to have them work on some projects for the rest of the year. The staff had already explained the projects, so now it was just a matter of babysitting the students while they worked on them. Well, there was a little more to it since they were in this school because of behavior problems. Babysitting might not be the right word, not really crowd control either. The ones who thought the projects were lame only came to school occasionally, on rainy days or the day before they had to meet their parole officer. The ones who did come liked the idea of the projects so they were motivated to work on them. I didn't have as much time at the computer, but I did have a more regular lunch and a few more snippets of time without students so I could work on my social life.

Occasionally Lawrence would call during the day. There was one call in particular that was overheard by the kid who made the announcement about my "bruise" to the class. What he actually heard of the conversation was put together with some embellishments about what he *thought* he heard to make a good story to tell all the other kids to continue to embarrass me. Luckily it stayed in the classroom and the administration didn't hear about it, or they didn't say they did, which was fine with me.

Tim was still complaining about losing the money for his bus ticket. I think he was realizing that he wasn't going to make it out here. He was giving me tips on things to see, and this time he wasn't including himself in the plans. He told me earlier that he had been to this area on vacation, which is why he wanted to come back to live out here. I hadn't been able to do much sight-seeing since I got here and that was pretty much all he did while he was here. He kept talking about all the places he went and all the fun he had. It just wouldn't be as much fun to do those things alone, if I could afford to do them. Tim suggested I get some man to pay for me to act like a tourist on occasion. Little comments like that made me think he had given up on the idea of coming out here. He knew things were not going well with Lawrence, and he sounded genuinely happy that I was making plans to go out with someone else.

Finally the work week was over. I cleaned up what I needed to in the classroom and headed home. There was just enough time to shower and change before Don planned on arriving. This time we were going on an actual date, in his truck. That was something I hadn't done in a while, probably not since I was with the idiot. Really it wasn't all that long ago, but it felt like a lifetime. I had a few minutes to look out my bedroom window to see when Don drove up.

I made it out of the door before he parked. When we both got settled in his truck, he asked what I thought about going to a drive-in movie. I had only been to one when I was very little. We saw *Bambi* and my cousin threw a fit because my aunt made her keep her pajamas zipped up. Yes, we were so little that we wore footy jammies and our parents had us in them to make it easier to put us right to bed after we got home from the movie because we were sure to fall asleep on the way home. It had been a *long* time since I went to a drive-in movie.

We joked about what most people think happens when a couple goes to a date at a drive-in. He noted that the transmission was on the steering column and the seats, including what the manufacturers called the middle seat, went all the way back to an extended cab so we would have more room to do things in the truck. Of course it would be dark so it didn't matter that his windows weren't tinted. When we got closer to the location he stopped at a gas station and asked if I wanted anything for during the movie. He ran in to get a soda for himself and a bottle of water for me.

We arrived after the opening credits of the first movie, but we didn't really miss much. Don got the audio on the radio, and said it would be all right if I moved closer to him. With an invitation like that, it was only polite for me to oblige. He put his arm around me and I felt like I was in a movie. I was hoping the movie we were beginning to act out wouldn't end up as one of those slasher, "don't get out of the car" movies. Luckily it was beginning to turn into a movie they would show late at night or on a cable channel.

His hands were all over me, and I wasn't complaining. It was exciting to be felt up in a somewhat public place. He found a way to get his hands under my shirt without making it look too obvious for people walking past on their way to the snack bar. We were parked in the middle so there weren't many people going past.

I don't want to compare experiences with different men, but this was different from a couple weekends ago when Lawrence and I were under the covers with the knowledge Rob could walk in at any time. This was a public place and people we had never met were only feet away from us and could walk past our windows at any time. When he heard something outside he would freeze. I guess he was hoping that the people walking by only looked at something that moved, and so as long as he didn't move they wouldn't look. At one point, his hand was over a very sensitive place on my body when he stopped. The giggle they must have heard would have drawn more attention than the motion of his hand under my shirt. Luckily there was a funny part in the movie at the same time so there were giggles from the nearby cars as well. Either that or everyone was enjoying a groping with a laugh.

Thinking about it later, Don must have liked public groping. The last time we had physical contact was out in the street by the school. There was probably less chance of someone seeing us then, but we were out in the open that night. Tonight we were in our own little place, but in a very public setting. Growing up, things like this were always done in a private place. This was exciting to me.

As the movie progressed, people stopped going by all together. About that time he turned his face towards me. I wasn't sure exactly what he was up to, but he had a look in his eye. Not something to be afraid of, because it was a look I had seen before. He leaned over and started kissing me. I remember seeing many one headed monsters in the vehicles in front of us. Not that I was really looking. When the picture on the screen got bright it was hard not to see through the windows of some vehicles, especially since his truck was taller than the cars that took up most of the spaces in the parking lot. A couple cars looked empty by this time. I'm sure if you looked long enough you would see a head or a hand or maybe even a foot above the seat every once in a while. I had better things to do, or more accurately better things were being done to me, than to play nosy neighbor in the parking lot. Lately I'd "seen" more movies than ever before in my life, but I couldn't tell you much about the movies I hadn't seen before.

It didn't take us long to go from being a one headed monster to disappearing below the seats once we put them all the way back. The sensations weren't new, but still very enjoyable. He still was fixated with my neck. I reminded him a couple times that I couldn't go to work with bruises like last time. This time he was more careful. His mouth didn't go far from my neck, but his hands were moving around my waist. He was testing the waters by running a finger or two inside the waistband of my jeans. I was trying to reciprocate the exploration along with trying to distract his hands

140

from going too far in. The newness of making out with someone hadn't diminished, but I was able to at least try to make him feel good. This was the first time I had made out in a car, but I was learning and trying new things. It sounded like he was enjoying what I was doing, so I kept doing it.

Before we knew it, the first movie was over and the second one was the third in a series. "Have you seen the first two?" He asked, with a strange look in his eye. He let me sit up and start adjusting my clothes and hair while we talked.

"No, I told you I don't see many movies."

"Then how about we go for a drive or something?"

"That would be fine with me, if you don't mind."

"I didn't see the first two either, so I have no idea what the third installment will be like. Right now I'd rather spend time with you anyway. Mind if we leave here and drive around for a while?"

"That's fine with me. Any ideas on where you want to drive to?"

"I lived around this area for a while. I've been talking about checking out some of my old haunts. It might be better if I could show them to someone else."

"That could be fun. I haven't been around the city much, except maybe when I was lost and looking for something. Driving around because you're lost isn't all that fun, and it's never fun driving around alone."

"Like I said, I grew up in this area. I can show you around a bit. Probably nothing really exciting, but something we can do while we talk. You are a very interesting and beautiful woman and I want to find out more, and have as much time as possible with you."

He drove around as promised. I saw the dispatch center where he worked, the schools he went to, and then he decided to take me to the apartment complex he grew up in. He didn't live there now, but it was one of those places that had a playground and a pool and something like a yard for kids to play in. It was late so we couldn't be too loud. Hopefully we could stay inconspicuous so no one would ask us what apartment we lived in.

Our conversation was mostly about what it was like growing up. The more I talked to people the more I was realizing that I didn't have a normal childhood. I grew up seven miles from the nearest "town" which had a population of 1,300 when I was there. We rode our bikes around our driveway or out to the woods, the neighbors were too far away and they didn't have kids our age anyway. I rode a big yellow bus to school every morning and home every night, from kindergarten through high school. My grandmother lived across the road (notice I didn't say street) otherwise we couldn't see another house from our yard.

Oh, yes, our yard. It took an entire day to mow it, more once a month or so when we took down the grass by the apple trees and other rarely used parts of our yard. We only had a walk behind mower so we took turns walking around the yard after the dew had worn off. Luckily there were several kids who could mow. Part of the yard I couldn't do because there was poison ivy and I was the most susceptible to getting a rash from mowing in that area.

Almost every day over summer, all the kids would pile in the car to go down to the lake for a swim. Not only was there no chlorine in the water, but there was mud you could sink into, reeds that grew nearby, and fish that would occasionally bite. Every so often we had to move to the side while a boat was launched.

Nights like this we would start a campfire and sit around it under the stars. The fire pit was to the side of the house, where the yard light—if it had to be turned on for some reason—couldn't reach. We sat around watching the fire dance under the twinkling stars telling stories and roasting marshmallows on sticks we just pulled off a nearby tree to make sure they were small and still green. Large rocks encircled the fire pit. Each of us had a rock that we usually sat on. The rock I insisted Dad get for me was from the low spot where water accumulated every spring. A corner of it had an indentation, just big enough to sit in. The rest of it would make a good table if you needed it, but it slanted down so you had to be careful what you put on it. The rock was almost a cube so if you wanted to sit on the ground it made an excellent back rest. We spent many a summer (spring, fall, and even a few winter) nights around the campfire just hanging out. Yes, I am definitely a country girl.

Don, like most of the men I was meeting, grew up in the city. It was impossible for them to get away from city lights on an average night. Another family lived within spitting distance, so stepping out the door was entering the public arena. Trees were planted by landscapers and watered with sprinklers. Out here the watering was done on certain days to make sure there was water for everyone. To cool off he would walk to the pool in the complex, and have to shower after to get the pool chemicals off of him. He rode his bike around the complex on the sidewalk, the ground wasn't all that even and he had bad experiences with holes in the yard. Occasionally they would find one of those holes when they played football in one of the larger grassy areas. As long as they were quiet they could play late into the night since the lights stayed on all night.

Speaking of getting late, we both realized it was already late for us. We both put in a full day at work and we were starting to get tired. Any time someone could come over and ask us to leave since we didn't live there. We had pushed our luck long enough. On the way to take me home, he started being suggestive, like he had the first time we talked. When we reached the street outside my house, he stopped his truck and quickly took my hand to keep me in the truck with him. It was late and the street was quiet. The only night lights left on were the ones that stayed on all night. It looked like everyone who went out was back home and sleeping. Don parked behind my Jeep, which was parked behind Rob's vehicle. We were parked in the little gap between our house and the next one, under a tree in what was a gap between the street lights. There were no lights on in the house so Rob must have been in his room as well.

Don moved his hand, with mine in it, to my lap. "I know it's late, but I really don't want this to end. You have no idea how incredible you are." He was sliding over to my side of the seat. We were just as close as we were while we were watching the movie, except this time he moved to my side of the truck so the steering wheel never got in the way. He pulled my left leg over his legs, and I let him. I was getting more and more adventurous, or some would say I was letting my gentlemen friends get more and more adventurous. My good girl-ness was disappearing, as his hand was disappearing into my jeans.

We were there, parked out on the street, for almost an hour. He never even suggested going inside the house, but he never asked about putting his hands inside my pants, either. Even with his hands in constant motion he started yawning. "Guess it's time for me to go. I'll call you sometime."

"Yes, I'm getting tired as well. You have my new cell number, right?"

"Yes, I have it in my cell phone. I really enjoyed your company tonight. Hopefully we can do it again soon." Regardless of what he said, I was pretty sure he would never use that number and this would be the last time I saw him. He was looking for a relationship that was more physical than I was ready for, as usual. It was just one of those feelings I had.

He jumped out and walked me to the door. Another of those one last kisses and he walked back to his truck. He waited for me to open the door, and then he was off. Before I went to bed I looked to see if there were any marks on my neck. There was nothing this time, as I expected, but I just wanted to make sure.

I never heard from him again, which didn't bother me one bit. For me he was entertainment for a couple of nights. Honestly he made me feel used. Later I would come to realize that I was more used by someone else, but for the time being Don was the chief user as far as I was concerned.

*****

The next day I waited by the phone, not for a call from Don, but some word from Lawrence. There was nothing from him. He told me to expect no contact while he was off to the east coast. This must be that time he was talking about. His trip was to take two weeks or more. How convenient that he would be gone and out of contact with me over my birthday. Although he got more than I was expecting on his birthday, it probably wasn't what he was hoping for. He hadn't seen me since then. Most of the calls that we actually connected were while I was sleepy. The e-mails were fewer and fewer, and there were no new pictures of him. He said it was because he was busy finishing up one job, starting another, dealing with his family, and whatever it was that supposedly took him just south of the Mason-Dixon line. The flower was starting to die no matter how much I tried to keep it alive. Maybe it was an annual, one of those plants that die after blooming only once.

Since there were only words—and those were sporadic at best—from Lawrence for a month, I decided it would be all right to start looking again. The first guy to respond was Otto, who was in town on business for a while. Actually, he was in a town just outside the metro area. His company was opening a branch there and promising a promotion along with a transfer to the new office for him. They sent him early to start looking for housing for himself and making contacts in the area for the company. They had a location for their new branch but were still looking for some of the things that keep businesses running. He was working out of a hotel room, and at times looking for company.

Thursday afternoon he asked if I would be willing to drive to see him for dinner. There was less than a month left of the school year, not the most productive time at any school. The kids were well into their projects or not bothering to come any more. It would be summer by the time the truancy officers came knocking, so they knew if they really didn't want to go to school they didn't have to. There were fewer incidents to write up, no lesson plans to worry about, and no worksheets to copy for tomorrow's lessons. Why not go for a little drive to a dinner out?

I met Otto at his hotel. He gave me the address since the directions I could get from the internet would be much better than any he, an out-of-towner, could give me. The town wasn't all that big and the hotel looked like a big house from the street. He was waiting for me in the lobby and asked if I would mind going to a Mexican place he found. This wasn't the first time I had Mexican food on a first date.

He looked like a traditional Mexican in American clothing. He had dark hair and skin and a bushy mustache that made his smile look even bigger when he saw me. He was a little taller than me, but not by much. I felt a little underdressed. It looked like he took off his tie and jacket but otherwise stayed in his business attire. I was in my work clothes also, just a very different line of work. His light blue shirt made his hair and skin look even darker than they were. My skin would never get that dark no matter how long I lay in the sun. There were no farmer tan lines like most of the men back home. His skin was dark from genetics, not sunbathing.

This restaurant reminded me of a small chain of establishments in Alaska. It was made to give you the feeling of what Americans think is the typical Mexican casa. The really ironic thing this time was that Otto was born in a little border town on the Mexican side. When he was very young his family moved to Los Angeles for his father's job and that's where he was being transferred from. As we looked at the menu, he told me about how what they served was different from the same dish in Mexico. I asked if the drinks were any different. His smile said he wasn't sure. When the server came around Otto asked if I would like a margarita to see if they were different. I was feeling adventurous so I agreed. I thought he would order one for himself, but he decided on a Coke instead. It made me feel a little uncomfortable that my drink had alcohol and would be so much more expensive than his. He also ordered our dinners, in what sounded like authentic Spanish. Also not the first time I heard someone order in Spanish, but it still sounded exotic to my fully American ears.

We continued to talk while we waited for our order. As the drinks came, he told me about his two kids. They were pre-teens and lived with him. His wife had been killed in a car accident several years earlier. Right now they were staying with his parents to finish out the school year down there. If he got a call and had to leave it would be either one of them or someone from work checking up on how things were going. I guess he wanted to make sure I didn't think I was one of many women he was entertaining while he was in town, or maybe that there was someone else back in LA and I was just an out of town fling.

I've always been interested in other places and other cultures. He started talking about how what is considered "traditionally Mexican" on this side of the border are different from how things truly are south of the border. He did say that he only knew about his little corner of Mexico and he only lived there until he was about three. He was in LA for Cinco de Mayo, and said he found it humorous that the biggest celebrations for the day happen in the United States. In Mexico, where he still sometimes goes to visit his extended family, they acknowledge the day, but more like we remember Civil War battles or something like that. Small remembrances in the places that were most affected, but no big parades, streets blocked off for cruising, and drinking for the entire weekend, or two if it happened to fall on Wednesday.

Our dinners came and he continued to tell me about truly traditional Mexican food. It wasn't as boring as it may sound. That stuff is interesting to me. He grew up in the middle of a different culture, not in a place that the tourism industry wants Americans to think is a different culture. He spoke English with an authentic Spanish accent, much like the native Spanish speaker I knew from college—the one who read Penthouse's Forum as bedtime stories to practice her articulation—not to impress me, but because that's the way he really talked. He, like my college friend, was trying to rid his voice of the Spanish accent to sound more like a US citizen. But I made sure he knew that I loved the way he talked and was very interested in what he was saying.

The server came back to ask if we wanted dessert or a box to take home what was left. Without asking me, Otto ordered another margarita since mine was almost gone. I wasn't planning on having one, much less two. It takes me a while sometimes, and it wasn't until I was driving home—later than I planned as you will see—that I realized what he was really doing. No one had ever tried to get me drunk before. This was another first for me. He also asked for one serving of fried ice cream.

"That better be for us to share."

"I'll have a bite or two, you said you liked ice cream and I want to treat you right."

"And you'll share that second margarita with me?"

"I have to drive back to the hotel, remember?"

"And I have to drive back to the city tonight, remember?"

"I was hoping you would stay with me a little while longer. We could go back to the hotel and talk some more to give you some time to wear off those margaritas."

So he didn't come right out and say it, but he was being honest about his plan to make me stay with him a little longer. Silly me, but I fell for the line about just spending time with him. Maybe it was the first margarita already taking effect, but I was really thinking he wanted to have a conversation with me. He was away from home and family and probably lonely. He spent weeks in the hotel room alone night after night, or at least that's what he told me. I was also very interested in how his life was different from mine. When he went back to visit his extended family he saw the Mexican version of the rural culture that I grew up in. Growing up and living in LA for most of his life he lived in a big city, very different from where I spent the first 35 years of my life. It was an

148

opportunity for me to learn about another world in a part of the country I had never visited. I spent 20 minutes in the San Francisco airport, all of it running from one flight that arrived late to my connecting flight which was waiting for me to take off. Other than that I had never been to California and I had never been south of the border. I was innocently willing to go along with going to his room to talk, after the fried ice cream.

That was a line, too. Well, he did have a couple of bites, but most of what he put on his fork ended up in my mouth. It may have taken me the entire meal, but eventually I noticed how quiet things were by our table. We were separated from most of the restaurant by a partial wall crawling with greenery. I couldn't turn my head all that fast without complications from the margaritas, but there was no one else in this part of the restaurant. We hadn't been there all that long that everyone else had cleared out. It was a Thursday night, probably not their busiest night. So why were we all by ourselves here? Maybe it was so he could take both of my hands in one of his and feed me ice cream. He was careful when he did, but I'm not used to being fed anything. I must admit, ice cream would be the best choice for something like that. Or maybe it was the alcohol kicking in. Eventually the ice cream was gone, the check was paid, and we were ready to leave.

"How were the margaritas?"

"Good, but a bit strong."

He smiled. It was about then that I put it all together. He had been staying blocks away from this place for a month. It served food that was familiar in name if not exactly what he grew up on. He seemed to know the staff here more than the typical out-of-towner. My guess was that he orchestrated the entire evening, maybe even arranging for stronger than average drinks for me.

"I probably should wait a while before driving home."

"I know of a quiet little place you can hang out for a while, to let your stomach settle."

At this point it was more my head I was worried about. Usually I can think about several things at once. If I just sit and watch TV usually I fall asleep, so I do things while keeping an eye on a show or movie. Now I had to actually think about thinking. Walking out of the restaurant I was glad Otto had his arm around me to keep me steady. I had to concentrate on sitting down gracefully after he opened his car door. This wasn't feeling so good to me.

The ride back to the hotel wasn't all that long, we could have walked but he probably was hoping I wouldn't be able to walk when we were done eating. That was pretty much the case. I'm not a big drinker and two strong margaritas in about an hour were making me feel very light headed.

There was only one time I was drunk, but that time I felt like I did occasionally when I got the flu. I must have been involved in conversations and activities—the activity was a drinking game. Someone came in with a movie for us to watch. I remember the opening credits and one scene, but before I knew it the closing credits were rolling. Kind of like the time I was in a play the night before I was hit by the flu. There I remember my opening line and shaking a box like I was supposed to do to end the play. Everyone said I delivered all my lines and even covered up when someone else forgot theirs, but I honestly don't remember anything in between.

This time my head was starting to spin, and I was hoping there was a place for me to sit down in his room. That right there should say what a state I was in. He was in a hotel room, of course there would be a place for me to sit down, even a place to lie down if I needed to. Maybe that was his plan.

"Is something wrong?" Maybe he noticed my hesitation getting out of the car.

"I'm not feeling so good at the moment."

"My room is close to the lobby. Do you think you can make it that far?"

"I should be able to."

"Let me help you just to make sure."

He put one arm around my waist and took my hand with the other. As we got to the door he let go of my hand just long enough to open the door. He repeated the process when we got to the door to his room. He guided me to his bed and helped me sit down.

"Is there anything I can get for you?"

"Some time for this to wear off."

"Sorry, that's one thing I can't get for you. Just sit back and let me take care of you for a while."

This was another of those places angels fear to tread. Here I was drunk, about an hour from home, in the hotel room of a guy I just met. I had never called in sick and I wasn't about to do that this close to the end of the year. It was also the Friday before my birthday. Otto didn't know that, but the people at work did. They wouldn't stop asking questions until they knew the whole story if I called in sick.

He turned on the TV. "There's probably nothing on, but let me check the movie channels."

Don't guys do anything but watch movies? I grew up an hour away from a movie theater and before satellite TV. The only movies we saw had commercials every 15 minutes or so, and we usually had to stay up past our bed time to see the end. But I didn't have the energy to complain. All I wanted to do was stop the room from spinning. My mind wasn't clear enough to contemplate what could happen, what Otto probably wanted to happen, in this situation. I guess I would have to count this as the second time I got drunk.

Otto was sitting on the other side of the bed. It would be hard for me to watch TV from this side of the bed. I fell back and flipped my feet from the side of the bed to the foot end. The plan was to sit up next to him, but my body wasn't quite ready for that yet. He found something that would work for him on the TV and fell back to lie next to me. It only took a couple seconds for his hands to slowly move under my shirts. I couldn't help but giggle.

"You like that, huh?"

I couldn't stop giggling, partly because I didn't know what to say to him, partly because at the moment I don't think I could talk at all even if I could think of something that made sense. My mind is starting to float just thinking about it. Maybe it was a good thing my mind wasn't working. If I thought about the situation I put myself in I probably would have gotten sick. Sometimes ignorance really is bliss.

I closed my eyes in hopes it would help the room stop spinning sooner. The problem was that it made it impossible to see what he was doing. He must have rolled to his side. I could feel two hands under my shirt, inching their way to my sports bra. He could have done much more since I was in no shape to argue. God must have been watching over me. Remember, this was a place where angels fear to tread so it must have been the Highest Power keeping me safe.

Sometimes being a big girl is a good thing. Although I hadn't had much alcohol in a while, my body seemed to be processing it quicker than normal. My head was beginning to clear, at least enough to stop his hand from going under my sports bra. If he had been faster things would have been different. God was really looking out for me that night.

"After all that, I don't even get to see you topless? I was a good boy, I could have done anything a couple of minutes ago but I didn't. The least you could do is let me see what's under all those shirts."

Was it only a couple minutes? According to the clock I had been there two hours. I sat up so quickly there was a breeze, which only helped me sober up.

"I have to be to work tomorrow, actually later today, and I have a drive to get home."

"You better call in sick, so you might as well stay here."

"Don't you have to be to work tomorrow?"

"There's no office for me to report to, and as long as I get all my tasks done before I go back there won't be any questions about when they got done."

"My line of work isn't so flexible. If I'm not there in the morning there will be problems *and* questions." Because of the nature of the school they didn't bother looking for substitute teachers. When one of us was sick, schedules were changed and phones were kept clear to call 911. The new person who enjoyed pretending she was in administration was looking for a reason to write me up. She was in on my interview last August and I think she considered me the lesser evil when she agreed to hire me. Things hadn't improved now that she was working with me. The questions would most likely come from the kids. They would want to know the *real* reason Miss Randi wasn't in school the day before her birthday. It was the better students who were still coming to school and I had been a little more open with them. They would expect the real story, unlike the one I gave them about the bruise on my neck. Calling in sick wasn't an option. "I really better get going."

"Are you sure you can drive in your condition?"

"I'm feeling much better. Time does wonders for that kind of sickness."

Living alone for so long, I had learned to do a lot of things on my own. One of those things was driving when I probably shouldn't have. I've driven in blizzards, on roads that were more like hiking trails, and when I had the flu. Driving with a leftover buzz was more illegal than the other things, but they helped me develop a "driving mode" in dangerous situations. I knew it was late and nearly the weekend. Law enforcement would be on drunk driver patrol, so I had to be extremely careful. Please do not consider this condoning driving while intoxicated. In a short time nature would have my blood/alcohol level below the legal limit anyway.

153

"Thanks for dinner, but I really need to be going now."

"I really think you should spend the night. You probably shouldn't be driving like you are now." Either he didn't notice that I was upright and not wavering or he was trying to make me feel sicker than I was to get me to stay. I started making my way to the door. He started out on the far side of the bed but rushed over to gently take hold of my arm.

"I'll be fine. I really need to get home to get a few hours of sleep before dealing with my little darlings at school."

"You could call in sick from here. They wouldn't know where you were and we could have the whole day together."

"No, I really have to be at work later. Thanks again for dinner. You have my number if you want to call me again." I was hoping he wouldn't call, but good manners say to always give people the option.

He didn't block my way out. He slowly walked behind me but he wasn't trying to stop me. I heard the bathroom door, which was right by the main door like they usually are in hotel rooms, shut seconds after the door to his room. I was awake enough to have a good idea what he was doing. That was probably another indication that I was no longer a good girl. My mind was starting to work like that of a man, constantly in the gutter.

There was a gas station not far from the hotel, or at least that's what I remembered from the drive up here. Once I found it, I parked the Jeep carefully and went inside. I took my time selecting the perfect drink to keep me awake and something to soak up anything that was left in my stomach. The lines on the floor where the tiles connected weren't waving so I was hoping I would be all right to drive home. I finished up the soda and the snacks in my Jeep before hitting the road again. Usually I have no problem with eating while driving, but I wanted to be able to concentrate better on what I was doing. There wasn't going to be any reason for someone to think there was anything wrong with this driver.

It was late and not quite the weekend, so the interstate was clear. I could take that to within blocks of my house. With the windows open it got a bit chilly, but that helped keep me awake and alert. Maybe the radio was loud, but they wouldn't stop me for that unless there was some other problem. I was being careful not to give them any indication of another problem. Hopefully they wouldn't see me as driving too carefully and pull me over for that. I've heard of that happening that time of the evening in some places.

I was too busy being careful to realize how lucky I was. Later when I thought about things, he really could have done anything while I was under the influence of the margaritas. God was protecting me. It had to be Him because that was one of those places angels fear to tread. There's no other explanation of how I got out of the hotel on my terms. I'm sure things didn't go the way Otto had intended.

*****

Just like with Don, there was no more word from Otto. I was more upset that there was no more word from Lawrence, either. When I told Tim what happened he called me a tease and said he was jealous that someone else got me drunk. That was supposed to be his job, after all.

The kids and staff were more interested in what I was planning on doing Saturday for my birthday than what I did the night before. One of the girls I was close to had her birthday on Sunday. I asked if there was anything she wanted special for her birthday that I could bring to school for her. When we were alone, she mentioned that she really liked tomato juice. When I drink it I usually add salt and pepper, never vodka. I didn't think anyone would object to me bringing in juice for us and everyone else on Monday. We had talked a while ago about how I don't usually celebrate my birthday. She wanted to make sure I was doing

155

something to acknowledge the day, so she was willing to share her special day with me. She was one of those kids who was 16 going on 30. The kids are really good kids who make many bad decisions.

I wanted to do something else for my birthday, something just for me. Of course Tim said if he were here he would help me celebrate. He wasn't saying as much about coming out here as he used to. Maybe in the fall, after he spent lots of time with his daughter over the summer. His daughter was a convenient excuse. Not having the money was a convenient excuse. Both of them could have been reasons, but really I thought he was afraid to leave. But remember, I did leave even with several excuses to stay.

Anyway, I was thinking of what I could get myself for my birthday. Ironically Friday was also payday. The check that came in the middle of the month always seemed a little bigger because rent came out of the end of the month check. I don't like shopping for clothes or anything else really. To me shopping is one of those necessary evils of living. There was a shop for bigger girls like me that I had seen last fall but never went in. It was fairly close to where the idiot who shall remain nameless lived. I tried not to frequent that area, but this was a special occasion. He wouldn't be anywhere near that shop so I decided to go for it.

I wasn't sure exactly what to expect. I hadn't been to a small shop in a long time. When I walked in the clerk asked if I was looking for anything in particular. There were a couple of other ladies in there, so she had to stay behind the counter unless called on to help someone.

The front displayed more professional attire. I needed clothes I could move around in—and maybe restrain a student in—so I looked for more casual clothes. Usually I wore a flannel over a t-shirt with jeans to work. We were required to keep a two-way radio on us at all times. As long as I kept mine in the chest pocket of a flannel shirt I wouldn't forget it somewhere and the boys wouldn't try to take it. The first boy who even pretended to make a grab for it was asked if he really wanted to reach out to that part of my body. There were enough students watching, so the story got around and no one tried to take it out of my pocket again.

As I went to the back for the more casual clothes, I noticed there was a back room. What I saw back there literally took my breath away. It was full of formal attire, at least what I saw right by the doorway. A couple of quick steps and I was running my fingers on the lace and sequins of a wedding dress. It was the fairy tale wedding dress of my dreams. My mom always said she would do the basic stitching for a wedding dress for me and my best friend said she would add the lace and sequins and fancy things like that. But here was a dress in my size already done up. It felt like fate. I had a proposal on the table and the feeling I would be married by the end of this year. Then I run into the dress of my dreams. It was almost too much. I wasn't going to ruin the moment by looking at the price tag. I just ran my fingers across the beads and sequins and lace, dreaming of the day I would wear a dress like this and walk down the aisle to meet my knight in shining armor. If it was going to happen this year, I knew exactly where to go to get the dress.

Further in the room there were outfits for after the wedding. That's what I wanted for my birthday present to myself, something black and lacy. They were separated more by color than by size. Let's see, nothing with garters. I was hoping for something totally see-through, so no satin. There it was. A teddy with a lacy black bodice and sheer skirt waiting for me to buy it. And look, there was even a pair of sheer panties as well. I don't know if those would be used, but I always like having choices. I didn't have a real pair of panties. These would definitely not be confused with my tighty whities. The first one I picked up was what I thought was my size. Can you try these things on? That's all right. If it doesn't fit I'll bring it back and say it was a gift. They wouldn't have to know it was a gift for myself.

I had to pause a little with it in my hand. I didn't want to look nervous when I paid for it. When I worked at a little grocery store in Alaska, we used to talk about the difference between the guys who confidently asked for the magazines behind the counter and the guys who tried to make it look casual and the guys who just looked at the back of every spot on the magazine rack looking for some personal evening entertainment. And the one guy who came in to buy a *Playgirl* really caused a stir among the employees. It was just another purchase, or should have been.

When I walked back into the main room, all the other customers had gone. The clerk was straightening out some tops near the check stand. She saw I was headed in that direction with something in my hand and quickly stepped behind the counter.

"Do you want a special box for this?"

"No, thanks. I have something to put it in at home." Actually I was thinking of the dresser drawer it would stay in for a while. But it was for a gift, after all. It was gift for me, but a gift none the less.

She put it in a black bag so there would be no problems taking it to the Jeep, or into the house once I got there. It was small enough I could have put it in my purse to take it in the house if I really needed to. Rob had his collection of panties, but I wasn't sure if he was looking for the whole ensemble or just the bottoms. He would *never* see me in it, and I didn't really want him to know I even had something like this. He didn't ask a lot of questions about my shopping, if he was even home, but it would be just my luck he would today.

"Have a good day," the clerk said with a smile. I remember working at the grocery store and selling condoms to guys. How do you end the conversation gracefully?

"Thanks, I will."

Now that I had my present, I decided to stop to pick up a sandwich and go to the lookout for a while. Tim called while I was up there. He remembered my birthday. If he were out here we would be going out tonight, or so he said. When I told him what I bought for myself he said that might be enough to convince him we should stay in instead. I wandered around up there for longer than I really anticipated, but there wasn't a lot to do back at the house. It was a beautiful, sunny birthday, just like last year. But so much was different from last year. A year ago I was getting ready to move back to civilization in hopes to be married soon. I could never have imagined how my life could have had changed in just one year.

*****

Before school that Monday, I stopped for tomato juice and a cake. The supermarket had what they called ice cream cakes—two layers of sheet cake with a layer of ice cream in the middle. That would have to work. The kids and I would be able to have cake and ice cream without having to carry them separately. I thought about getting something for the kid who was lactose intolerant, but then I remembered that he was not above eating the regular cake and giving the ice cream to someone else, maybe even in exchange for something, if he could swing it.

During lunch they asked what my family got me for my birthday, but never what I got for myself. It was a good thing I bought two containers of juice. I was surprised to find out that several students liked tomato juice, or maybe it was something different for them. This school was for students who had abused drugs and/or alcohol in the past so some of them may have imagined it with vodka in it. Of course, the cake was gone a couple minutes after it came out of the freezer.

We started talking about memorable birthdays and birthday traditions. I told them about my birthday last year when I froze my feet wading into a lake in Alaska only to find out that I had a flat tire on the Jeep from the 12 miles of gravel road it took to get to the lake. First I had to move the Jeep off the rocky shore to a level spot to change the tire, hoping I didn't damage the wheel in the process. I was out of cell phone range and well beyond where there was lots of help for things like this. After changing the tire all by myself, I looked up to see that a moose was watching me. As I slowly put everything back in the Jeep, not too concerned with putting things where they belonged for the moment, I walked to the driver's side, where the moose was, only to see a porcupine watching the moose on the other side of the road.

Since we could change the schedule as we cared to, the kids got a little extra time for lunch. Talking about birthdays got some kids emotional. We had talks like this around Christmas time, too. The kids talked about being forgotten or worse yet, beaten on their special day. It turned into an impromptu therapy session which made them forget to find out what I all got for my birthday.

No word from anyone but Tim that week. On Friday I was complaining to my teaching assistant how my social life had cooled down. There was no real birthday party for me. A year when I actually wanted to celebrate my birthday and there was no one to celebrate it with; that's the way things go for me. You can't count getting drunk two days before my birthday since the guy who got me drunk didn't know it was my birthday. Al, that was her name—short for Alejandra—said they had planned on inviting Rob over for some drinks that evening and invited me over as well. She was the one who set up our arrangement. Rob, her husband's uncle, had a house and wanted to split rent with someone and I was that someone.

The house she and her common law husband were building was almost done, and in about two weeks they would be moving from their third-story apartment to their own house. This would be the last night they could do anything special for a month or so since next weekend would be spent packing, the next moving and the next few ones unpacking and setting up the house. Her husband had been injured on the job a couple of months ago and he was going to go back to work in a couple of weeks, just after the weekend they planned on moving. She wanted to have an evening to just relax before all the work started. She asked if I wanted to come over and join them. The plan was for me to go home and she would pick me up. Rob would drive over when he got done with work. Her husband, Raul, had his uncle coming over and she wanted to have a friend as well.

I had met Raul a couple of times when he came to the school. For Thanksgiving we had a traditional dinner and kids and staff were allowed to invite family. For some that was the only turkey they had that week. Al, Raul, and their two kids ate in my classroom, not that there were a lot of choices. He came to school occasionally when his leg was healed enough for him to get out of bed but not good enough to go to work. At first he was bored with sitting around the apartment they shared, and when he was finally cleared to drive himself he took advantage of it. Raul would never leave until he got a chance to say hello to me. I thought it was just good manners, that weekend I was to find out it may have been something else.

Al and Raul had been living together since their nine-year-old daughter was born, so in almost any state they would be considered to have a common law marriage. Some of the time she used the computer in my class, she was looking for romantic places for a ceremony. What she really wanted was a big church wedding with all the frills. They were waiting for the money to have the wedding of her dreams and the longer they put it off the more things she decided she needed, putting it off even more.

She was the one person at work I told how drunk I got the week before. My reputation at school had started out as a shy, quiet, good girl. The stories of my escapades were greatly exaggerated by the students. The staff knew they couldn't all be true and didn't question me on how many actually were. I still had somewhat of a good girl image since the kids had never heard me cuss or complain about being hung over. The "bruise" of a couple months ago wasn't forgotten, but it could be explained as a momentary indiscretion since they never saw another one. I was seen as the good girl player, if such a thing existed. Maybe it was just that my social life was my only rebellious area. In other ways I was still the good girl the staff hired and the kids knew from the beginning of the year.

At our weekly staff meetings they joked about me buying things from and/or for the students. Once the dean of students was saying how the staff deals with frustration without chemicals, "You don't see Miss Randi getting high in the hallway," really got their attention. Everyone thought it would be funny to see me inebriated, especially Al, who I worked with the most. She thought it would be funny to see me drunk. I thought she was kidding when she said that, little did I know. . .

Just as she picked me up, there was a call from Rob. The pizza place he really liked was conveniently just blocks away from the house, but he wasn't. After he called in the order he realized he would be a little later getting done with work. It would be better for him to go straight from work to the party so we stopped at the pizza parlor and he stopped at the liquor store. We drove around to see the outside of the new house, but with the pizza still warm we decided to get that to the apartment and come back at a later date for the grand tour.

Rob was there when we arrived. He had picked up plenty of the beer they usually drank and a few other things from the liquor store. Raul was, of course, there. He had broken his leg and torn up his ankle on the job. The leg had healed quickly, but the ankle took more time so he had been home for months now. They had two kids who were both sleeping over at their respective friend's house, so the adults could be as loud and obnoxious as the apartment complex would let us.

The guys greeted us with a beer for each of us. Al took hers and went to the bedroom to change into more comfy clothes. Raul gave me the low down on how he injured his leg and how it was almost healed as he encouraged me to drink my beer. It wasn't my usual, if I had a usual, and he wanted to make sure it was acceptable for me. Al must have told him about last weekend because he made some comment about building up a tolerance to alcohol. Rob was asleep when I got home last weekend and I never told him about my adventure so he must have heard it from Al. When she came back out, she went straight to the kitchen to get the pizzas organized including getting some ranch dressing to dip the crusts in. I was more of a marinara person, but I could adapt. I didn't know where anything was in her kitchen and the guys were no help at all.

We decided a movie wasn't a good idea. All of us were tired and that would probably just put us to sleep. For a while we just chatted about the kids at our school, things going on at Rob's school and job, and Al's and Raul's new house. It was convenient that Raul was off work while it was being built so he could go over there often and see what was going on.

After the pizza, we decided we all needed a cocktail to wash down the beer. I was handed a glass, which Al said contained good things. Not exactly what I would prefer, but not all that bad compared to some I had tasted in the past. It was part alcohol and part energy drink. I'm not a big fan of the energy drinks, either.

Eventually they decided they would teach me a drinking game. But first, we all needed a drink. The guys went into the kitchen to make them up as Al started to go over the rules of the game with me. I had only played a card type drinking game one other time—that one night in college that I got drunk.

I had played a game similar to what they were playing but for fun without drinking. The guys came back with a glass for each of us to start with. After the glass was done, we would have our choice of beer or another drink to continue the game. It was one of those games that wasn't fun unless you had four players so there was no getting out for me.

The apartment wasn't all that big and they didn't have a lot of chairs. Rob, Al, and I sat on the floor. Raul still had to be careful with his ankle so sitting on the floor for an extended period of time —and then getting up from that position—was still difficult. He sat on the couch. So there we were, the four of us—and the youngest of us was in her late 20s—playing a drinking game on a pretty pink

163

Little Tikes table we borrowed from their daughter's room. I don't think the cup holders were meant for something with alcohol in it, but we used them for that anyway.

The game included the opportunity to make others drink. Being the new kid in the group I was "given" drinks by everyone. Luckily during the first round we only drank when we lost. That gave me an opportunity to get the rules down while I was still somewhat in control of my faculties, at least as in control as I would be for the rest of the night. The others playing knew the rules, so I don't know if they were purposely playing badly as an excuse to drink, already affected by the drinks we had with the pizza, or just no good at the game. In any case they were drinking a lot more than I was, not that I was complaining or even bringing attention to that fact.

The three of them were ready for another drink a couple of hands before I was. Raul offered to get them since he was sitting on something other than the floor. He came back with four beers.

"I'm not quite ready for another." They could all see that my glass wasn't quite empty.

"You will before long, and that way I don't have to get one for you when that happens." Another man was trying to get me drunk. This time it was a "married" man so I wasn't thinking about the possibilities.

He knew what was coming up. Any time someone could give away a drink it was to me. The beer ran out for all of us at about the same time. The pizza must have done more in my stomach than the Mexican food last week, because the room wasn't spinning yet. That and the fact that it's easy to wet my lips with the can tipped, making it look like I was taking a long drink. They were all too drunk to notice things like that. After a little while, I traded my full can with the one Al had finished. She knew she was on her second and since the empty was by me, I must have already finished my first. Sometimes she wasn't all that observant sober and now she was even less so after a few drinks.

Raul decided to get everyone two beers this time since we were all getting bad at the game. I was actually sitting closest to the kitchen and when Raul sat back down, he was closer to me than to Rob who was across from me at the table. My first innocent girl thought was that this way he was closer to the kitchen when he needed to get more materials for the game. About half way through the next beer I noticed Raul's foot was on my leg. My first innocent girl thought was that it made things more comfortable with his bad ankle. I had some problems with my foot and when I was sitting for any amount of time at school (like staff meetings or when I was required to attend group therapy with the kids) I was allowed a pillow and an extra chair to keep my foot up.

As time went on, the game got slower as we had intoxicated conferences about the rules, or how each of us remembered the rules. Then Raul's foot was moving up my leg. Before I knew it he had it right in my crotch. In working with kids you sometimes get body parts innocently in otherwise inappropriate places. I shifted on the floor to let him know I knew where his foot was. I thought he would quickly move it from between my legs, maybe with a comment about how he didn't realize where it was. Instead, I got the beginning of a massage from his foot. He knew exactly where it was and that it was not exactly appropriate. At this point I didn't really care. There I was sitting with a friend/co-worker on one side and her common law husband sitting on the other rubbing his foot between my legs under the table. This is not where a good girl finds herself.

After that round of beers disappeared, we took a little break. The guys needed a cigarette. Al and I took the opportunity to chat some more about anything but work. She convinced me that things were over with Lawrence and all the other guys I had talked about since the beginning of the year. She was going to think of some guys she could set me up with. Rob was too old for me and Raul was hers and never thought of any other woman, or so she said.

She was in the bathroom as the guys came in. All I could catch of their conversation was something about a three way. When the door closed their conversation quickly ended. There was a little dance as the guys tussled to get to the bathroom first and Al was trying to get out. Everyone was very happy.

Al and I were sitting in the living room. Raul must have won the race to the bathroom because he was in the kitchen making up another round of drinks. This time he gave me mine first, then Al hers, then went back to the kitchen for his, letting Rob get his own. We drank these without the pretense of a drinking game. Instead we were flipping cards over trying to guess what they were before they were shown along with talking about nothing in particular.

Raul said he was getting warm and went to his room to change his shirt. Ten minutes or so later, Al went in to find him passed out on the bed. That seemed like a good indication we should all call it a night. Rob was a gentleman and let me sleep on the couch as he put a pillow on the floor to catch some Zs. No one was in any condition to drive.

I slept through the morning, which is unusual for me, even for a Saturday. Around 1 pm I sat up, which got Rob's attention. He had planned on making something for a party he was invited to that evening, but he still didn't feel up to driving. So I drove his Jeep home. On the way home he tried to play big brother by giving me a lecture noting that Lawrence hadn't been over in a while. I deserved better than that.

*****

Tim had called while we were out. That was the only call on my phone. If Lawrence was telling me everything honestly, he should be home by now. If he really wanted to marry me, he would have called to let me know he was home. But I knew it would never happen. My second real promise of marriage was gone, but I was still grasping at straws since he never really said it was over. There was nothing really new from Tim. It was a holiday weekend so he knew I had more time on my hands.

I went to one of the local libraries with my laptop to check on things. On the website I noticed Lawrence had re-activated his account. That sealed it for me. I was done with him. It was a game to him. It might as well be a game for me as well. Since he wasn't really serious about marrying me, I had no guilt in sending out some more first contacts with guys in the area.

One of the guys who happened to be online at the time was, ironically, named Randy. I just had to see if he wanted to chat, and he did. He lived in that town Tim originally said he was from, which was about half way between where Otto was staying and the metro area I lived in. Since it was a holiday weekend, he already had plans. Maybe we could meet next weekend. We could chat online and on the phone until then, if I gave him my number. What the heck, it was just a cell number. The library was closing soon, so I had to go. He promised to call in a while, giving me time to get home.

But there was another call. I answered it as I started looking for a parking lot to pull into. It was Lawrence on the phone. His trip took longer than anticipated because once he got there other people asked to talk with him. At least that's what he told me. Now they were really behind with the new job so he would have to spend the holiday weekend on the new jobsite to start making a plan to get things back on track.

While he was away he was thinking about things. If I wanted kids he was more than happy to do his part in making them (and we could start on that right away if I wanted to) but once they were born they would be my responsibility. He realized he could be a grandfather soon, and so he wasn't going to change diapers or get up for early morning feedings any more. Of course he would have enough money to take care of everything, and I wouldn't have to work so I wouldn't have to deal with "those delinquents" any more. My first thought was then I could sit around the house waiting for him to be horny. My real job would be to make sure he was sexually satisfied. I didn't say that out loud, but maybe I should have. While we were talking, a call that came through and went to voicemail.

After about an hour, Lawrence told me we would be meeting next weekend, so I should call him on Thursday. After all, we had to talk about our wedding. I told him about the tidbit I found out when researching who can perform a wedding ceremony. In the state we were in it could all be done without clergy or witnesses or anyone but the couple to be married. He thought that would be good, and commented that I can be sneaky at times. He liked that and asked if I had looked at rings. I had been through this too much to think it was actually going to happen. He didn't mention my birthday and I didn't ask why he re-opened his account on the website. I could play the game as well as anyone.

I actually waited until I got home to check my voicemail. Yes, it was from Randy. I called him back and ended up leaving a message saying it took me longer to get home because I stopped somewhere. I didn't say it was in a parking lot to talk to someone who said he wanted to marry me. I found out later Randy had his own secrets.

Eventually he called me back. He was looking forward to meeting next weekend. He would decide where that would be and would get back to me. We chit-chatted about nothing. He collected different things that he found at garage sales. It was like a treasure hunt for him. I do the same, but looking for different things. I get excited when I see a certain type of glasses and I'm always on the look-out for a certain pattern of dishes that my mother is trying to make sets of for each of her children. If we would meet it would have to be up by him, but I liked driving around, especially now that I had driven through the area once already.

*****

Since it was a legal holiday, the libraries weren't open on my extra day off so I couldn't go online there. There was a coffee shop nearby that said it was a Wi-Fi hot spot. I quickly checked what I needed to and went back to the house. I wasn't really waiting for a call, but I had planned on using this time to get ready for my upcoming trip to Alaska. Both Tim and Randy called to see what I was up to, but otherwise there was time to get a lot of things done with my plans.

I was going back to teach Bible school in the community I lived in only a year ago. Some other people were going to get the supplies we needed. It was my job to decide what we needed. They were making lists for the food we would need and basic things that should come along with us but the stuff for the specific crafts and things would also have to go on the list soon. After a busy Friday night, the long weekend was pretty calm.

It was the last week of May. I had turned another year older, but still no closer to a real, lasting relationship. Tim was talking about coming out in the fall, maybe. Lawrence's games weren't fun anymore, and he was hardly playing anyway. It was way too early to call Randy a relationship, much less a lasting one.

I was preparing to go to Alaska again. There wouldn't be anyone coming up to share my vacation time with me, but I could spend that time with my friends up there. The couple who let me stay in their guestroom many a night said I could use it as a home base when I needed to. They had internet access so I would probably have more time to chat up there than I did for the moment living down here. Yes, there is almost always a time difference, but that only meant I didn't have to stay up as long to chat with lonely guys well into the night for them.

The feeling that I would be married by the end of the year was still there, even though the year was almost half over. What I didn't know was that I was on the edge of the month that would change my life forever.

Chapter 7 — Back to good?

June was here. There was only a week and a half to deal with the kids. I had already gotten my notice that the new staff member got her way. All of us who were hired this school year could re-apply if we wished. Our names and resumes would be put in the stack with all the other ones that came in when the jobs were posted. It was a convenient way to get rid of certain members who didn't fit into her idea of a perfect school. In any case, the pay wasn't nearly worth the amount of time and bruises (the real kind from when the kids get out of control) I had put into the job. I had the entire summer to get another job.

In the meantime I could get unemployment on top of my salary, since my pay was split into 24 payments rather than just over the school year—something else the new staff member told me I was wrong about. One of those things she kept talking about, saying she thought I was wrong but would check on it. When she checked on it and found out I was right, it was never mentioned again. She really didn't like me, but that was her demon, not mine.

Since I wouldn't be around for two weeks I decided to wait to start looking for a new job. If the schools wanted to do interviews right away and I was in Alaska it wouldn't look good. Lawrence would be happy, if he ever even found out that I would be getting another job.

Tim was complaining about the summer heat already. We were both in places that got hot over summer, but he was living in a house with air conditioning. As long as his sugar mamas kept paying the electric bills for him, he would be fine. I was living on the second floor without air conditioning. It was already starting to get warm during the day, but the only days I had to endure the heat was on weekends. I was spending more time at the library during those times. That way I was in air conditioning and was able to use my laptop to chat with guys.

The first weekend of June was warm, but I found someone to spend Saturday with so I didn't need the library to keep me cool. Little did I know that Saturday morning what an adventure was in store for me. It was so funny. If someone told me it happened to them I wouldn't believe them, but it makes a good story. Actually, it almost sounds like one of those stories attached to a chain e-mail sent around by the two or three people in your address book that forward things like that.

Before I really start the story, here is an update on Lawrence. I called on Thursday like we arranged, but only to leave a message. I wasn't really expecting anything. Lawrence was probably done with me since I was going too fast by wanting to be a part of his family and too slow on being his booty call. He still said he wanted to marry me, but only at the very end of the last conversation after telling me how I would have to follow his rules in a relationship. I'm not good at strictly following rules set by someone else and imposed on me. I left another message Friday afternoon, just saying that I was done with work. In truth, I was pretty much done with Lawrence as well. His profile was back on the website so I had no guilt for chatting with other guys.

So, what happened that weekend?

Friday Randy sent me a message saying he still wanted to meet on Saturday morning. He worked at a grocery store as a butcher during the afternoon to evening shift. Most days he started working about the time I got off work so if we were going to meet it would have to be a weekend. He asked if I could drive up to meet him. To get to his town from my house I had to take the interstate up a ways and then turn off onto a county road. There was a little mini-city by the exit of the interstate. We could meet there so it would be about half way for each of us. That was the story he told me Saturday morning when he called to confirm our date.

We met at a coffee shop. He didn't have quite as far to go and got there before me. It was a beautiful, sunny day so he sat outside and waited for the Jeep I described on the phone. He looked pretty much as I expected. He mentioned he was originally from southern California and he looked like an aging surfer dude. His shirt was a large floral print with unnaturally bright colors. Over his legs were a pair of baggy cargo shorts and on his feet were a pair of flip-flops. His hair was too short to put in a pony tail but long enough to get in his face when there was any type of a breeze with curls that ended about on his shoulders. He could have been in any beach movie, but he was a little older than the average beach bum.

I nervously walked over to him for formal introductions. Yes it was him, but he was wondering if I wanted to talk with him here, or maybe go somewhere else to get to know each other. I wasn't really in the mood for coffee. Even an iced one wasn't what I really wanted. There was a 1950's themed diner in the shopping center. We could get a shake and share it since they would make it in one of those big metal glasses and bring it all to the table for us to enjoy.

It was the usual first date chit-chat. He talked about his ex-wife a lot more than I was really comfortable with. It seems they did a do-it-yourself divorce since they had no kids and very little assets. He didn't say exactly when they officially separated, only that the divorce wasn't quite final but would be when his next check came in. He was also still her first call when she needed anything. She was mentally challenged and her routine had become to call him at the first sign of trouble. Even though they were legally separated he still took her to doctor appointments and such because he didn't want her to feel like she was being abandoned by him. Not exactly sure on what the word "separation" meant to him, but I wasn't going to judge. He was helping out a friend who just happened to be married to him in the past.

He was also interested in my sexual history, since I really had none. At least in my mind I was still a good girl no matter what happened with Lawrence. I explained how I was a loner growing up and always working for the church at one level or another during my adult life. Lately I had been more socially active, but that didn't necessarily mean sexually active in the fullest sense of the term. I told him how I learned to talk dirty while still being a good girl. Several guys I talked to over the phone said I could easily get a job talking to guys who pay by the minute. Part of it was my voice and part of it was how I said things. "Mischievously innocent" was my favorite description of my voice.

After all that our shake was gone. He asked if I would be willing to move our conversation to his van. I knew it wouldn't be much of a conversation, but I agreed to spend some time in his van. There wasn't a lot of room in it. He was using it as a mobile storage unit for his collecting and hobby. I should have put the pieces together, but I was still innocently naive. More on the reality of the situation later, the rest of this date was way too funny to skip over.

His van was legally parked in an unused part of the lot with an empty spot between it and my Jeep. They were sitting out in the middle of nowhere, about half way between the coffee shop and a doughnut shop. By this time in the day shoppers were thinking about lunch, not breakfast, so our vehicles were sitting conspicuously apart from all the others in the lot.

So there we were, in the front seat of his van. He moved some things around in the back so he could put my seat back, then climbed in on my side. For some reason he took his shoes off when he got in, not that the sandals on his feet really counted as shoes for me. As you may have guessed it was impossible for us to share the seat. Since I was already lying back, he just got on top of me. Let me remind you, we were both fully clothed, except for his shoes. He was kissing me and I don't even remember what our hands were doing. His were probably trying to keep his balance on top of me in the seat. I had never gone "parking" as a teenager and this was my second time in as many months. All the lines were running through my head. If this van's rocking don't come knocking, things like that. As usual I was enjoying the sensations and trying not to notice his growing excitement. We were both caught up in the moment.

That all came crashing to a halt with a knock on the window. Randy lifted himself up and turned his head to see who was knocking. All I could see was a flat, slanted hat on a head that seemed to be nothing more than a holder for a large pair of sunglasses. Then again, from where I was that was about all I could see besides the sky. Randy started to roll the window down.

"Is everything all right in there?"

"Yes, Officer. Is there a problem?"

"Only if there's one in there."

"No problem in here, Officer."

"Would you mind stepping out of the vehicle?"

He got out of the van as gracefully as he could. Once out he found his sandals and threw them on the ground to slip his feet into them.

"Can I see your ID, sir?"

Randy reached back for his wallet and fumbled through the cards to get his driver's license. I was trying my best to stifle the laugh that was building up inside me.

"Are you all right, miss?"

"Yes, I'm fine." If I said more than that it would have been in a flurry of laughter. Before I could get my composure to explain that my ID was in the Jeep right next door, he was off to the squad car with just the one.

The look on Randy's face said that he was about to burst into laughter as well. This was *way* too funny. I had heard of a couple

175

that got a parking ticket for "parking" but they never saw the officer. It's hard to see someone put something under the windshield wiper when you are lying across the back seat. Not to mention the fact that they were a bit distracted by what they were doing in the back seat.

The officer came back and handed Randy his ID. "Thank you, sir. We had a call of a suspicious van and had to come and check it out. Stay safe, both of you." He tipped his hat to me and was off. Once the car was safely on its way out of the parking area we both doubled over in laughter.

"At least you know I'm not wanted for anything," Randy said through bursts of giggles.

Eventually we settled down.

"Guess I should be going so I'm not late for work."

"Wouldn't want you to get a speeding ticket, now would I?" Even with most of my giggles worked out I still couldn't get the smile off my face.

"I'll call you when I get a chance. Sometimes I can sneak a call in during my breaks and stuff." He walked me to the driver's side of the Jeep and gave me a quick good-bye kiss. Maybe he was afraid that any more than that would get him arrested, or maybe he was still laughing so hard and didn't want me to know it. We had been kissing for a while any way so I wasn't too disappointed.

On the drive home it hit me what the actual call might have been that went into the police station. God had always watched out for me, so situations like that were an after-thought of what could have been. In the moment I don't think of things like that. Maybe I should start, but my country girl innocence prevented me from seeing the dangers of some situations. I grew up before "stranger danger" became part of the elementary school curriculum. That's all part of going where angels fear to tread. "No fear" can be a convenient excuse for "no brains" or unbridled innocence.

*****

Randy did call, about every other day or so. We talked about my upcoming trip to Alaska. Of course he said he was jealous that he would never make it up there. I told him I would bring him pictures next time I saw him. There were plenty of pictures of Alaska in my stuff from the previous years, but it didn't sound like we would be seeing each other again before my trip.

Tim sounded like he didn't believe me that I was going to Alaska again. Since he didn't ever go anywhere outside his little town any more, he didn't believe that anyone else would travel I guess. One day he would tell me how he was saving money. The next day some emergency came up—like he needed a new pair of shoes because his "old ones" were stained green from mowing the lawn—so he had to use that money. I had been saving money to go to Alaska since I started making money again after moving down here. There were still a couple churches that helped out with some of the expenses. At this point I was getting my paycheck and unemployment when I got back so I wasn't worried about money at the moment.

There was another unexpected call. Ken called to say he would be in town this weekend and wondered if I wanted to see him again. This would be the last weekend before I left for Alaska, but I could spend some time with him. While we were talking I mentioned what I bought myself for my birthday. That really got his attention. He had mentioned getting something like that for me when we were talking about a road trip during spring break, so his reaction didn't surprise me. He was scheduled to arrive in town Friday morning, but it would take him most of the day to take care of all the stuff required with each trip. We could get together sometime on Saturday and see what happened.

In my mind there was no reason for guilt. The only guy who mentioned something permanent wasn't talking to me, not even the Thursday night "call me tomorrow" call at 2 am from him. The guy I met last weekend said nothing about exclusivity. I was on a dating website for heaven's sake. Even my innocent country girl mind figured that the guys I was talking with were at least talking with other women. So this was a little more than talking, but men do stuff like this all the time on TV. Then again, I'm not like most of the women seen on TV. In any case, I didn't see a date with Ken as a problem. I would still be a good girl. We would just mess around a bit like we had in the past. In my mind an outfit like I was going to show him would be something for him to look at. I had been topless with him after all. This time I would have a little less on. In my innocent mind that would be all right, with nothing else expected. I should have known better.

The teddy didn't feel right under my other clothes. It was a little out of my ordinary to have something like that on instead of my usual cotton undies. The little skirt-like thing was bunching up under my jeans and the stitching that connected it to the lace on top was itchy. The lace didn't give much support up on top either. I should have taken all that as an indication not to do this, but hindsight is always better. I needed something to distract me from packing for a while anyway.

The next weekend would be spent in airports for the most part. I was a little nervous about facing all my friends in Alaska. The last time I saw them everyone thought I would be married soon. I'd have to explain to each and every one of them, individually, why that didn't happen. Not exactly something I was looking forward to. I was hoping for a nice little—flirty—chat. That's not exactly what Ken had on his mind and the two ideas were about to clash.

Ken was finishing up something online when I got there. We talked for a little while, but it was obvious what was on his mind. We hadn't really talked in over a month and I was on my way up to Alaska. He had been to Alaska to work on a fishing vessel over summers for a while when he was younger. He knew really rural Alaska, places you have to fly into or take a ship to visit. My little town you could drive to, but it was still considered rural. We were sitting on the couch, and it didn't take him long to start feeling what was under my shirt.

"Do you want to see the whole thing?"

"Only if you're comfortable with that."

He helped me take off my shirt. He took a few steps back to put it on the couch and stood there while I dropped my jeans. It was obvious he liked what he saw. I didn't think I was capable of getting that reaction from a man. Then again, based on the pictures in his bathroom and what I saw on his computer over his shoulder when he was trying to quickly close windows, he really liked lace when that was all that was covering a female body. I was expecting to sit down on the couch and continue the conversation, maybe pick out a movie or something like that. See how my good girl mind works? I think almost anyone else would have expected what happened next, but at this point I still didn't see it coming.

"Have you ever seen my bedroom?"

"No, that's the one room I don't think I've ever seen."

"Let me show you then." He took my hand and led me to his bedroom. I can't believe how stupid I was at that point. A few months ago I refused to go to a guy's bedroom. But I had become desensitized. I really don't know what I was thinking right then. Looking back I see how it must have looked to Ken. If I ever see him again, I would apologize profusely.

He indicated I should sit down on the side of his bed. He followed and sat next to me after he took his shirt off. At the time it didn't faze me that he didn't take his shorts off, then again, I wasn't really thinking clearly. His lips and hands hardly left my body for the next few minutes. As usual, it felt good to me. As you might expect, Ken wanted to feel good, too. He expected one thing, and I knew that wasn't going to happen. We wrestled a little, arguing about who would win without using words. In my mind we could do things without doing "the thing." After all, I had done that before. I don't think Ken ever had. Finally he gave up trying.

179

"I think you better leave now, before I do something we would both regret."

I really didn't know what to say to that.

He got out of bed and put his shirt back on. "You are beautiful and I want to be able to stop while I still can so I don't hurt you." He walked out of the room.

I stayed on the bed for a moment to figure out what to do. After a minute or two I followed Ken to the living room. I got my clothes as quickly as possible trying to figure out what to say.

"I'm sorry I disappointed you."

"This is just a thought, but maybe you should just find someone guy in Alaska and do it with him. That way you can just get your first time over with and never have to see him again unless you really want to."

I couldn't believe he said that. When we were talking on the phone I'm sure I mentioned my desire to make my wedding night the first night I allowed a man to fully express his love. He thought I should "just get it over with" with some stranger. That's just sex, not making love. If I wanted to "just get it over with" I could have done that several times already. That was not my intention. He must not have heard the part about my wedding night. He was probably too busy thinking of the Fredrick's of Hollywood catalogue when we were talking about it. He grew up on the streets and I'm guessing he just got it over with early in life and expected that everyone else should, too.

He didn't bother to walk me out this time. A quick good-bye at the door and I never saw him again. I was too stunned to really think about things at the time. I went over there as a short distraction from preparations for Alaska. It was quicker than I thought, but now I had time to get a few more things done.

*****

I was in emotional shock and going through the motions the rest of the weekend. I got things pretty much ready for the trip. Randy called a couple times that weekend. I told him, and Tim, that I would be in the classroom this week and then teaching Bible school in the mornings next week.

I didn't have much time to talk during that week. I had to have everything done to wrap up the school year by Friday, the new staff member was insistent on that. I wanted to have everything done anyway, but she was annoying about reminding me about it. The kids were done with their projects. The ones who were still attending school played a lot of football in the lot next door and took a lot of walks in a park at the end of the block. The teaching assistants and a couple others from the corporate office took care of most of that, giving me time to get grades and all the paperwork done. There wasn't a lot of time for chatting with guys, and now wouldn't be the time to start something new anyway. Then it was a matter of cleaning off my desk and getting all my personal stuff out of the classroom before handing over the keys on Friday.

Everything got done and I was on a plane headed for Alaska late Saturday morning. I had to focus on the Bible school the first week I was up there. The people who came up to help me overheard me talking to one of the locals about what happened last fall. I was pretty much at the point I could laugh at it all now. I saw with that 20/20 hindsight the things that just didn't make sense to me at the time. I could explain things better to people who saw the beginning of the situation and people I had just met.

It would have been nice to take a little time off of dating, but that didn't exactly happen. Well, it did to some extent. The only calls I got were from Tim and Randy. There wasn't time to start anything with someone new. I was enjoying playing tour guide for the people who had never been to that corner of the world before. It's a beautiful place and watching people see it for the first time is like watching kids open presents on Christmas morning or when babies realize that they can control those things on the end of their arms to reach for toys.

We were staying in the gym of the little school in the town. When I wanted privacy I had to go outside. Since there was so little darkness that wasn't really a problem, and the reception was better out there anyway. I felt obligated to show my helpers around the area, but they gave me time occasionally to make personal calls.

There were some calls that were totally personal during that week. I wouldn't exactly consider calls from Tim as dating, but he still called almost every day. Now there was an even bigger time difference so he could call later in the night for him and still have it be a respectable hour for me. There was no way to really prove I was in Alaska. My phone didn't take pictures and he didn't know any of the voices I could use as evidence I had actually taken the trip. He had no reason not to believe me, other than the fact that he would never have the guts to do something like that.

Randy called many times as well. While teaching, actually all the time I was awake when I was up there, I kept my cell phone in my pocket. It was small and things can come up fast and unexpectedly up there. In reality, I was afraid that if I set it down anywhere I would forget to take it with me when I left. The only reason I don't regularly lose my keys is that I need them to drive home from where ever I happened to be. Since I had a phone, I kept it with me, in case a moose stranded me in an outhouse. Don't laugh, the first year I was up there that actually happened to someone in my group. Anyway, when I called Randy back Wednesday afternoon, since he mentioned it was his day off, I mentioned that he made the phone vibrate while it was in my pocket because I shut the sound off while I was teaching. He asked if I wanted him to call him more often so it would vibrate more. Thursday it went off several times in the morning with only one message from Randy, "Hope you enjoy the vibrations."

Other than that there wasn't a lot I could do as far as dating was concerned. The only computer access I had was at the town library, which was open four hours a day at most. When I lived up there I volunteered for the library so I had a key at the time. That meant I could go in any time the library wasn't open and use the computers as long as I wanted. Patrons were limited to half hour blocks on the computers. Over the winter you could usually get longer times. With all the seasonal workers in the town living in tents or cabins with no electricity, the half hour limit was usually all anyone could get. Just about the time you get a good chat going your time was up. To add to that, the connection was dial-up, which means everything is pretty slow compared to how things are in civilization.

Mornings were spent with the kids at the Bible school. Most afternoons were spent playing tour guide for the other people who came up to help me or talking with friends I hadn't seen in a year. There wasn't much time for a social life anyway.

*****

Friday morning the Bible school was over. My helpers went off to the hotel rooms they were going to stay the weekend in and I went to the friend's house I was going to stay at next week. We took most of Friday night catching up, so it wasn't until Saturday morning I had time on the computer again. There was a week's worth of junk mail, as expected. I had a few e-dresses to check. One I use for the dating site, one for keeping in contact with my family, and one for when I need to give an e-dress for something online. Cleaning them up didn't bother me.

There was a message from Randy, however, that did bother me. He told me the real reason why he didn't want to meet at his place the weekend before I left. It seems his now finally officially ex-wife was still living with him at the time. He said the divorce was amicable, but not that they weren't really separated. This message was that she finally found a place of her own and was moving out. The tone of it was positive, but that didn't make me feel any better. I was upset. He may not have been wanted by the authorities, but it

183

seems he was still wanted by his ex-wife to some extent. He never said how long they had been separated, turns out he really wasn't. From that point on I knew our relationship wasn't going anywhere. If I were busy with real potential relationships I would have ignored him all together. As it was I was bored and he offered something to do when I got back. If I got a better offer I would definitely take it. Like with Tim, he was someone for me to pass time with until I found someone to spend the rest of my life with.

*****

The family I was staying with pretty much left me alone when I wanted time to myself. They were busy with other friends and family that had come up. They understood I would be in and out of the house visiting my friends. They knew I would be kept busy and they didn't have to entertain me. They also didn't spend much time on the computer. The computer was upstairs where my room was, and their room was downstairs along with the kitchen and all the living area. Most of the time I could do pretty much whatever I wanted to upstairs and they wouldn't know it where they were. She was the only one who would come up anyway, and while I was there she would make a lot of noise to let me know she was coming. Usually that was enough time to let any guy know I wouldn't be alone for a while so he didn't have to wonder why messages weren't as instant as they usually were.

During that week I was on vacation in Alaska I met a couple very interesting guys. The first one was Mark. He was from the Midwest and very young. I met him on a different dating sight, but he said he loved my picture and wanted to me to call him. Did I mention he was young? We were both on summer vacation from school only he was a college student and I was a high school teacher. Eventually I did call him, and all he wanted to do is find out what I was wearing and where my hands were at the moment. I knew this wasn't going anywhere, so I played along. As I was going along with him, I started thinking maybe I should charge him for this call. Since I most likely didn't have a teaching job lined up for fall, maybe I should see if I could get a job at a call center for lonely guys like Mark. If they charge by the minute just think of how much I could make, just talking with my mischievously innocent voice.

As he claimed to explore his body, I claimed to explore mine. He kept asking about how I looked. He said he was tired of the bronzed bodies everyone was trying to create. That's good, I have a good Alaskan tan. By the way, that means I have no tan—think of how tan Mr. and Mrs. Claus are. They also have good Alaskan tans. During an Alaskan summer the sun is out most of the day, but never really high in the sky. It would be like trying to tan when you can only get out in the sun from about 5 pm to sundown.

He liked the rosy red cheeks in the picture I had online and asked if I wore a lot of makeup. I hate makeup. It never goes on right, which only accentuates my asymmetrical face. Once on it has to be taken off, usually with scrubbing. My skin is so sensitive that some cleansers can make it break out so I don't want to have to use a lot to clean it.

Once all that was out of the way, he got to what he really wanted to do. He must have just finished a biology class in college because he was asking me about certain body parts using the medical terms for them instead of the usual slang. Maybe he was trying to impress me with his knowledge of the female body. Made me wonder how much he knew from experience and how much he learned from books, or more likely magazines or movies. A few moans sprinkled in here and there from both of us, and he said he needed to clean up a few things.

He called often that week, and several times the following weeks. Most of the time he had to leave a message, begging me to call him soon. This wasn't going anywhere and I was just having fun pretending. When we would actually talk, it started with a weather report from where he was and ended with him having to clean things up. He never asked if I wanted to meet face to face. Occasionally he would see me online and start to chat. He always wanted me to see his webcam. I didn't have one and if I did I wouldn't have let him see me. It was easier to type or talk my way through a sexual encounter for him. I wasn't getting anything out of it but practice using my voice as an instrument of pleasure. He was young and far away and not something I was really interested in. I guess that meant I was playing him along, but I don't think he really cared. He got what he wanted out of any conversation we had so he was satisfied.

I didn't think of my talks with Mark as taking away from my good girl-ness. It was still all talk after all, like the chats I had online in the classroom. He may have been doing something while we talked, but I wasn't. Even if I did, it was to myself. Good girls can do things to themselves, they just don't tell other people about it.

Of course I wanted more than just conversation or at least the promise of more once I got back home. I needed someone more my age to share past experiences with. I needed someone who wanted me for something other than just phone sex. Of the many conversations I had while I was in Alaska, one gentleman continued to converse with me. It somewhat started out with phone sex but at least he expressed an interest in something else. The good girl-ness was being worn away in some ways, but in one way I was still a good girl and that was the way I was looking at things. Now, who was that gentlemen?

The Monday of that week I was online for the first time in a while. The weekend was busy with catching up with friends I hadn't seen in a year. The little time I was online was spent cleaning all the junk mail from my various e-dresses, and of course finding out that Randy's wife moved out of his place. Monday I logged into my account on the dating website. Usually weekends are better for trolling for conversations, but sometimes you get lucky and find someone at work or for some reason at home and bored.

The profile that caught my attention had the screen name of "another knight." I've always been intrigued by fairy tales and things like that, so I read on. He was a little older than me, not enough to make a difference now, but he was in high school while I was finishing up elementary school. He listed his location as a legendary city in American mythology and his occupation as a singer/songwriter. His picture showed a gray, scraggly beard that was probably trimmed to look that way. I liked the beard, and the gray in it just made it more interesting to me. He was online, so I thought I would try to start a chat with him while I was looking at openings for teaching jobs in the metro area.

It didn't take him long to answer my invitation. The introductions took on a medieval twist. He referred to me as Princess. There are rumors in my family about being nobility, but after leaving the home country because of a bar fight it would probably be hard to prove one way or another. In any case, I was happy to be his princess, and he was interested in being my knight in shining armor, or no armor if I was willing to wear nothing but my pointy hat with the long scarf at the top. There came a point in our flirtations that I had to let him know my secret.

He went totally chivalrous on me at that point. We continued to chat about castles and dragons and such for a while. Eventually he had to go, but he asked if we could chat again. We exchanged e-dresses so we could chat on Yahoo later. I went back to concentrate on looking for a job until I had to leave for another dinner with a family who invited me over.

The next day when I logged on, he was also online. He picked up right where we left off yesterday, instantly flirtatious. He asked for my phone number, and must have called as soon as he got the message. The instant I heard his voice, I knew there was something special here. I've often used my voice as a toy, pretending to be other people or playing with them like I was doing with Mark. He hoped to make a living with his voice, and I could understand why.

There was just something about it. The really funny thing was that he said he liked my voice as well.

The more we talked, the more interested we became in each other. He was staying with a former lover because he couldn't find another place in that town. He was thinking of making a change soon anyway, so he mentioned that he was interested in coming to the metro area where I lived. He had lived in that area once before, but he lived in many places before. The slightest hint that he may move there to be with me sent me spinning. I had moved to be with someone who I had known for two years and it didn't work out. Now he was saying he may move to be with someone he barely knew two days. This couldn't be happening. Maybe in the fairy tales there was love at first sight, but not in the real world. We hadn't even seen each other, only pictures, and who knows if the pictures on the site were real or not. Knights don't come in and sweep princesses off their feet in the real world.

The next day we IM-ed and talked again. He sang a song he was working on, saying he had stopped working on it until yesterday when he heard my voice. Hearing the song made me melt. His voice was a deep baritone and I was getting my own personal concert with a love song I rekindled in his repertoire.

When he told me a little bit of the story behind the song I had a few reservations. He said he was married twice before and had all but given up on finding another woman to permanently share his life with. That was pretty much what Lawrence said. I had signed up on the website to find a spouse. Now I realized what Lawrence wrote in his bio was more the case. He said he was looking for "a friend, a lover and maybe even a wife." That theory didn't work that well for me last time, but as usual, I was hoping this would be different.

My knight was still talking about moving to the metro area. He really wanted to get away from where he was. I knew he wouldn't be staying at my place, and he didn't really ask. He just mentioned that he had already checked how much a bus ticket would cost and he had that much. He was working with a franchise store and didn't think there would be a problem getting a transfer to a branch somewhere in the metro area. This was *way* too fast. I agonized for months before moving to the area for a man. Now he was talking about moving there after only a couple of phone conversations and some online chatting. The woman he was staying with was coming back, so he had to go. We set up a time to chat tomorrow. He would meet me online and see what happened from there.

There was time that afternoon to talk with my host. She was very interested in how my social life was going. Actually, that was the main topic of conversation for most of the time I was up there. Everyone wanted to know what happened with "that other guy" and if I had found anyone else.

I mentioned that I had a picture from Christmas on the website, but that was just a head shot. The place I was staying was out in the country with lots of trees that were in bloom so she suggested we go outside and get some more pictures of me. It was fun to play model for a while. When she had time she was going to send the pictures to me so I could put them on the website, or whatever I wanted to do with them. By the next day they were in my inbox, so I put them on the website. It was one of those that let you post pictures besides the one that showed up next to your profile. I picked the three best of my poses to share with the guys who wanted to see more of what I looked like. At the time it seemed innocent enough, but later I was to find out what some men really thought of them.

Wednesday I met my knight online again. We started typing suggestive messages. We decided it was too hard to type with both hands and do what we were saying, so I logged off the computer and went to my room. The door closed just as the phone rang. Of course it was my knight, still trying to sweep his princess off her feet. The conversation turned quickly to what he would do to me if we were to meet. It was easier to do what he asked now that we were talking on the phone, with at least one hand free. And it was easier for me to talk to him the same way instead of having to type it all out. His voice was soothing and sexy even when he wasn't singing. I wasn't singing either, but he liked the sounds I was making. He stopped singing for a while to join me. I was comfortable enough with him to imagine we were doing what we were talking about. This wasn't the pretending like with Mark. This was real phone sex. Maybe it was being away from home, maybe it was being on vacation with no job to come home to, maybe it was the thought of "just getting it over with" as Ken suggested. His voice was just too inviting to resist.

After a while we continued a real conversation. He was asking what part of the city I lived in, hoping he could find a place nearby. So he was still talking about moving to be near me. He also had a few more songs to sing to me. We talked about lots of things, and nothing at all for hours.

The next day was my flight home. As usual with flights out of Alaska it was a late night departure. There was time to get online again. My knight was there, but something was odd. He didn't want to talk, but we IM-ed for a while. Of course I knew it was because of what we had done yesterday, but he said it wasn't. He had a ticket to leave town the next day and arrive at the bus station by me on Saturday. After our phone conversation yesterday he had a lot of questions about my sexual experience. As usual he didn't believe that I was still a virgin at my age, especially the way I was talking. Online dating is notorious for stretching the truth. In my mind I was telling the truth, but that was too much for most guys to believe.

He sounded excited to leave his current living situation, but maybe he was nervous about the new one. We had briefly discussed him staying with me, long enough for me to shoot it down. I wasn't going to let Tim stay with me if he ever showed up so I certainly wasn't going to share my room with someone I met online just a couple of days ago. Maybe that's what had him upset. Eventually I had to pack and get ready to leave.

I said my good-byes to my host, and made a few stops on my way to the airport. There was one of those feelings again, this time that I wouldn't be coming back to Alaska next summer so I was also saying good-bye to my mountains on the way up to Anchorage. There were a few souvenirs I wanted to pick up for my family members. Since this might be the last time I was in Alaska at all, I had to make sure there was something for everyone including the youngest members of the family who would only have the hand-me-downs of t-shirts and stuffed toys from the Last Frontier.

As I was repacking my luggage to accommodate the new purchases, my phone rang. When I saw the number I realized what day of the week it was—Thursday. The call was from Lawrence. With the time difference, this was a bit early for his usual but still late if I would have been at home. I told him I was in Alaska, but on my way home. He said he would have this weekend free and wanted to get together again. He didn't mention what he was doing the weeks we hadn't talked, and I didn't say what I was doing. He asked if I had been looking at rings. I was intentionally evasive of the question, saying I wanted to do that with him. Maybe that was something we could do this weekend when we got together. He still hadn't been paid for the last job, some snag in the financing, so it would only be window shopping. Then we could go back to my place and see what happened. I will never forget how he ended the call. "I want to marry you. I'll call you when you get back so we can get together again. I love you."

Those were his last words to me. Maybe I'm a little on the clairvoyant side, but at the time I knew they would be his last words to me. I wasn't going to wait by the phone for a call from him when I got back. Yes, I would let him know I was back, but that would be a message because he wouldn't want to answer the phone when I called. That's the way things had been going the past two months and there was nothing in the conversation with him that indicated this time would be different.

*****

I arrived home mid-morning. I let my mom and the people in Alaska know that I was safe back in my house and fell asleep for several hours. When I woke up I let Lawrence know I was back, by leaving a message as I figured would happen. Even when my phone rang, I knew it wasn't him before I saw the number.

It was my knight. He told me that the phone he had was from the ex he was currently staying with, and he wouldn't be bringing it with him when he came to town. I shouldn't call him on that number because she would answer it and then she would have my number and she was, well, a little unstable to put it politely.

He seemed to be getting serious about me. So if he was coming all the way over here to be closer to me, he deserved to know about the call I got last night. When I told him, he was devastated. Remember, he was married twice before and had several relationships. All but one that he mentioned ended with her cheating on him, according to what he told me.

I told him that the call last night may be the last time I ever talked with him, but that didn't help. All he heard was that someone I had a near sexual experience with (something he may call an actual sexual experience if he knew exactly what we did) called me. If I was anything like the pictures I sent him, no man would be able to resist me. If a former date was calling, it was to restart the relationship. No matter how many times or ways I told him there would probably be no more contact between me and a past fling, my knight wasn't buying it. He now wasn't sure about leaving, but there wasn't really anything keeping him there. His last words to me were that he would call if he came into town, but I shouldn't call him at that number under any circumstances.

I had no way to contact him. He didn't want me to call. Since there was no internet at the house and my job was done, the only way I could log into my IM was to go to the library. If he was traveling that wouldn't help anyway. He didn't say anything about where he was going to stay when he arrived or if he would have internet access there. My knight disappeared.

This was getting too hard for me. I was supposed to use the time in Alaska to relax. Now I was back not even a full day and the stress was back worse than it was before. Maybe it was a good thing I would have to go to a library to go online. Some time away from the chat rooms might do me some good.

*****

Saturday I went to the Greyhound station to see when the bus from his town was coming in. By the time I got there the first one had been in for a couple of hours and the next one he could have been on was scheduled for much later that night. They couldn't tell me if my knight was on either of those busses. I wasn't sure he would be coming anyway. The last time I talked to him he was incredibly upset with me. He may not want to see me even if he did use that bus ticket.

No call from Lawrence, as expected. No word from my knight. No word from Randy, but after I told him what I thought about him not telling me he was still living with his wife I was almost hoping to not hear from him again. No word from any of the guys I met online except Tim, who would never be in my physical world. That was a pretty quiet weekend and the last weekend of June.

The year was half over and there was no man in my life. The feeling that I would be married by New Year's Eve wasn't looking accurate. Maybe that was God's way of making me rest a little before the wild ride I was about to go on in the month of July.

193

Chapter 8 — Too hot to be good

July has always been an enigma to me. First as a student, then as a teacher, it was the one month with no school. It started out with the highlight of the month with fireworks on the 4th of July and then dragged on with hot, steamy days that never seemed to end. June was the beginning of summer with all the hopes of the season. August was the end and usually by then I was ready for the hot weather to be gone and some nights it would get downright cold. July was stuck in the middle with nothing to do but work the summer job I usually had and dream of cooler days. This July would go down as the wildest ride to date.

Monday of the first week I went online again. My six month subscription was just about up, but there was enough for this month. Hopefully that would be enough for me to find Mr. Right. There was a message from a guy with the screen name of HighFlyer. He also happened to be online when I was at the library. I hadn't brought my laptop that trip so I could only chat for an hour before my time on the library computer was over. He was a pilot in the Air Force, but retired for a couple of years. He never really said what he was doing now, other than looking for someone to share his life with. At least that's what he told me. Actually I think it was more someone to share the night with, but let me get on with the story.

It was hot and my room on the second floor with no real ventilation wasn't comfortable. I decided to take my laptop to another library and spend some time online where I wasn't restrained by the time limits of the community computers. When I lived in Alaska I spent a lot of time at the library when it wasn't open. The good thing about being in a large metro area was that libraries were open longer hours and there were several to choose from.

The house was hot so I was looking for something to do in air conditioning and spending time online was a good way to spend those hot summer days. My excuse was that I was looking for a job, but really I was looking for a husband. I didn't want to frighten guys off by telling them that, so if anyone asked, I was looking at school websites and other job related things. As long as I was online I may as well see who else was and have a chat with them, right?

The second library for the day was closer to home and a newly opened facility. The best places to access the internet were on the second floor. Luckily there was a study room that was available so I could have some privacy. You never know how these conversations are going to go and I didn't want some Nosy Nelly looking over my shoulder while I'm having cyber sex. Not that I was really planning on anything like that, but the way things were going for me you never know. I never really planned on something like that, but it happened more often than I care to share.

HighFlyer had sent me a message with his Yahoo identification so we could use that to chat. He was also online again so we chatted some more. He had seen all of the pictures of me and wanted to see me in person. It was already late for a meeting tonight, but we made plans on meeting the next day. There was one question he had for me:

HighFlyer: Are you sure about your age?

Randi: Yes, I'm really as old as my profile says I am. Why?

HighFlyer: You look so much younger in your pictures.

Randi: Lots of people say that. Do you have a problem with it?

HighFlyer: No, I think you look great. Usually people take away years, not add them.

Randi: I haven't done either.

HighFlyer: Then how much did you touch up those pictures?

Randi: Other than taking out the red in my eyes from the one picture, nothing.

HighFlyer: Are you for real?

Randi: Yes, those are really me, taken last week when I was in Alaska.

HighFlyer: All of them?

Randi: The one by my profile was taken in December, but the other ones were all taken last week.

HighFlyer: Now I really can't wait to meet you.

Someone else who didn't think I was real. Let me guess, tomorrow he will ask to meet at a Starbucks by his house so he can leave if he doesn't see anyone who looks like the pictures. The library would be closing soon so we didn't have time to make definite plans. He would be online again tomorrow so he could think about where to meet tonight and give me directions then.

By now my room should be cooler, and I thought I still had some ice cream in the freezer to cool the inside of my body. In any case, the library was closing so I had to go home.

*****

It was after noon by the time I got to the library and back online. I could get used to these lazy summer days of not having to get up early and be off to school. I had a couple of resumes to send out before getting ready for another cyber social session. HighFlyer thought I had ditched him. I wondered how long he was waiting for me on the computer. I explained that I rarely have days when I don't have to get up and out of the house for something, so when I

197

do I take advantage of them. He agreed that leisure mornings are best.

He was ready to meet any time. As predicted, he mentioned a Starbucks that he frequented. I wasn't sure if it was close to his house or not since he was evasive about where he lived. It was on the other side of the city so it would take me a while to get there once I got home and changed into more presentable attire. He said anything I wore would be nice, but probably nothing looked good on me. Yes, he was getting flirtatious. He gave me his phone number in case I couldn't find the place. I told him I would be there in about three hours. That would give me time to get home and changed and find my way to a new part of the city.

As we were chatting I was looking where the place was. I had been down that main drag a couple of times before looking for a bookstore for something I needed for my classroom last year. That was the "new downtown area" that had a few of the older shops left but mostly it was bigger strip malls and lots of parking lots. I never liked that type of atmosphere. Not quite an outdoor mall, but not the quaint little shops either. He said he knew the area pretty well and had some ideas of what we could do if we wanted to do something after our initial meeting. Since I still considered myself new to the area, I didn't even know much of what was just a block from my house so it was better to meet where at least one of us knew the area. If I was going to have time to get everything done before our meeting, I had to get going. He described what he would be wearing so I would be able to recognize him when I got there. I started trying to think of what I was going to wear, but he said he will never be able to forget the face he saw in the pictures. He would be able to identify me by that so I didn't have to decide right then and there what I was going to wear.

I decided not to change my clothes, but I did grab something from the fridge so my stomach wouldn't growl later. It was rush hour on Wednesday, but the 3rd of July so traffic wasn't bad.

Once there, I looked for the car he described yesterday. I found something like it with HIGHFLYR on the license plates. It must be his. When I walked in the door he stood up and motioned for me to join him at a table.

"What would you like to drink?"

"Something cold and fruity would be nice." We had already discussed how I wasn't really a coffee drinker but now they have so many different drinks that don't have any coffee in them.

"You stay here to keep the table and I'll be right back." He disappeared behind a display for a while and then reappeared with a drink in each hand. I was guessing the pink one was for me and the brown one was for him. "Hope you like this."

"Looks good. Exactly what I asked for. Thank you." I wasn't expecting something that big. Usually the smallest size is good enough for me. Now the trick would be drinking it without my version of a brain freeze. We talked about what happens to me when my mouth gets too cold. Instead of a headache, my throat stops functioning. I can't swallow, or talk, or do anything. He said he would keep me talking so that wouldn't happen.

Our conversation started with questions about 4th of July traditions. Growing up, that's when we would light some sparklers and ground fireworks along with a campfire. The grand finale was when we would light last year's Christmas tree before letting the fire burn itself out. One of my nephews used to think that *Oh, Christmas Tree* was a campfire song and wondered why we sang it in church during the Children's Christmas Service. When my brother, who was a volunteer firefighter, and his family moved into the place I grew up in, he would have everyone over on the evening of the 3rd for a fireworks show around that same campfire pit surrounded by the rocks.

The last several summers I'd been up in Alaska for the holiday. It was hard to enjoy fireworks when you couldn't even see stars at night. Up there New Year's Eve was the big night for fireworks if they had them at all. The big thing for the 4th of July where I lived

199

was the Mt. Marathon race. It started years earlier as a bar bet and now it was one of the biggest events in the area. The rule was you had to run up the mountain, but coming down could be any way you want. Legend has it that someone once rolled the entire way down. No one could put a year on it so I doubt it actually happened. I was pretty much done with the story when he interrupted me.

"I can't believe it."

"Can't believe what?"

"You are for real."

"Of course I'm for real, what were you expecting?"

"Nothing like what is sitting in front of me. And I mean that in a good way." My drink was almost gone and warm enough by now that a throat freeze would be difficult, so he started to talk. He told me about his adventures with online dating. Most of the women sounded like me at first. When he met them he found out what they were less than totally honest about. I had to show him my ID to prove my age, but as he said earlier, most people lie to make themselves younger not older. Ironic how people want to be right around 21, right? If they are younger they lie to be older and if they are older they tell you they are younger than their actual, chronological age. Many of the women he met had old pictures of themselves or put photo shopped pictures on the website, according to him.

All that was left of my drink was what had filled in the ring at the bottom of the cup. In a situation like this it wasn't worth all the trouble to get it out. Instead I was playing with the cup, rolling it from one hand to the other across the table. He waited until the cup just left the hand closest to him before surrounding my hand with his hands.

"So, what would you like to do tonight?"

"I don't know. What did you have in mind?"

By this time the sun was almost down. Neither of us was really hungry, but we didn't want the evening to end just yet. The vibes I was getting from him made me nervous. He must have felt that because his hands softened around mine.

"There's a park nearby, maybe we can go there and talk some more. We may even be able to see some fireworks from there." The wink in his eye gave me an indication of what fireworks he was looking for that night.

He walked me to my Jeep and pointed out his car. It was dark, but rush hour was over so I should be able to follow him a couple of blocks to the park. There wouldn't be a big rush to the park anyway. As long as I stayed close we should be fine. With all my travels in Alaska I was usually the lead vehicle, but I was flexible. He made sure not to go too fast on the winding streets to the park.

We ended up in a small parking area near a grassy field. Just beyond the street light put there to make the parking lot safe was a baseball diamond with a small set of bleachers on the far side of a high fence. We got safely around the fence and almost to the bleachers when there was a funny sound, followed by a spray of water. The sprinklers must have been set to go off when no one would be there. We giggled and ran to the other side of the bleachers, the dry side. That was also the side that was totally out of the light, so we had a little more privacy. Not that it really mattered since we seemed to be the only ones in the park.

He started holding my hand while we talked about nothing in particular. Soon his other hand was on my leg. He was moving slowly, but steadily. In the distance we would see a colorful spark or two from early 4th of July celebrations. It was nice being able to see the colors and not have the loud boom ringing in my ears for the next few days. Before I knew it there was a tongue in my ear.

"What would you think about going to your place for the night?" This time I knew what he had in mind, and it wasn't going to happen.

"I live all the way on the other side of town. What about your place?" I had a feeling that would be my out. He was incredibly evasive about his living arrangements, which made me think he was

201

thinking he would either be sleeping with me or his wife that night. He picked the place to meet without really asking my thoughts on a location. It was in a place that was several blocks from anything residential, and on the side of town closest to the ritzier suburbs. He had already retired from one career and never said how he spent his time during the day. Now, I would see how he gets out of this one.

"My place isn't really set up for guests." Why, only one bedroom and his girlfriend was already there? In my mind that was the only thing it could be. My encounter with Randy made me more than a little suspicious about this situation. "It's kind of small, and you said you had a big room all to yourself."

I had been a naïve good girl for most of my life, but things were changing. Experience had made me a little wiser. I was putting it all together. He asked me a lot of questions but didn't answer any about himself. Instead he would ask me another question or give me a story about life in the Air Force. I had always been full of stories and very willing to share them if someone was willing to listen. Sometimes I had to consciously think to ask someone a question to make the conversation two ways. Thinking back on the conversation that was ending, I didn't do a very good job at that. He kept me busy talking about myself without sharing much about himself. That would be a convenient and easy way to hide his personal information, like the fact that he was married or living with someone and just wanted a little fling on the side. I wasn't going to go through that again. I would be a disappointing fling any way.

"My place isn't really set up for guests, either. I have no furniture and half of the space is just storage for boxes of stuff I need to go through to see what I can get rid of."

The conversation didn't last long after that. He decided his pants were too wet to be comfortable after the sprinkler incident. We walked back to the parking area and he opened my door after I unlocked it. Another promise of a call soon that I knew would never come. The kiss was something to remember, but I knew more of them would come at a price I wasn't willing to pay. The last thing I saw of him was his "highflyr" plates illuminated by the street light in the parking area.

It was a good way to spend an evening, but I was getting frustrated with these meetings with guys who only wanted what I wasn't prepared to give. Where was that knight in shining armor to take me away from all of this? He hadn't called me either, and maybe he never would.

*****

I didn't plan ahead enough to see the fireworks in town from the lookout. By the time I drove up there it was too crowded in all the good spots. Since I drove up there so late, I got a nice show on my way home. I hadn't seen fireworks on the 4th of July for four years, so any display would be better. I drove as slowly as I could to enjoy bursts of color in various parts of the city. One of the parks on my way home had some when I drove by so I stopped for a while to watch what I could.

The next day the libraries were back to open so I could get back to looking for a job and a husband. I got there as the library was opening and was able to get into one of the study rooms. It was a good thing schools were taking applications online. I think I left my printer in Alaska, or at least I hadn't remembered seeing it after I set it on a table when I was packing the U-Haul up there. I could sit in the library with just my laptop and send my resume to schools and fill out any online application.

As usual I checked my e-mails and the dating website first and occasionally while I was working just to see who was online. I also had my Yahoo Messenger open just in case my knight would be willing to chat with me again. Maybe he never came to town, maybe he found someone else, or maybe he just stopped looking.

All I knew was that he wasn't talking to me. Lawrence hadn't called since I was in Alaska, either. This was too frustrating to be helpful.

Eventually there was a message from Mark. He wanted me to call him again. I said I was not at home and this wouldn't be a good time. I didn't know we could do this, but he called me over my computer. I had a headset with a microphone like the telemarketers have. It was something leftover from when I took some classes over the internet in Alaska. I don't think Mark understood what I meant when I said I wasn't at home. I was sitting in a public library. Yes, I had a room to myself that was somewhat soundproof, but it also had windows for one entire wall facing the main stacks of the library. What he was asking me to do is something I couldn't do in that situation. It got to the point where I just played along like I had done before. He was too busy thinking about the one thing he wanted to realize what I was saying. It didn't take him long this time, and he remembered something else he had to do. This was going nowhere and only wasting my time. I decided to block him from my IM and never heard from him again. Well, he did try to call a few times but cell phones with caller ID are nice for things like this. Eventually he stopped calling all together. Maybe he started paying for such conversations.

A notice came up that I received a new message from someone on the dating website. The message was from a guy with a screen name of Mr. Clean. The picture next to it explained why. His eyebrows were black, but as far as the number of hairs on his head they were similar to Mr. Clean's total. He said he saw my pictures—the ones that were taken in Alaska—and wondered if I had done any modeling. After I stopped laughing, I started typing a message back. Before it was finished, there was an invitation to IM with him. That would probably be easier than an e-mail.

He claimed to be a portrait photographer who worked out of a home studio. His specialty was women who wanted to feel sexy. He asked if I wanted to go to his studio and let him find my inner Aphrodite. That would be a long way for me to go for pictures I would never show anyone. As we chatted that day I realized he was one of those stereotypical photographers who take some pictures to pay the bills to afford the equipment necessary to take the pictures he really wanted.

We chatted a few times during the next week, on a commercial format rather than through the website where we met. Each time it was interrupted by a woman coming over for an appointment. Sometimes he would send me the pictures. They started out with fully clothed model and the clothing would come off picture by picture. He said he would do that for me. Start with some good pictures and then, as I became more comfortable with him and the camera, clothing would come off. He implied that many of those photo shoots end in him shooting something else either alone or, preferably, with her help. He kept assuring me that everything was consensual and reciprocated if desired. None of this had anything to do with the fee schedule for the session, and the model would get all the pictures that were taken. The pictures he sent to me were only with the "model's" permission, or at least that's what he told me.

There was no way I could afford a trip to his studio. He said we could meet in the middle and he could turn any hotel room into a studio. The question I never asked was if he would be paying for the room by the hour. He would bring all the props we could think of using. He could teach me what it would take to be a full figured model. He claimed there was somewhat a demand for that kind of thing. I wasn't working now. Maybe it was time for me to switch careers.

He was very flattering, but not very realistic. At first I was skeptical. Soon I was fully aware of his plan. There must have been some complaints from other women on the dating site. I never sent a message to the profile police, but before the last time I IMed with him his profile disappeared from the website. Not the first time someone disappeared after questionable behavior.

Tim agreed that I could be a model, but this guy was using photography to get something else he wanted. According to Tim he probably used the pictures taken later in the session when he had to fly solo. He also said he would pay to see pictures like that of me. He could be such a charmer.

*****

That weekend Randy called. He said he missed talking to me and was sorry he wasn't totally honest about where his now ex-wife was living. The holiday had messed up his schedule and he actually had a weekend off. Of course it didn't matter now that I wasn't working.

He asked if I had met anyone else on the website. At the time I was still IMing with Mr. Clean, but I knew that was going nowhere. I told him about my knight, and that I hadn't heard from since just before he was supposed to get on the bus over here. He asked if I wanted to spend an evening with him. This time I could meet him at his place where we would have to be *really* loud before anyone would call the police to interrupt us. He reminded me that he had air conditioning at his place—that settled it.

Finding his place wasn't hard. It was one of those apartment complexes where all the buildings look alike and made a square around an open area tenants could use as a yard. The square was almost big enough for a football game. Hard to miss, but confusing to find a parking spot when you aren't sure of the exact apartment you're looking for. I gave him a call and he met me by my Jeep. It was way too hot for either of us to stay outside for a long hello.

Just stepping into his apartment made it clear he was a collector. It wasn't big and there were things everywhere. I'm not sure how to classify some of them. It wasn't one of those places with stacks of stuff accumulated over a lifetime like I had seen in some with some of the older church members I had visited in Alaska, but the place was full of stuff. There was enough room on the couch for both of us to sit, and it was in the line of cold air from the air conditioning.

For some reason, Randy was sweating. He said he did that often as he got a fan from the bedroom to cool us even more. The air conditioner just wasn't enough to cool the entire apartment, but sitting right in front of it was better than sitting up in my room.

Before I knew it we were lounging on the couch. My back was resting on the arm rest and my legs were on Randy's lap. He was sitting between them. He had taken his shirt off and implied I would be more comfortable topless as well. Yes, I probably would be cooler but I didn't think that would be appropriate in this situation. I was learning. Taking my shirt off would have implied something to him that I wasn't ready for even if it was innocently done to keep cool.

We talked for a long time. I was running my fingers through his hair and he was rubbing my legs. He told me more of what happened since the last time we met and asked me a lot of questions about my past. I was intentionally vague, as usual. Based on what happened the next day, he was filling in blanks with some wild and crazy adventures I was never a part of except in his imagination.

He had worked all week and must have been tired. At one point he asked a question that took me telling a longer story to answer. Somewhere in the story he must have dozed off. I sat there for a while with a man sleeping between my legs and then realized my room would be cooler by now. If he was that tired it was time for me to leave, anyway.

"Sorry I fell asleep. I really do want to spend time with you."

"Maybe some other time. I have the rest of the summer and who knows if I'll have a teaching job next fall. I'm sure we can get together again."

"Hopefully next time it will be cool enough for us to continue where we were when the cop interrupted us the first time we met."

He got up and offered me a hand. On the way up his hand brushed unnaturally across my chest. I smiled to let him know I got his message.

"It's getting late and I should let you get some sleep."

"We could get some sleep together here."

"If I stayed I don't think we would get a lot of sleep right away."

"I think I could stay awake long enough to make it worth your while to stay."

He was standing right in front of me by the door. One arm went behind my back and the other hand pulled my face to his. Once his lips were firmly planted on mine, that hand went behind my head to insure a long kiss good bye. The hand around my back eased to the front and I wasn't fighting it. When his hand started easing downward I knew it was time for me to go. With both of his hands were busy I reached for the door. He didn't argue once the door was opened. Although it was dark we could hear kids playing in the square. I guess he didn't want one of them to call the cops on him for not letting a woman out of his apartment.

"I really hope to hear from you again."

"I'm sure you will. Give me a call next time you get some time off."

My room was cool enough with the fan on. I drifted off to sleep wondering if my knight was in a place with air conditioning. Funny the thoughts that run through your head as you ease into dreamland.

After church the next morning I took a drive to the lookout for my usual Sunday picnic lunch before heading to the library. Not a lot of schools posted job openings over the weekend, so Sundays there was more time for e-dating. Since it was a weekend the guys who were online usually weren't called away from the chat to work, usually.

Mr. Clean was working. At this point he was still trying to convince me to meet him somewhere for a "photo" shoot. Our IM session was frequently interrupted while he would take a picture or two. I kept thinking how unprofessional it would be to have someone IMing with someone while taking pictures of someone else. He said he was on the computer to download the pictures so his client could see them right away. Then her friend agreed to have some pictures taken as well. Then the three of them decided to play with some of the props. He took a couple of pictures with them playing that he was describing to me since they weren't comfortable showing me their pictures. From what he was describing I would be uncomfortable just playing with the props much less having someone take pictures of it. They were going to give the pictures to their respective boyfriends. That was the last day I IM-ed with him. I was looking for something serious and he definitely wasn't that so there was no need to continue conversing with him.

That's when I noticed that his profile was taken off the website. As I was searching, I also noticed that Randy had changed his profile. In his bio he started rambling about a woman who claimed to be a virgin but the way she acted indicated she probably wasn't. What? He was talking about me! That pissed me off! I couldn't believe he was questioning me. He was on a dating website while still living with his wife and now accuses me of not being totally honest? He spent part of a Saturday morning making out with me in a parking lot while his wife was at his apartment, and I'm the one who isn't telling the whole truth? His apartment only had one bed, he didn't say anything about sleeping on the couch and my past is in question? That was just too much for me.

When I calmed down enough to type something to him, it wasn't a friendly message. Part of it was the questions that went through my head as I was reading his manifesto. Part of it was that he put stuff about me in his bio. No one else would know it was me he was talking about, but I was still upset. In the e-mail I mentioned that if he wanted to keep the length the same, he could take out the stuff about me and put in how long it had been since he lived with his wife and explain that situation to prospective dates. That would be a better indication of what he thought of honesty.

The first time he called after my message, I answered the phone to let him explain. He apologized again for not giving me the whole truth to start with. Then he apologized for questioning my honesty. Then he gave me all the reasons he had for not believing me. I knew he really didn't believe me. After that he was only allowed to leave a message. We hadn't IM-ed outside of the website and I didn't think of blocking his e-mails to my regular e-dress. Occasionally I would get something from him. It was always something that he sent out to everyone in his address book without thinking about who was all in it. Eventually I asked him to take me out of his contact list. I was slowly weeding out the men who didn't live up to my ideal.

*****

Some friends from back home were making a family vacation into a visit out to see me. This would be a good time for me to take a break from working on my "Mrs." degree and spend some time with my best friend and her family. They were only in town a few days and had lots of things they wanted to do. Part of what they wanted to do was spend time in the pool. While they did that I stayed in their air conditioned room and used the hotel internet access to get my computer work done. I sent out a few more resumes and applications, but I was also trolling a little. During that time I met one gentleman that stood out from the rest. This Robert was from southern California, and I could tell.

Our chats quickly took a turn to the wild side. He started asking what I was wearing, and then admitted that he enjoyed wearing women's undergarments. Ironically his were more decorative than mine. The next day when I spent time in their hotel room, he was talking about what he and a male friend did the night before. He was concerned that I would think of him as a weirdo. Why would I think any less of him because he wore panties and had what some might call sexual relations with another man? Actually I didn't, I also knew I would never really meet him or I wouldn't have continued the conversation. As long as it was just for fun I could let him talk about whatever he wanted to and join in a little.

The next day he asked if he could come to see me. He would bring along a female friend for me if I wanted to try something new. He would be more than happy to watch as we got to know each other. I was playing along—playing is innocent, right?—until he said he mentioned he had some time off. Was he really serious about coming to see me and introducing me to a new friend? He knew that I was unemployed, so I couldn't use the "I can't get time off" excuse. He also knew I was using a borrowed internet connection. I excused myself for the day, hoping he would forget by the next time I got online.

What was I thinking? A horny man would never forget plans for a sexual escapade. His first question to me the next day was when he could come to see me. It was the last day in town for my friends and there wasn't much time to chat. At least that was my out that day. After that I made sure not to get online that time of day. There were a couple e-mails, all left unanswered. I figured out how to make myself invisible to some people while online and waiting for messages from my knight in shining armor.

*****

There was still nothing from my knight. Funny how a fling of less than a week where we never even saw each other had me so upset. Some guys I was trying to avoid and others I was upset when they didn't call. I was trying to avoid Randy and Robert. They wanted something I did not want to give them. I wanted a call from my knight. Maybe it was just that the relationship didn't get far enough for me to be mad at him. It just didn't seem like the story of my knight in shining armor had an ending yet – happy or otherwise. It felt like I was still in the middle of the fairy tale and I wanted to know how it ended. Even a call that said it was definitely over would be some closure.

Speaking of calls, something funny happened. Most of the time, I didn't answer the phone if I didn't recognize the number. Then there was a call from a number I almost recognized. I answered it. Ken's voice was on the line.

"Sorry I didn't get to my phone right away. What did you want?"

"What do you mean?"

"Didn't you just call me?"

"No."

"Now I feel pretty silly. So how are you doing anyway?"

"Still looking for a job."

"Did you find a man in Alaska?"

"Depends on what you consider finding a man."

"Did you do what I suggested?"

"No, I couldn't do something like that."

"I didn't think you would. Not that it's a bad thing, but you're too much of a good girl."

It finally hit me that he must have wishing I had called and that's why he called me. "How are things going with you?"

"Remember that woman I was talking about who works at the office?"

"Yes, I remember you talking about her."

"Well, we are going to be married in September."

That threw me for a loop. I must have just been on his mind, but instead of his fiancée? That was weird.

I will never understand men. The guy I wanted to call me won't talk to me and the guy who doesn't really want to talk to me is calling me. It was flattering that he was still thinking of me, and still had my number in his phone. The notion that I might really be attractive was sinking in. Not attractive enough to keep a man like

Lawrence, but the more I thought about it, the less I really wanted a man like him.

The conversation with Ken ended with me thinking to myself about what I really wanted in a man. I was looking for someone who would sweep me off my feet and into "happily ever after" land. I was definitely not someone who just wanted a sex toy. It had taken many months of many e-dating experiences, but I was figuring things out little by little.

That was the last I heard from Ken. I never found out if he actually did get married. Unless he's reading this, he never found out how my life changed between that call and the middle of September. He wasn't the first guy to disappear slowly but surely from my life.

*****

It was the middle of a hot July, and I was still waiting for my knight to come back from his own crusade. Tim was complaining about how hot it was by him. He didn't seem to hear me when I said it was hot here, too. Now he was going to save up the money and come out with his daughter before the end of summer so she could start school out here. Of course, her mother wouldn't hear of it, and Tim, understandably, couldn't convince her otherwise.

I was at the library having a rare IM chat with Tim when someone else from the website asked if I would like to have a chat with him. His profile didn't look too scary, so I accepted his invitation. When he told me his real name I laughed. Robin. It was the same name I used for an alter ego in high school. It turns out his mother was an incredible Winnie the Pooh fan. His father wouldn't let her name him Christopher Robin, but they could both agree on Robin Christopher.

Robin was a little older than me with gray hair to boot. Then again, Lawrence and my knight, or at least the picture I saw of him, also fit that description. Maybe I was fated to marry someone a few years older than me. He was born in Calgary and moved down here for work a couple of years ago. His son was also here, going to college somewhere in the states. He never really said what happened with his wife, and I wasn't about to ask. All I knew was that he listed his status as divorced.

There was the usual "getting to know you" chat for a while. Robin said he had enough online chatting. He wanted to meet in person. It wasn't that he was desperate, or so he said, but it was Sunday and if we didn't meet today we wouldn't be able to meet for another week.

I had done that one other time, met a man I hardly knew because of time restraints. That one turned out disastrous. Later I found out that I was in the early stages of a nasty flu that night, but it didn't help that he called the waitress by her name more than he used mine and told me he thought we should split the bill *after* it came.

Robin wasn't asking to go out to eat, just to meet at a coffee shop. I could handle that, and my stomach only had the usual first meeting butterflies.

I typed good-bye to Tim, who wished me luck. It took a bit to log out and get the computer ready for bed for the night. The Starbucks was between the house and the library. There wasn't really time to go home and change. I had already told Robin what I was wearing so he would know it was me.

Finally I found how to get in front of the coffee shop and parked where I could see the door. Walking in, I immediately noticed a tall gentleman with distinguished white hair standing on the other side of the room. That must be him. He was wearing longer cargo shorts and a loud floral print shirt. He looked like the typical tourist. As I approached his table, he gave me a big smile and asked if I wanted something to drink. I got something cold and fruity and sat down across the table from him.

We talked about growing up without a lot of technology. It always seemed ironic that I did most of my dating online but didn't have cable TV, the internet, or even a landline in the house. He was at times a consultant for various educational facilities so he needed all those things at home.

His main job was as an instructor at a local trade school. We taught at different levels, but had a lot of the same frustrations. He said he felt a bit sorry for people teaching where I had been for the last school year. When students have to pay for classes they usually take things a bit more seriously and behavior is not really an issue for him.

This was new territory in my dating world. Finally, I found someone who could carry on an intellectual conversation. I found someone who understood some of the challenges of teaching. I found someone who kept up with current events. I found someone who was interested in my mind along with my body.

Yes, the conversation turned very flirty at times. He was the same in the real world as he was in the cyber world. He mentioned more than once that if he had a teacher like me in high school he probably would have flunked the class just to be able to stare at my chest for another semester. Finally he asked if we could go somewhere more private so he could do more than just stare at it. As he asked, his hand reached over the table to take mine all the time keeping his eyes glued to mine. He sensed my hesitation and started talking about growing up in a place that offered a lot of privacy if you wanted it.

His hand stayed on mine. His eyes went to my chest a few times, but for the most part he kept them up with mine. Once when I caught them drifting down he said that he was trying to be a gentleman and not put any pressure on me, but he was really interested in seeing what was under my shirt. I mentioned that it was another shirt, and he couldn't help but smile. He had a genuine smile, not something he put on long enough to get my clothes off, which just made me more comfortable with the thought of doing that. After a couple of hours of good conversation I was ready for a little action.

215

"You are really who you said you were." I was trying to figure out a way to ease into something physical.

"Funny, I was going to say the same thing. You are a sweet, innocent girl."

"I'd like to think I'm still innocent, but I'm not sure that would describe everything I've ever done."

"You have to be more innocent than most of the women I meet on the website. You haven't once asked to go to my place or if I wanted to go to yours. Granted, we've known each other for less than a day, but you are the real thing and we can move our relationship as fast or as slow as you want. You're in the driver's seat and I'm happy to come along for the ride."

This was getting to be too much. "How about we take my Jeep behind the building where no one was parked when I came in and continue our talk? One drink like this a day is enough for me and pretty soon we are going to be considered loitering here."

"I think they let people do that in places like this, but I'd be happy to move this conversation to a more intimate setting."

He went around to the back of the building to make sure the coast was clear as I brought the Jeep around. I was wondering what he had in mind, since he had to make sure there was no one else back there, but the way the conversation was going I really trusted him. He seemed to be able to sense my uneasiness about things before I was aware of them. He understood that although I was 37 years old, I was a teenager as far as dating went. It was one of those paradoxes. Since he didn't just want to get me alone I was willing to be alone with him.

We talked for a while again. Looking back I should have seen that he was trying to get me back to the way I was feeling in the coffee shop without seeming too eager. He wanted something physical as well, but he was willing to wait and let it happen when I was ready.

"I know this is not private enough for you to show me what's under that shirt, but maybe I can show you what's in my shorts." A bit forward of him, but it is where our conversation was bound to go. He started reaching for his fly, and I didn't stop him. After a few adjustments in his seat, I could see a bit of flesh poking out. He reached over to take my hand and guide it to where his other hand was still adjusting things on his lap. The look in his eyes said he wanted something other than my hand. I started to oblige him. At first he enjoyed it. I couldn't see his face, but by the sounds he was making it was obvious. Out of the blue he started to push my head away.

"Pretty soon I won't want you to stop and this isn't as private as I would like."

"Want to go somewhere else?"

"It's early and I can go into work late tomorrow, so did you have a more private place in mind? With my son staying with me for a couple weeks it isn't really a good place for privacy or I would suggest we go there."

"How about my place?"

"Are you sure about that?"

"It's not that far away and even if Rob is around, which he isn't much over the weekends, he says he can't hear anything that goes on upstairs in my room."

"So we could do anything we want?" His eyes had a glimmer I had seen before, but this time I was much more comfortable with it.

"He's never complained that I have the TV or radio up too loud and the only time he comes up there is when he wants me to trim the back of his hair. And when he does that he announces himself at the bottom of the stairs before he takes one step up."

"Sounds like a place I wouldn't mind going to at this moment."

"Just remember, half of it is pretty much storage for my stuff when I had a house in Alaska. And I don't make my bed."

"We would just be messing it up soon anyway." He had a reassuring smile that was as mischievously innocent as my voice

217

was said to be. "How about I follow you to your place and we go upstairs and see what happens there?"

"Ok, but the only piece of furniture I have up there is my bed."

"That's all we are going to need. I'll bring my car back here so you know what it looks like and then I'll follow you home."

I gave him the street I lived on just in case we got separated and he disappeared. Soon after that a little white car appeared.

The little two car caravan made it to the house quickly. Rob wasn't home, or at least he wasn't parked out front. I pulled up far enough for the little white car to pull in behind my black Jeep and jumped out.

"Looks like a nice neighborhood." It was in the older residential part of town. "Where I live all the houses look alike. Do you think your housemate is home?"

"Over summer the only reason he uses the garage is on the day they sweep the street."

"So we're all alone?" By this time I was unlocking the door.

"That would be my guess." He reached around me to open the door for me. I didn't hear any noises from the kitchen. "But we can go right upstairs anyway."

The stairs were just to the right of the door so we didn't have to go through the house to get to my room. It had been a while since I had a gentleman up to my room. This one didn't pull my clothes off right away. We got all the way to the bed fully clothed. We sat on the edge and he took my hand. He must have sensed my nervousness.

"We don't have to do anything you don't want to."

"You're probably going to be disappointed. I'm kind of surprised you actually followed me here."

"I'd be happy if you just did to me what you did in your Jeep. You don't even have to go any further. But maybe I should make you feel good first. Mind if I see what's under that shirt?"

"It's just another shirt." I was getting a bit flirty. Again I was going where angels fear to tread. But I was still not thinking of this from his point of view. I was just having fun, entertaining a friend up in my room. I had already told him I wasn't going to go all the way, or at least I thought I told him that. Maybe he had been told that before by other women who had changed their minds after a while with him.

"Want to come to my place?" means different things to men and women. To women it might be a cup of coffee or extending a conversation. To men it means sex is imminent. In this case I knew it would be more than just a cup of coffee and I knew he remembered it wouldn't be sex.

Before I knew it we were oppositely naked. His shorts and my shirts were on the floor. As promised, he was making me feel very good. My mind was racing to not so good things. How far was I going to let him go? This wouldn't be the first time I was naked with a man, if it got that far. But we had just met. Would a good girl be naked with a man she met just today? Then again, could I still consider myself a good girl at all?

After being lost in my moment for a while, I remembered what he asked for. By the time I got into position he was lost in the moment. He let me know he was feeling really good, and then quickly excused himself for a minute. I wasn't going to ask what he was doing in the bathroom. It didn't take him long.

"That was more than I was expecting."

"Hope you enjoyed it, even though you had to finish things yourself."

"I very much enjoyed it. Now what can I do for you to enjoy?"

"You've already done something I enjoyed."

We talked for a little while longer. He has been having problems with his neck, which is why he didn't think he could reciprocate. He had been seeing doctors and chiropractors since he moved from Calgary and the pain was just getting worse.

As we sat there, the sun started shining through the crack in the shade. He looked down at his watch and started talking about getting back to his son. It seemed his son was staying with him at least for a while during the summer break from college. The time for his son to leave was getting close so he wanted to spend as much time as possible with him. I could understand that. He promised he would contact me again soon. He got his shorts on quicker than I could fully dress. I followed him to the top of the steps and watched as long as I could. As the front door was closing I was running to the windows facing the front of the house. Since I had my shirts on, I could lift the shades to wave good-bye.

*****

Nothing much happened that week until Wednesday when Robin called me again. I was hoping for a call from another knight, but no such luck. Tim called about every day to complain about the heat and his ex-girlfriend and the woman he was staying with, the usual for him. I took the calls just to have someone to talk to for a while when he called.

Robin's son was going to be sight-seeing out of town with some friends and he didn't want to eat alone. At least that was the story he told me. He asked if there were any ethnic restaurants by where I lived. I hadn't been to any, but thinking of the places near-by that had their street signs in Spanish I figured we could find something. He didn't like chain restaurants that pretended to be ethnic. He wanted to go to the real thing. I jokingly asked if he was going to pay in pesos. He said his credit card would do the conversion for him if necessary. It was nice to be able to joke with someone who understood my sense of humor without getting all uptight about it. He had a few hours before his next meeting and would like to have lunch with me.

When he came to pick me up, I realized what kind of a car he had. I had never ridden in a BMW before. The people I hung out with had a domestic car or something that was imported from the Orient, not Europe. It was purchased from a dealer in Calgary according to the sticker on the back, so he didn't just get it.

We went to a little hole in the wall I had seen several times driving around the area. Neither of us knew much Spanish, luckily the staff was fluent in English. They asked what language we wanted for our menu. I was tempted to say something off the wall like Tagalog, but he answered English before I could open my mouth. While we were waiting for our order, or waiting to see exactly what we ordered, we started talking.

This time it was a real, intellectual conversation. Over summer he just did his consulting work since the trade school he teaches at doesn't offer his class during the summer. We talked for over an hour about the state of education here, and a little of it in Canada. We talked about how different it was growing up somewhere other than the big city. We talked about how students have changed since we started teaching, and were students ourselves. This was more like the dates I was used to before online dating. There were a few flirty comments here and there, but otherwise nothing all that sexual.

It was a good conversation, but it had to end. He had to get back to work soon. As we drove to my place, he told me how much he enjoyed lunch and wanted to do it again soon. He also hinted that he would like to do what we did this weekend again as well. By that time he was walking me to the door. I had lunch with a true gentleman. I'd gotten used to going out with men who thought mostly with their little heads. A meal out with a woman was just to get things started before a physical encounter for most of them.

I thanked him for lunch. He promised he would call some day when he had some extra time before hurrying back to his BMW and driving away.

I wasn't expecting much. After the way my social life was going this was almost a disappointment. He didn't try to grab anything, didn't make comments that made me turn every shade of red, and didn't ask to go back to my room. Yes, I was disappointed.

Then again, maybe this was more of what real dating should be like, two adults having a nice time with each other.

*****

There was plenty of afternoon left so I decided to go to the library and spend some time on the computer. On the way there Tim called to tell me he was working on his ex-girlfriend to try to talk her into letting his daughter move out here with him. Like that was really going to happen. He wanted to get out of the heat and he didn't believe me that it was hotter where I was. When I told him I just got done with a date it only made me feel worse. He kept saying all the things that could have been done on Robin's lunch instead of just having lunch. According to him something could have been done in the car without anyone knowing about it and with plenty of time for lunch as well. Most of the things he mentioned I wouldn't do until after my wedding if at all, but it sounded like he enjoyed talking about it. Then he abruptly said he had to go. No excuse or anything. He just said that he had to go.

In the time it had taken me to get to the library there was an e-mail from Robin. He enjoyed himself and was wondering if I had some time on Friday about the same time. He had an early working lunch scheduled, but he wanted to know if I would be up for something else during his lunch break. So he was still interested. He also gave me his phone number. And he explained that he really wanted to see more of me but he had a meeting about next school year that he had to go to. He was at the meeting supposedly taking notes on his computer when he was typing out the message to me. I sent a message back with my phone number, which I thought I had given him before.

As long as I was at the library I logged into the website and there was a message from a new guy. I wasn't so sure about answering since I was hoping something would happen with Robin. We never said anything about being exclusive, and since we met on a dating website he must know I might still be looking. The message was just a quick hello. I wasn't going to put all my eggs in Robin's basket.

There was nothing much exciting going on after sending out a few more resumes. It was getting a little disturbing that summer was half over and I still didn't have a job for next school year. People say that someone in my area of teaching should have no problem getting a job. Maybe it's because I had been out of teaching for three years before teaching for the last school year in a non-traditional setting. Maybe it was because of my out of state training. Maybe it just wasn't time for me to have a job. In any case, looking for a job was a job in itself, and I was trying to do my best at that job.

Tim kept saying that I could go back to where I got my training. So was he really looking to come out here or not? Who knows with him? He claimed to be looking for dates, but spent all his free time on the phone with me. It was very encouraging to talk with him. He thought it was a good sign that Robin drove across town just to have lunch with me. This time there was no innuendo or any reason for him to think it wasn't just lunch. Since he asked for my phone number after that, he must have still been interested. According to Tim, this one looked promising.

The next day was about the same as the previous afternoon. There was another message from that new guy. He said he was looking for someone to spend the rest of his life with and had a few of those, "Should we even try this" questions for me to answer before we met in person. He said he wasn't good at doing things over the internet and preferred to be face to face or on the phone. Right now he was in the middle of something at work and said maybe we could talk in person next week. That gave me some time to get rid of him if things went well with Robin.

Speaking of Robin, there was another message from him letting me know to expect a call from him tonight. His son was going to be with friends in the evening, but he wasn't sure how long. They were planning for another weekend getaway so he might want to make some plans for the weekend as well. He enjoyed our intellectual conversation, but would be interested in some not so intellectual, not so conversational interaction if I would be interested. Of course I was interested. I hadn't had a lot of online encounters lately. My guess was that guys were on vacation and not on the computer as much.

There was also nothing from my knight, which had me more upset than not having a job. Yes, once I disappeared from someone's life, but he asked me to. My knight disappeared because a guy made one last call and I wanted to be honest about it. It had been almost a month since I last heard from him, but I couldn't really get him out of my mind. I had never actually seen him, but his picture was in my head more than I thought it would be. The memory of his voice sung me to sleep many nights since I last heard it. It was one of those things I couldn't explain, but I couldn't forget.

An entire day in the library and I was ready to leave the computer for a while. I hadn't been up in my room but two minutes when I got a call from Robin. He said he had an early lunch meeting, but was wondering if I would be interested in a visitor after that. He wanted to make up for how quickly he had to leave after lunch on Wednesday. I assured him that I understood, but he didn't want to disappoint me. I never told him he had. It was just another way he showed how well he knew me even though we hadn't really known each other all that long. That was encouraging. Maybe my knight was just another "could have been" and I was supposed to be with Robin.

We talked for quite a while. Of course the conversation went beyond even PG-13 several times. He liked my voice, and that I was talking about what I bought myself for my birthday. He wanted me to model it when he came over the next day. That I could do, with pleasure. And he promised to pleasure me if I did.

This was the kind of conversation I used to have to type out with an IM chat. I was moving from being a cyber slut to phone sex. I had done that before, just not as much as I was now. Robin acknowledged and respected my dream of waiting until my wedding night for the actual thing, but he listed several things we could do in the mean time as well as what we could do to make the dream come true when the time was right. Hopefully this would turn out better than things did with the last man who talked about things like that.

After all the time I spent online with guys who only wanted to chat with someone to fuel their fantasies, it was good to have a real conversation with a man. The conversation was "adult" in both senses of the word. At times we were discussing what goes on in classrooms, and other times it was about what goes on in bedrooms. It was just like when we were physically together. One time it was all about some type of sexual encounter and the other time it was lunch and conversation in public. Maybe this was more of what dating was supposed to be like. For me it had always been all or nothing. This was a pleasant mix of the two. I could get used to this.

The call was so enjoyable we didn't realize how late it was getting. He had to get up early for meetings in the morning before that early lunch he talked about. We decided to call it a night and continue the conversation the next day in person.

The next morning I didn't bother getting out of bed until fairly late in the morning. I wasn't going to be going over to the library right away so I took the opportunity to linger in bed. There was no rush, so I took my time in the shower. The black and lacy birthday present had to go on a totally dry body or it just didn't work right. Just after I got it situated, the phone rang. He was done with lunch and on his way to my place. I threw on a pair of baggy shorts and t-shirt so I could answer the door.

"That wasn't exactly what I was expecting."

225

"I couldn't answer the door in just my birthday present. Let me go upstairs first and follow in about a minute."

"I should be able to wait that long."

I started up the steps and he started counting out loud with a huge smile on his face. Quick like a bunny, I ran up the stairs and took off the extra clothes before he got to 30.

"Ok, I'm ready now."

I could hear him starting up the stairs. "Good, because I was hoping I wouldn't have to wait that long. And I'm really glad I didn't." He had made it to the top of the stairs just in time to see me strike a pose. "You are incredibly beautiful in your birthday present, or your birthday suit." He stood there, just looking at me. I wasn't used to that.

"Are you planning on just standing there?"

"I want to enjoy this moment." He started walking toward me. He took the two steps he needed to so that he was close enough to touch me. Electricity went through my body as his hands went first around my waist to pull me closer to him. I could feel his excitement through the lace. He was a bit taller than me so his excitement was about at my belly button, but it only made me giggle thinking about it later.

His hands started to caress my back. As we started easing to the bed he put his lips on mine. By the time we were to the bed his lips had moved to my neck and his hands were on my chest. The electricity was still there, with shock waves running through me as he touched certain parts of me. I was on my back laying on the bed. He took his hands off me long enough to take his own clothes off.

"I know you said you didn't want to go all the way, but how far are you willing to let me go?"

Now that was a question. It wouldn't be fair to have him do what he wanted until I say stop. Each step he would think he would have two more, and in the end he would be very disappointed. He must have sensed my confusion.

226

"How about I do some experiments and if you want me to stop, just say so." Since he suggested it, I figured it would be all right.

I liked his way of experimenting. I'll let you use your imagination, just like he used his. All I'm going to say is that he pretty much got what he wanted and I could still say that I was a good girl in some sense of the term. Soon after he left I realized it was time to wash the sheets, but it was about time I did laundry anyway.

He apologized for his quick coming and going, but he had an appointment that afternoon. He was going to see a specialist to see what could be done about his neck pain. It was a little disappointing to me that he couldn't stick around for a bit. He said he was disappointed that he couldn't give me as much pleasure as he got. He tried to do some things, but the experiments with things like that made his neck worse. I didn't mind. What he did felt good. Of course he didn't believe me that what he did was more than most men had ever done for me before.

It was the message I got from him later that afternoon that really disappointed me. Again he mentioned that he felt bad that he couldn't do everything he wanted to me. The word from the doctor was that his neck wasn't going to get better without surgery, and then with a lot of time if at all. He felt it wasn't fair to me to be with a man who couldn't fulfill my every desire. I should look for someone else and forget all about him.

My response was that I enjoyed our conversation as well as our activities, and I wouldn't mind continuing that relationship, but I never got a response back from him. I guess he felt that if we couldn't have a fully sexual relationship we shouldn't have any at all. Looking back I understood what he was saying, but I was still disappointed. Finally I met a guy I could have an intellectual conversation with, and he dumps me because he can't be as physical as he wants to be. I was satisfied with what he did. In the end, it was his decision, not mine. Maybe that was a convenient excuse, an easy out for him.

227

I didn't really have time to think about it. At first I didn't want to think about it. He was another man who wouldn't talk to me. At least this one told me it was over and I wasn't waiting around wondering. I guess my knight said it was over as well, I just didn't want to accept that.

With all that going through my head, I wasn't really paying attention to what was going on. Maybe that's why things fell apart like they did. But I'm getting ahead of myself.

*****

There was another message from the new guy. His name was Mike. Based on my answers to his questions, he wanted to meet me. He worked some pretty weird hours, but he had some time off coming soon and was wondering if we could get together then. Until then he had a few more questions. He happened to be online so we could chat about those questions. I let him know that I was looking for a husband and not interested in having sex without that. Just the fact that he was asking all these questions told me that he was interested in finding something other than just a fling. Then again, he worked for a mental health facility so he knew what questions to ask. I never got a degree in psychology, but I had some training in counseling. I could see some of what he was doing as what some of the dating sites do to try to make matches. Since I made it this far I guessed I was passing his tests.

I also mentioned that I was having a little trouble with my computer. He said maybe we could meet somewhere for a bit. My guess was this would be one of those meetings to see if I was for real. He had a little of that free time tomorrow. We set up a time to meet at the coffee shop near my place, actually it was the one I went to when the library was closed or I didn't feel like driving as far.

When I talked to my confidant, Tim, I told him about the new guy. He said something didn't feel right to him. He told me to be careful. Men who seem too good to be true usually are. It wasn't that he sounded too good to be true, just that he seemed interested in something long term. Maybe that's what Tim was concerned about. He wanted me to be unattached in case he actually did make it out here. It was only about a month before school started again and he was still talking about his daughter going to school out here. That only reminded me that I had less than a month to find a job for this school year. He tried to change the subject to what he was going to do when he came out here. I should be ready to have someone sweep me off my feet. Of course I said that would be wonderful, but really I wasn't holding my breath.

The next day I met Mike at the coffee shop. I just had time to get my computer up and running when he came to my table outside. He had seen me when he parked, but I was focused on the laptop. Suddenly there he was, hoping he had the right person. I hadn't seen his picture, but he described himself pretty well. His curly hair was difficult to style so he just left it short. His facial hair was meant to look scraggly. It was nowhere near gray, but it looked good on him. He was about average height, probably just a bit taller than me if I had been standing. He had on a big white t-shirt and orange cargo shorts. The colors together probably made him look younger than he was, and he was already younger than me.

He started asking about the processor and stuff like that. Soon I just turned it his way so he could see for himself. Computers are like cars for me. I know how to use them, but not why they work and definitely not how to fix them. He started defragging it, which as anyone who knows computers knows, takes a while. We had some time to talk while the computer was busy.

We had never talked about age. He knew that I was a few years older than he was. In my family that wasn't unusual so it didn't matter to me.

"You look younger than me anyway." He was very flattering.

"People have always said I looked younger than I am."

"I bet we would get carded if we went out for drinks."

"Aren't we out for drinks now? Did they card you for the coffee?" My sense of humor can sometimes be overwhelming, so this was a test to see if he could handle it.

"As a matter of fact, they did card me. I think it was more to check if the credit card I used was really mine, but they did ask for ID." His smile let me know he understood I was joking. "How about you?"

"I used cash so with a little extra they didn't ask for ID."

He asked about my family, what brought me out here and assorted other follow-ups to questions he had posed in past chats. According to him there are some questions you need to see the facial reactions to in order to get the "real" answer. Seems this guy knew his e-dating. He was very open about the fact that he was analyzing me as we were getting to know each other. I had been accused of overanalyzing the idiot who shall remain nameless. He was afraid to be analyzed, but he didn't really complain until I started pointing out his demon. I was interested to hear what someone else had to say about me.

"So, would you be comfortable sharing the results with me?"

"I'll need some time to get the report ready." It was fun to have a silly conversation with someone. "Actually, I do have to get going for the afternoon. My weekend starts on Wednesday, how about we plan on meeting again then?"

"That works for me."

"We can chat some more before then, and I should have that report after work tonight. I can e-mail it to you and you can decide if you still want to talk to me."

"I'm sure I will. Thanks for looking at my computer."

"You know I didn't come to look at your computer. I came to look at you, and I wasn't disappointed." He gallantly kissed the back of my hand.

"Flattery will get you everywhere."

"I'm hoping so. But now I have to get going or I'll be late to work."

This was encouraging. Nothing physical happened, but maybe that was a good thing. He was somewhat intellectual, and at least got my jokes. Maybe he wasn't as close of a match as Robin, but that door was closed. And except for a few chats, on the phone with Tim and on the computer with Mike, so was the month of July.

I should be getting ready for another school year. There were several interviews, but it seemed like most of the schools had someone else in mind but had to interview a certain number of people for each job. They wanted people who had worked in the regular school system. My three years away from school and one year working in a non-traditional school didn't add up to the experience others candidates had, usually at the school they were interviewing for but not in the area they were they had the opening. It would be easier to replace them in their former subject than the area that was open.

August was very different—some good and some bad. My mom was coming for a visit. Maybe there would be some big news for her when she got here. I hadn't told her much about my social life so far. Part of it was that I was hoping she still thought of me as a good girl. Part of it was that I thought that if I told her she would be expecting something and if it didn't happen she would know how upset I was. Part of it was that she might tell my siblings and even though I was far away from them, I had done too much to them while they were dating and didn't want to risk any paybacks.

In any case my family didn't know about my social life, and I was hoping for it to stay that way.

Chapter 9 — Taking the bad with the good

I woke up on August 1st full of hope, but it was definitely not a good day. In fact, it turned out to be the worst day of my life. The month of August was really a roller coaster for me.

I went to the library early. I figured that if Mike worked a late shift he wouldn't wake up until late in the morning, if he saw the morning at all. There was a message from him that he was planning on meeting me somewhere in the early evening. He would call me in the late afternoon to let me know where and give me a better idea of when. There were no messages from anyone else. I was getting a little discouraged. Even though I was involved with someone, it was nice when I was getting lots of messages from guys. I had probably turned down so many or let them run their course that now my profile was way down the list. That's how it goes in the online dating world.

There were some messages from schools. I should have been concentrating on getting a job rather than a husband. Summer was coming to an end and I didn't really want to have a school year of subbing and unemployment. One school asked about an interview early next week. I didn't think Mom would mind if I took a little time out of her time with me to do an interview. I stayed at the library a little while longer looking at job sites and lingering on the dating sites. There was nothing encouraging from either of them, so I decided to go home to see if Mike would call. Oddly enough, there was no call from Tim for over a day. Usually he says something when he's busy and isn't going to be calling.

The call from Mike came soon after I got to the house. He asked for my address so he could come and pick me up. He thought maybe we could hang out at my place for a while and then go to dinner when we got hungry. As we talked he Map Quested my address and said he could figure out how to get to the house. He was finishing up getting dressed and would be over in a half hour or so. It would be the beginning of rush hour, so I figured it would be a bit longer than his predicted half hour. I had time to actually make my bed, something I don't normally do. If we were going to be talking in my room it would probably be good to have a made bed to sit on since I didn't have any other furniture, except the folding chairs I used for a night stand and a TV stand.

After a half hour, I went outside to wait on the steps leading up to the porch. I even remembered to take my phone along with me in case Mike needed directions. A car stopped in front of the house and my phone rang at about the same time. It was Mike letting me know he was here. So he had a sense of humor as well.

He quickly got out of his SUV and jumped up the steps to make it to me before I could stand up. His curly black hair bounced wildly as he bounded up the steps. He was wearing something like I would wear—jeans with a t-shirt and a long sleeve shirt over it. I usually choose a flannel shirt for the top, but it was summer and flannel tends to be a bit too warm for most people. Even I was just in a long sleeve t-shirt. I wasn't sure what kind of place we would be going for dinner.

"See, I told you it wouldn't take me long to get here." It had taken a bit longer than he said, but I wasn't going to argue a few minutes. It was, after all, summer when time isn't as rigid as it is during the school year.

"Since I don't know exactly where you live I didn't know how much of rush hour you would have to deal with."

"It wasn't all that bad. Since my schedule is so crazy I rarely have to drive during the official rush hour. My guess is summer rush hours aren't as bad."

"Yes, but summer is almost over."

We talked about my job prospects as we went up to my room. When we got to the top of the stairs I felt the need to apologize again for my living arrangements. He was evasive about where he lived. For some reason he didn't want me to know where he lived or who he lived with. At least he didn't share that information with me voluntarily, and I wasn't going to ask. He was asking all the questions and there wasn't time for me to do anything but answer.

I was telling all kinds of stories and monopolizing the conversation without realizing it. That seemed to be exactly what he wanted. He answered my questions with a word or two and then would ask me something that would lead me to another story. He told me he hadn't had the time to write up his report on me and wanted more information to make it more comprehensive.

The questions quickly turned to my sexual past. I had answered most of his questions. I wasn't embarrassed about what I had done, but there are just some questions you only want to answer once per person. There were also some things that I felt were too personal to share with someone I had only recently met. The thing I was most self-conscious of was what I hadn't done.

The rate of conversation changed so that he was now doing most of the talking. He would describe a sexual situation and I would have to say that I hadn't done that. I thought I had done a lot that I maybe shouldn't have, but my activities were tame compared to what he was asking. Based on the "have you ever" questions he was asking either he had a lot of experience or watched a lot of porn.

He announced that he wasn't hungry yet. He suggested we do more than just talk for a while. He assured me that I would enjoy it.

We could maybe try some of those things he described. According to him, a good girl like me deserved someone who was good to her. He was more than willing to be that someone and do lots of good things to me. He started to put his hand up my shirt. I closed my eyes. He had given me permission to just lay back and enjoy what he was doing, so that's exactly what I started to do.

Before I knew it my shirt was on the floor, and so was his. Every step along the way he assured me how good the next step would feel. Pretty soon our pants were on the floor not that far from the bed. It didn't really matter that I made the bed anymore. The blankets were on the floor and the top sheet was in a ball in a corner.

He promised to make me feel good, and he was following through. His hands were exploring my naked body. He slowly removed the last stitches of clothing I was wearing, then his. I was starting to think how to tell him to stop while I still had the energy to think. What I thought were signals for him to slow down weren't being received. He had gotten about as far as I wanted him to go but he didn't seem to be taking my hints. Instead he kept telling me how good I would feel at that next step.

"What if we made a deal—you make me feel good then I make you feel good. After that we can take a break for a while." He might as well finish what he was starting with me. After all, he just got done saying I shouldn't feel guilty about being pleasured. I had made men feel good in the past so I should be able to follow through on my promise when the time was right.

"If I go first you promise to take care of me when I'm done?"

"Of course, that's what I said I would do." I have always prided myself in following through on promises. I was nervous about the idea, but it wouldn't be the first time for me to make a man feel good. The thing that concerned me the most was that I didn't have as much experience as the girls who did some of those other things he described earlier.

My thoughts had me a bit distracted so I wasn't paying attention to everything he was doing. Doing two things at once in this case meant thinking about my lack of experience and enjoying what he was doing to me. That was more than my mind could handle at the moment, so I decided to stop thinking and just enjoy what he was doing. He gave me permission to do that after all. It would just be doing what he asked me to do.

His lips started down my torso until they finally reached their destination. It did feel good, and I let him know it. It felt so good I didn't realize that his left hand was not on my body any more. My eyes were closed so I didn't see him reaching for something of the floor in his pants pocket.

"Done already?" I was too naive to know what he was up to. He was the third man I had up in my room. The other two stopped when I asked them to, and I assumed he would as well. God had been with me those times, His angels watching over me. I had taken chances with the other guys and it worked out. As his mouth came up to mine, I began to realize my luck had run out. I had gone too far. The angels refused to go where they feared to tread.

"Not done, but I have an idea that will make us both feel good at the same time."

"I think you better stop, are you hungry yet?" I was trying to get out of this.

"No, I just ate. Now it's time for some physical activity."

"Maybe I want something to eat."

"No, I know what you really want." It always bothered me when people said they knew what I wanted or what I was thinking. This time it was scaring me more than a little.

"I want to make you feel good." There was starting to get a tinge of desperation in his voice, or something else I didn't recognize. Mike wasn't really listening to what I was saying. He obviously had something on his mind, and wasn't going to stop until he got what he wanted.

"Don't be scared, it's going to feel really good for both of us if you just let me do what I want."

I started to tell him I wanted him to stop. He put his right hand to my mouth with so much pressure I couldn't finish my sentence. There was a soft click on the side of the bed. When I turned my eyes to see what it was, I saw his left hand put his open pocket knife on the folding chair I was using as a night stand. "Something of mine is going inside you, exactly what is up to you. I hope you let me decide. What I want to put in you will make us both feel good. You said you just wanted me to feel good, right?" He let me shake my head yes while keeping his hand over my mouth so not a sound could slip out.

What happened next, I really don't know. I remember turning my head to see the blade of his pocket knife glowing red with the light from my clock radio. The next thing I remember was seeing a red trail from my body to the drain of my bathtub. Was the blood from a cut, or was the blood from…

All I could hear was the water coming out of the shower hitting my knees, which were pulled up to my chin. If he was still in my room I didn't know it, but I had the feeling he was already gone. He had what he wanted.

I started putting together the pieces. It was like putting together the pieces of a dream. Based on where I was hurting and the trail of blood to the drain, I stopped thinking. I decided I didn't want to think any more of what happened. I was hoping that, like a nightmare, if I didn't think about it I would totally forget about it. It would become like all the other forgotten bad dreams. If it never came to mind, maybe it didn't really happen.

I remembered that play I did when I had the flu. I must have done things, but I have no memory of them. There have also been times when I went to sleep while riding in a car. I remember getting in the car and then pulling into the driveway at home. The night I got drunk in college I remember the opening and closing credits of the movie, but only one scene in between. This was kind of the same feeling.

I remember being on the bed with Mike on top of me, and the next thing I remembered was being in the shower alone, hurting and bleeding. When I realized what must have happened all I could do was cry.

I was so alone.

I don't know how long I had been in the shower, or how long I stayed there. Eventually the water turned cold and I decided to get out and see what time it was. Mike was gone, and so was everything he brought with him.

There was a message from Tim on my phone, but I wasn't about to call him back right then. His hunch had been right, to watch out for this guy, but I didn't listen. I really didn't know what to do. I had invited Mike up to my room. I had helped him take my clothes off. I willingly let him do something sexual to me. But I had asked him to stop. Then came the knife. Mercifully my memory was wiped clean of the details of what happened. I had pushed my luck too far, but God was still looking out for me in a way.

When something similar happened to my roommate in college, she went to the police, who didn't do anything but write her story down. They would ask me to try to remember everything that happened. As long as I didn't remember it maybe it didn't happen. I was hurting, but if I went to a hospital they would have done tests and told me what happened. I wanted to stay in denial. As long as nobody said the words, maybe it didn't really happen. Maybe it was good that I was so far from family and friends who would have asked about my date. As long as nobody else knew, maybe it didn't really happen.

I decided to get dressed and take a drive. There was still a bit of sunlight left. By the time I got to the lookout the sun was about to go down. I sat on the rocks, trying to figure out what to do next. It was the middle of the week over the summer so there weren't many people at the park. The families had gone home with their picnic baskets and the teenagers weren't yet looking for a place to make out. Only an hour or two before that started, and I knew I had to be gone by that time. I sat there for a long time thinking of nothing and everything at the same time.

A year ago this time I was still living with the idiot. We were talking about marriage, but I was starting to see that something wasn't quite right with our relationship. It would be a couple of months before I moved out. One year ago I was just starting to get over the traumatic events that brought me out of Alaska. At the time I thought that was the worst thing that had could happen to me. Now I wish I could go back. I wouldn't do many things differently, just a few this past month. A year ago I was a shy, quiet girl who turned red when I saw a man wearing just a towel. Now several men had seen me naked. A year ago I could count how many men I had gone out with on my fingers. Now I had dates with different men every weekend. My life had changed so much in just one year, not even a full 12 months.

I had changed as well. A year ago I was a wall flower, willing to hide in the shadows when it came to dating. Now I was initiating contact online and suggesting to meet men in person, knowing, or maybe hoping, it would end with some form of physical contact. It was my turn to realize I was different from most of the men I was contacting. Maybe it was that I was different from most of the women looking for men, online or otherwise. I was a country girl lost in the big city. It was more than just lack of sexual experience. I had come from a different world and now I wished for the simpler place that I came from, but could I? I had changed to the point where I probably wouldn't fit in there, either.

I had become a tease. I realized that I was attractive. In the big city there were lots of men who were interested and even excited by bigger girls. I was willing to do things that excited them even more. I got their engines started, then wanted to shut them off before they could go anywhere. The way I was talking they expected something. I talked slutty. When they realized I wasn't going all the way they figured I was too much work for too little reward. They could get their reward from many other girls without having to work so hard.

I guess Lawrence said it best in his profile, "I'm looking for a friend and a lover, and maybe a wife." The order was wrong for me. The friendship had to come first, but it should be husband then lover. The men I was meeting recently weren't willing to talk marriage with someone they hadn't slept with. I didn't want to sleep with a man unless I was positive it would be a permanent relationship. Maybe that was it. To me marriage was permanent, but most of the men I was meeting already had one temporary marriage. Since no relationship was permanent to them, it was all right, if not expected, to sleep with women even if they weren't really interested in marriage with them.

I decided to take some time off from dating. Some of the time would be spent deciding what I was really looking for, and then I could start taking the time to look for a man who had the same thing in mind. I would have to really think about what I wanted to say in my profile. It would have to be something that said what I really wanted without sounding like Puritan Prudence. I had some time to think about it.

Mom would be here late the next afternoon and I wasn't going to be dating while she was here. Not only would it have been bad form, but I didn't want to give her too much information to take back to my siblings. There wasn't really all that much they could do compared to what I did when they were dating, but I still wanted to keep my private life private even from my family.

When I heard a car pull into the parking lot, I decided it was time to leave the lookout. It was just getting to the point where I needed my headlights to see as I took my time driving home. I took the long way around. I wasn't ready to see my room again just yet.

The library was open late on Wednesdays, so I went there to see if I could get on one of their computers. This late in the evening there were several open computers. The library closed in less than an hour, so there wasn't much time.

I thought I should take one more look before taking my break. There was a message for me from Mike. The nerve! Was his name even "Mike"? How could he think I would want to see him again? I wasn't sure if I wanted to open it, but if I did I could see what he had to say while I was still upset rather than getting upset all over again tomorrow. He thanked me for a "good time" and said he would probably call me tomorrow to see if I wanted to get together again.

No way in hell!

I had to stop myself from saying it out loud in the library, but I thought it really, really loud. I decided to block any further messages from him. He was not going to be able to contact me online again. This was one bridge I was willing to burn.

*****

I called Tim back the next day. My loyal back up guy friend. He could tell I was upset but didn't ask much about it. Instead he wanted to talk about what he was all going to do when he got out here. Again. All talk, that guy. I reminded him that Mom was coming so I probably wouldn't be talking with him until she went back. He was jealous that she was coming out here and he was stuck back there.

So that was it for online dating for a while.

All my time at the library was spent looking for a job. Then I went back to the house to get my room ready for Mom. There was enough for me to do to keep my mind off what happened. I was thinking of how I would answer the interview questions for the interviews I had set up that next week. Finding my letters of recommendation and transcripts took up some of my time as well. Before I knew it I was at the airport waiting for Mom.

We had an understanding that my social life was a "don't ask because I'm not going to tell" situation. There was plenty for us to do and plenty of family members to talk about. We talked on the phone at least once a week but it wasn't the same as the slumber party talks we had every night while she was visiting.

My body was still hurting a bit and sleeping on the floor so she could have my bed didn't help, but I wasn't about to let her know. Tim took the hint and no one else called while she was there. I didn't check my e-mails a lot, except the one I used for finding a job. The time away from dating went by quickly.

Eventually it was time for her to go home. There was the usual teary good-bye at the airport. This time it was her getting on the plane, which was a bit different from the norm. When I flew away it was a bit easier. My mind would be busy with what to do during the flight, how to get to the next one, and then driving home. Now all I could do was think about all the things that could go wrong with Mom's flight. I liked it better when I was the one in the air.

*****

God has incredible timing. Typically things would happen just when I started wondering what I should do next. The schools where I interviewed said they probably wouldn't have an answer until next week. But I needed some rest anyway. It had been a long two weeks for me.

On the way home from the airport, I started to get hungry so I stopped at a place that had blueberry milkshakes, just like I used to have when I was in high school. Eating by myself wasn't as much fun as the late nights with my friends after a game or just for something to do if there wasn't a game that weekend. Some ladies at the booth next to me were having an interesting conversation and didn't notice me eavesdropping. Not something you would

243

really call entertainment, but it did pass the time while I finished my shake and burger. And I wanted the time to pass.

I tried to keep my mind occupied as much as possible. I didn't want to have time to think about what happened just before Mom got there. It had been two weeks. In those two weeks I was playing tour guide and had someone to talk to all the time. But now, I was alone again, and for who knows how long.

My subscription to the website ran out earlier in the week and I decided right there that I wasn't even going to try to find the money to start it up again. I probably could have found the money, but I needed to take some time off from meeting potential new boyfriends.

I had gotten too far away from who I really was. I needed to do it God's way. Too many times I had gone where angels feared to tread, and I got caught. If God really had someone for me He would send him in His time. As I was quietly trying to get every last drop of the shake, I resolved to really let it in God's hands. If I was supposed to have someone in my life, He would send somebody in an unmistakable way. I had to be patient and let it happen in His time.

As I was waiting for the server to take care of the check, I decided my "rumschpringe" was over. That is the tradition where some Amish communities allow young adults to experience life outside the community for a while. They would be allowed back with no questions asked and confidential medical care for anything that needed attention. They were released from the rules of society for a while so they would realize they wanted the safety and security of being bound by those same rules.

As I made my way back to the Jeep, the plan started to form. I would go back to being so busy with other things I wouldn't have time to have a romantic social life. The person who knew the most details of my escapades had a new job in a school where I would never work, so it should be almost easy to put my wild days behind me and go back to being a good girl for real.

My mind kept working as I drove back to the house. Of course Mom had suggested I move back to my family. Maybe if the school year started and I was still out of work, I might consider it. But I was sure I could find something to do. The church I was going to was bigger than the one I grew up in, so there must be some way they could use my experience and talents. There may even be someone who could help me get a job. If I didn't go to my actual family, I was sure there would be enough to keep me busy at least until I could figure out what God really wanted me to do.

Eventually I was almost home. For a second or two I contemplated going to the library again, but I still didn't feel like it, so I kept going. Just as I turned off the engine, my ring tone emanated from my purse. Mom wasn't home yet. Tim wouldn't be calling. The caller ID said it was the number was restricted. I had no idea who it was, but I answered it anyway—and I'm so glad I did.

"Hello, Princess." An audible gasp escaped my lips when I realized who was on the other end of the call. It was my knight. It took him a while, but eventually he called me back. And his timing… well, he showed up right when I had given up hope.

At first I didn't say anything mainly because I didn't know what to say. "Are you that mad at me that you don't want to talk to me?"

"No, I'm just surprised that you actually want to talk to me. I thought you would be just another guy who talked to me for a while and stopped for one reason or another." That has happened to me more times than I care to count. At first it was a vacation or busy time at work that took them away from the computer for a while, never to return my messages. Then it was phone messages that were never returned. In this case, he told me not to call and in fact made it impossible for me to call since he changed his phone number. Now he calls out of the blue and I'm supposed to be able to have a deep conversation instantly?

"I haven't been able to think of anyone but you. It's been a while since we last talked. Are you still single?"

"Yes. That guy who I told you about hasn't called since before we talked. I've been out a few times since we last talked, but none of them want to talk to me anymore either."

"Their loss."

"Did you ever get on that bus?" I was hoping to get the conversation off of me for a while.

"Yes."

"So where are you staying now?"

"With a friend."

"Just a friend?"

"Yes, she is just a friend." I wanted to ask more, but didn't have the nerve. He didn't seem to want to talk about it. I had to think of something else to talk about. I hadn't heard from him in over a month, and I wasn't going to let him go that quickly.

"When did you get into town?"

"A while ago." He paused for a bit before attempting to explain. "I thought I wasn't going to talk to you again, but I just couldn't get you out of my mind. Now that I have a job here I thought maybe you might talk to me again." He talked slowly, like he was searching for just the right words.

"I would talk to you even if you didn't have a job. I still don't have one for next year."

"I'm sure you'll get one soon."

We continued to talk for a while. There were a few awkward moments, like when he asked if I was still a virgin. He must have heard the quiver in my voice because he changed the subject quickly. He said he didn't want to call me when he didn't have a job. As he said in the beginning of our conversation, he wasn't going to call me ever again. He said he had too many bad memories of women cheating on him. But then he kept thinking of me, or so he said, and had to at least give me a call now that he had a job.

We talked for a while about nothing at all. He asked for my e-dress again so he could put it in his phone and we could use some

246

IM program when I was online. He also asked if it would be all right if he called me again when he got a chance.

Eventually I made it into the house and back up to my room. When he asked if I was alone in my room; there was something in his voice that sounded familiar. Up in Alaska we had some very intimate conversations. It was like the time since then didn't exist. His voice was comforting. It was exactly what I needed at that moment.

He started asking about what I was wearing and where my hands were. After the shock of him actually calling back wore off a bit, I played along. The conversation got very intimate, too intimate to share with just anyone, even someone who has read this far into the story. Use your imagination to figure out what we did while we talked, each of us alone in our rooms. Maybe my rumschpringe wasn't quite over.

*****

The next few days fell into a routine. My knight would call around the time I was waking up and we would have an intimate conversation. Then I would go to the library where he would look for me online, and we would chat while I looked for a job. I didn't check the dating website very often any more. I was still hurting from the last guy I met there. Although I originally met my knight there, he sent off different vibes, good vibes. Once in a while I would get a message from one of the guys I met before, but I was careful not to get too suggestive with them. I had learned my lesson, and well, I was saving that for my knight. My subscription ran out so the things I could do on the site were very limited. It didn't matter since I wasn't looking to start something with someone new.

Even though we had never met in person, there was an unexplainable attraction to him. For the first time, when I checked the dating site I felt like I was "cheating" on him. I wasn't ready to take my profile off the site just yet, but if I was going to start anything it was going to be with my knight. It was time for me to go back to being a good girl again.

The job front was moving at a snail's pace. That last interview turned out the same. The job was earmarked for someone in the district but they had to interview a certain number of people. It was getting close to the opening of school, but last year at this time I was still looking for a job so I wasn't giving up yet. I had a couple more interviews set up, and this time of year schools have hired all the planned openings. Now it was the teachers that left because they found a different job over the summer. Schools were a bit more desperate to have a full staff hired by the first day of school.

By the early afternoon I would be back at the house trying to stay cool. My knight would call again. It was warm, so I was usually wasn't wearing much unless I went downstairs to get some ice cream or something cold to drink. He liked that idea but our conversations couldn't get intimate because he was on a break at work.

After a few days I got up the nerve to ask him why he was blocking his number when he called. He said he didn't think it was. He gave me his number so I could call him when I wanted to. The next time he called his number showed. He really didn't know he was blocking his number and changed the settings so I would know it was him when he called.

Eventually he asked if I would mind coming over to see him. He was living all the way across town, literally. I lived blocks from the western edge of the big city and he was living where the city was growing to the east. I had nothing better to do, so I thought a little road trip on the interstate across town could be an adventure.

He wanted me to meet him where he worked. His "friend" wouldn't take too kindly to a woman coming over to visit him. We talked a bit about her. They met on the same site we had, but it had quickly turned into more of a business relationship, according to him. He said he was going to move to the city and she said she had a spare room he could use until he got on his feet. I'm guessing at some point she thought it might turn into something else. According to him it never did because he thought of that as cheating on me. Instead of spending time with her he would sit in his room listening to a particular break-up song over and over, thinking of me. She had realized there would never be anything between them and was understandably upset.

His situation reminded of my own. It had been a little over a year since I left Alaska. I moved 3,000 miles to someone who said he wanted to get to know me before we got married. It took him about four months to decide he knew enough of me and wanted to keep things were they were. I wanted to get out of that situation as soon as I could without him knowing how close to gone I was. I took boxes out one at a time when I went to work or filled the Jeep with them when I was alone at the house. I started taking the boxes to a storage area even before I met Rob and decided to share a house with him. I had a lot of stuff so it took me a while to get everything out of the idiot's house without him really knowing about it. He must have seen the stack of boxes getting smaller, but he never asked. One day he said there were some things he wanted to say before I left, and I told him it better be that day because I would be leaving for good the next morning.

Later I found out my knight was in a similar situation. He wanted to get out of there, quickly and quietly. She was a woman scorned and as long as he had to go home to her things weren't pleasant. He was a dead end as far as a relationship with her was concerned, so she criticized everything he did. But at the time I didn't know that. All I knew was that he wanted to see me in person.

He told me what street the store where he worked was on. The next big question was when we would meet. The day he mentioned it was his day off, so he asked if I would be willing to see him the next day. He started work later in the morning, so his lunch break was early afternoon rather than right at noon.

As we talked more, he made one request that took me a little off guard. He asked that I wear a dress with nothing under it. I had never been in public without underwear unless I was wearing a bathing suit, so I was a bit hesitant. Actually, I was almost more uncomfortable about wearing a dress than having nothing under it. The only time anyone caught me in public in a dress was when it was job related. Part of our intimate conversation that day included what he would do if I showed up with no underwear and he had his whole lunch break to get to know me. It made me a bit more nervous, but I was also feeling adventurous. I was seriously thinking of doing what he asked. After all, what could happen in a parking lot at a shopping center in a vehicle that didn't have tinted windows in the 30 minutes of his lunch break?

I would park in a very public place. The first time I made out in a vehicle others could see, the police came to see if I was all right. The other times I had made out in a vehicle the guy knew he couldn't do too much. I was sure I would be safe enough to indulge his wish and give him a little fantasy to think about when he went back to work for the afternoon.

It had been a while since I had any physical attention, and that wasn't a good experience. A little public display of affections couldn't get out of hand, could it? Didn't I need help easing back into physical affection? I knew nothing would really happen, but it would be a funny story if anything came of this meeting if I dressed as he requested.

Do you think I actually slept that night? My mind wouldn't stop thinking long enough for me to fall asleep. It was supposed to be warm again the next day. Maybe wearing a dress with nothing under it would be cooler than jeans. I was thinking of all the things that could happen when we actually met. It wouldn't be a real date. It would be just a meeting. We would see each other for the first time and then hopefully he would still want to talk to me. Maybe it was better when I set up meetings with a guy only hours before it happened. I didn't have an entire day to think of all the possibilities.

*****

I couldn't concentrate on getting a job the next morning. I was too busy getting ready and thinking about what I wasn't wearing. Of course I had a change of clothes, including underwear, along with me when I left the house.

The highway was nearly empty so I made good time, only to find out it was in the wrong direction. Remember when I went to meet Connor and the road he told me to take didn't go all the way through town? The street my knight worked on was like that. It started where I went to meet Lawrence in a southern suburb but the store that my knight worked at was at the other end of the street at the far north part of town.

I got to the south end about ten minutes before we were to meet. I drove north, knowing soon I would be back in the city limits and thought the store would be right there. Imagine my surprise when the road curved to the left to merge with a parallel street before continuing north or hitting the city limits.

By that time his break was scheduled to start. I was nervous about what I was wearing (and what I wasn't wearing) and now I had no idea where I was going. I pulled into a parking lot and took out the map to find out that the street disappeared for a while before continuing on the other side of an industrial district. As long as I was stopped I gave my knight a call.

He finally gave me the cross street nearby so I could find it on my map. If he had told me that right away I would have been there on time. As it was now I might get there by the very end of his break if at all. I got all dressed up (or not) for nothing.

I told him I was on my way and would be there as soon as I could. There was an obvious disappointment in his voice, but there was nothing I could do now. At least he knew I was on my way. He would be there all day working the rest of his shift. If I didn't make it during his lunch break we could still meet during his short break and decide if he wanted me to stick around till the end of his shift. There must be somewhere else we could go to talk if he still wanted to talk to me.

The street restarted a few blocks from where I stopped. From there it was a straight shot, but with lots of stop lights. Each one seemed to turn red just as I approached. I may as well have been on a bus stopping every block or two. The clock in the Jeep seemed to run faster and I was running out of time. Eventually I got to the cross street. He was supposedly somewhere around that parking lot waiting for me. His break was almost over and I was just finding my way into the parking lot. I pulled into a parking spot at the far side of the lot where it was kind of empty at the moment.

I took a deep breath and was going to get my phone out to let my knight know that I had eventually made it. Before I could do that, I noticed a gentleman walking up to the Jeep with a big smile on his face. He looked like the picture I had seen on the website. As I stepped out of the Jeep, his smile got bigger. It must have hurt to smile that much but he didn't seem to mind. He came over and closed the Jeep door when I got out of the way. Then he wrapped his arms around me.

The last few minutes of that break were the first minutes of the rest of my life. . .

About the Author

Randi Zohr was born and raised in rural Wisconsin, where she started her teaching career. She moved to Alaska to take an extended sabbatical from teaching. While there, she fell in love with the mountains, so when it was over she moved to Denver and resumed teaching. Eventually the events that inspired this novel led her to her soul mate. Together they are living in Reno with their three princesses where she is teaching, ironically for an online school